Hard Look Back

A Stephanie Hart Novel

F. J. Talley

PROLOGUE

The smell still burned his nose, but Caleb Spool didn't care. He was too focused, too driven. He had a lot of work to do. Maybe in Port Angel things will go better. Maybe this time they'll like it and he won't have to be so tough. *Not unless they force me.*

CHAPTER ONE

"Let's assemble, people," said Sergeant O. C. Boyd, shift supervisor for the ninth precinct. Boyd was in his late forties, a powerful Black man with a no-nonsense attitude and a brusque manner. "We have a lot to tell you." Boyd was joined at the front of the room by Captain Andrew Shoemaker and Lieutenant of Detectives Samuel Perkins.

The officers sat in their stiff chairs and continued their conversations until Boyd interrupted them again. "The captain and lieutenant are here to talk about the child abduction statistics. Look at the briefing at your tables. It'll show you more of the statistics on missing children, both in this state and in other major cities like Port Angel. The statistics are depressing."

Boyd looked up and Captain Andrew Shoemaker took the podium. "These statistics are frightening, and we have to be diligent that this epidemic doesn't spread to Port Angel. Increasing community awareness is key. As we know, most child abductors are non-custodial parents, but recently, there have been more kids abducted by strangers. This is not just an urban problem—it's something impacting kids all over the country." Shoemaker stepped back from the podium. "And that's one reason we're pushing for Operation ID this weekend. This is important."

Officer Stephanie Hart groaned, and got the attention and her friend, Danny Novak.

"Problem, Steve?"

Hart shook her head. "I'll tell you later."

"You got something, Hart?" Boyd asked.

"No, O. C. I'm just not my best with little kids."

"Is that all?" Boyd teased. "I figured you'd be all over that, being a woman."

"Yeah, that sounds like Hart," came the voice of another officer.

Hart turned toward him. "You sayin' I'm not a woman, Canady? Is that what you're saying?"

Mike Canady laughed. "Never."

"Some parents and parent groups are pushing us to do more," Shoemaker continued, "and Operation ID is one way to do that. At your seats, you have the schedule for staffing in the public schools on Friday and for picking up additional kids you missed on Saturday at the Mason Soccer Complex. We'll have three stations there."

"Isn't this the weekend of the soccer tournament?"

"It is," Samuel Perkins said. "We'll have more traffic on that day than usual, even during soccer season. It's an ideal day for Operation ID, and we're conducting this along with other cities that are targeting their own fall sports tournaments, like field hockey and volleyball."

Hart leaned over again to Novak. "With lots of kids underfoot the whole time."

Novak frowned. "Not your thing, huh?"

Hart shrugged. "I never thought about it, but I can't say I'm into little kids. As they get older, I'm fine with them. But ..." Hart and Novak brought their attention back to Shoemaker.

"Those of you working in the schools on Friday are to be there toward the end of shift. If you're working Operation ID at Mason on Saturday, we'll be sharing duties with personnel from the twelfth precinct. That should reduce the burden on you and allow you to circulate. Uniform of the day is Class B to allow you more freedom. Only officers on shift will be armed. The rest of you are in Class C dress." Shoemaker looked up. "Any more questions?" No one raised a hand. "Remember, this event is a great opportunity to connect with community members and increase our presence in the neighborhoods. Let's place our best feet forward. Questions may be addressed by Sergeant Boyd." Shoemaker turned and nodded to Boyd. "Yours, O.C." Shoemaker and Perkins left the room.

"You heard the captain, people," Boyd said. "We need to make this work as we explain to parents how important it is. Department policy forbids us from taking ID pictures if the parents aren't there or if they haven't already sent in the signed permission slip."

"Any idea of how many people that'll be, O. C., in round numbers?" Novak asked.

Boyd shook his head. "I can only tell you the number for each of the schools—there aren't many sign-ups for the soccer tournament yet. If you want to stop by the office on the way out, I can give you the approximate number for each site. Assume some kids won't show up and others will show up on that day with their parents as walk-ins."

"Got it."

Boyd continued the briefing, detailing the most recent crimes and incidents within the precinct before finishing the briefing twelve minutes after it started.

Danny Novak intercepted his friend as they approached their cruisers. "Are you that bad with kids, Steve?"

"No. I mean, I don't hate kids, but I've never been the motherly type, you know?"

Novak smiled. "Oh, I think you'd be an awesome kick-ass mom. That would keep the boys away from your daughter."

"Already happened with my own mom and me, thank you very much," said Hart. "But no matter, tomorrow should go just fine."

CHAPTER TWO

Alejandro Martinez sat at the head of the dining room table with his wife and two daughters as he blessed the meal and started serving. "The soccer club director told me that some girls are worried about the tournament, Lacey," he asked his younger daughter. "Are you good?"

Lacey, all eight years and seventy-five pounds of her, smiled. "Sure. That's why we practice, isn't it?"

"Way to go, Bug," Lacey's sister Alicia said. "You show 'em on Saturday."

"You're coming?"

"We're all going to be there, Lacey," said Patty Stevens. "This is a really big tournament, and who knows, you might score a goal this time."

Alicia rolled her eyes. "Lacey's a defender, Mom."

"It could still happen."

"I guess we'll find out on Saturday," Martinez said. His gaze caught Lacey squarely in the eye. "The point is to be prepared, right?" Lacey nodded. "So we should get a good rest tomorrow night."

"But don't forget the ID thing at school tomorrow," Lacey said. "We have to do that."

Alicia laughed. "People tell me you shouldn't want an ID so much, Bug. Then you've got to worry about people asking to see it all the time." She looked up at her father. "It's true. People talk about a police state all the time."

"I doubt there's much of a police state in the third grade, Alicia. Plus, Operation ID is a good idea, and Lacey's never had one before."

Patty shuddered. "Do you think it's that important?"

Martinez nodded. "It is, hon. It helps in case something happens—it doesn't mean something actually will happen, and—"

"Oh," Patty said. "I just realized."

"What?" Martinez asked.

"I've got that dental appointment at two thirty. I'm not sure I can get to the school on time. Can you go?"

Martinez's eyebrows furrowed. "I probably can. I need to check my calendar." He turned to Alicia. "You don't need either of us with you, do you?"

"I got it," Alicia said. She pointed to her sister. "Plus, Bug really wants one of you there."

Martinez looked eyes with Lacey. "Guess I'll be seeing you at school tomorrow, Pumpkin."

Hart exited her cruiser and approached her colleagues, Angela Marin and Mike Canady. Several cars idled in the parking lot with adults standing near them and at the school entrance. Hart looked over at the school building and shook her head. "I don't remember elementary schools looking so little when I was in school."

"That's how it's supposed to be, Steve," Canady said. He looked at Angela Marin, the smallest of the three. "Now if Gee had said that, I'd be surprised."

Marin rolled her eyes and turned toward the school. "Enough, Canuck. Let's go inside and get set up." The officers entered the school building and found the office.

"Good afternoon," Marin said. "I bet you can guess why we're here."

The secretary behind the front desk was young and very energetic. "Absolutely!" she gushed. "The teachers are preparing to take their students to the gym. Their parents should be arriving soon, too. How much time do you need?"

Marin looked at Canady and Hart. "Right. Some parents are already outside. We don't need much time, maybe twenty minutes total. Tell the teachers that and if we have trouble, we'll let you know."

"All right." The woman nodded toward an older student, probably a fifth or sixth grader, who was sitting near her. "Mark, would you please escort these officers to the gym?"

The boy stood and smiled, and walked toward the door with Hart, Canady and Marin following. At the gym, he pointed toward three tables at the far end. "They told me you'd be over there." He frowned. "Do you need cords or anything?"

"We should have enough," Hart said. "Can you stay for a bit so we can check?"

"Sure."

The officers unpacked the Operation ID materials and set up their tables, confirming the number of extension cords they carried with them. Hart turned toward Mark. "Do you have an ID already?"

"I got mine last year." The student dug in his pocket and pulled out a mangled card. "But I was hoping to get a new one—my mom left it in the washer once."

"No problem," Hart said. "We can give you a new one to test our equipment."

The boy smiled. "That'd be great."

"Good, give me the card, and you can have a seat while we turn everything on."

The boy sat on one of the chairs to the side of the Operation ID tables and Canady turned to Hart, smiling.

"What?"

"Nothing, Steve. But you aren't nearly as bad with kids as you think you are."

Hart waved Canady away. "Whatever." Five minutes later, Hart had entered Mark's information in the software and was ready. "Come on over, Mark." The boy came over and sat in the chair in front of Hart's station. "Let me get everything lined up first." She fiddled with a few items, pulled the table back a foot, then looked again in the viewfinder. She looked back to Mark. "Got it. Now give me a smile."

The boy complied, and Hart took the shot. She frowned a little at the picture, then smiled to herself. "This is a good shot, Mark. It shouldn't take more than a couple of minutes to print."

Five minutes later, Hart gave Mark his new Operation ID card. "You can head back to the office and tell them we're ready, okay?"

"Yes, ma'am." Mark didn't see Hart wince with the word *ma'am*.

"You're getting older and older here, Steve," said Canady.

"And what does that say about you, Mike?"

"Touché."

The sound of several small and large shoes outside the gym interrupted their banter. The sound stopped as teachers held the students and parents at bay while one teacher entered the gym.

"Are you ready for us?" she asked.

Marin checked with Canady and Hart, who both nodded. "Bring them in."

The crowd of children and their parents was large but orderly, and most of the kids were excited to be getting official ID cards. Each parent or student presented a form to the officer with height, weight and other information, then the students posed for pictures as Mark had done. After the first fifteen minutes, they had settled into a nice rhythm and Hart looked up as a Hispanic man in his thirties with two young daughters walked up.

"Who do we have here?"

"I'm Lacey," one of the girls said, "and this is my sister, Alicia, and my dad." Lacey held the Operation ID form in front of her like a sign.

Alicia was standing quietly, but seemed bored with the whole exercise. *Thirteen*, Hart thought.

"Is this only for you, Lacey?"

Lacey nodded. "Yes. Alicia already got hers at her middle school." Lacey's smile was infectious.

"May I have the form, please?"

"Yes," Lacey said as she handed the form to Hart. "My mom had to sign it because we have different names from our dad."

Hart glanced at the form, noting "Lacey Stevens" as the girl, Patricia Stevens as the mother, and Alejandro Martinez as an authorized guardian. She looked up at Lacey. "That doesn't matter, Lacey. What matters is that you get your new ID card. Are you ready for that?"

"Yes, ma'am," said Lacey, and Hart heard Canady chuckle.

"Good," Hart said. "Let me enter this information into the system so we can take your picture." She glanced again at Alicia. "And you got yours today, Alicia?"

Alicia was suddenly attentive, and she smiled. "Yes, ma'am. I go to Eastern Middle, and we finished classes early to get our pictures taken. That way I could stop by Spencer to pick up Lacey." Alicia's friendly manner surprised Hart after her ultra-bored appearance. *What's it like to be thirteen now?*

"That sounds good." Hart entered Lacey's information into the computer. She looked up at the younger girl. "I'm ready, Lacey. Sit over there and I'll take your picture."

Lacey sat in the seat, and Hart noticed her shin guards for the first time.

"Picture on three, Lacey. One, two, three." The flash was minimal and Lacey's smile never faltered. Hart turned to Martinez. "Take a look." Martinez and Alicia looked at the picture and both smiled.

"It looks good," said Martinez. He looked at his younger daughter. "It's a great shot—you'll like it."

"Can I see it?"

"Of course." Hart waved Lacey over.

The little girl saw the picture and smiled. "It looks like me."

Hart, Martinez, and Alicia laughed. "Well, I should hope so," Hart said. "Now, give the machine a couple of minutes and you'll have your ID, which I'll give to your dad, okay?"

"Okay."

"I see you play soccer."

"We both do," Lacey said. "Alicia almost played on a travel team, but she didn't want to practice that much."

"Are your teams playing in the tournament on Saturday?"

"Yep."

Hart smiled. "Well, that's fine. I'll be there too." She handed Lacey the ID card.

"Thank you, ma'am." Lacey looked up at her father. "Do we go now?"

"Yes, Pumpkin," said Martinez. He looked at Hart and smiled. "Thank you, officer."

"No thanks necessary," Hart said. She turned to Lacey and Alicia. "I'll see you girls on Saturday."

On Saturday morning, several officers from the ninth and twelfth precincts worked traffic and crowd control at the Mason Soccer Complex. Two hundred players from a variety of teams and clubs were scheduled to play throughout the day, and the police department thought having Operation ID stations would serve the community. Several precinct captains had also assigned officers to the tournament to strengthen community relations.

Stephanie Hart and several other officers worked the crowd for community relations, meeting parents and players and helping to keep the event safe and family friendly. She was paired with Novak, her friend and last field training officer when she joined the department.

"This event is nice, Steve," said Novak, a tall, very Irish-looking man one year older than Hart.

Hart surveyed the event before turning to Novak. "It is. I didn't know what to expect, but also didn't think it would be a problem. Have there been problems in the past?"

"No. But sometimes people can get out of hand. The biggest issue at these events is parking. Teams and players have to come and go and getting a space is always a hassle."

Hart laughed. "I'm glad we aren't working parking today."

"Not yet, you mean."

Hart and Novak continued walking and interacting with parents and players. As she walked between two fields near a parking lot, Hart spotted Lacey Stevens with her team. Lacey's father appeared to be her coach; he was wearing the same orange T-shirt as the team. *Fathers and daughters,* she thought. Martinez' players listened well to this coaching and cheered at the end of his remarks. Hart smiled then kept walking with Novak, checking out the other fields and their fellow officers.

Hart was walking with Carson Poole during the third round of games when she heard Martinez shouting to his team.

"Pressure, Andy, pressure!" Martinez said, then, "Nice! Way to back him up, Stu!" Martinez turned to the players on the sidelines. "We're on fire!"

Poole suppressed a laugh. "I remember when I played soccer years ago. Not every coach sounded as positive as that guy."

"I got you," Hart agreed. "My dad was an assistant coach for my volleyball team, and he was the most positive of the bunch. It makes a difference."

"Not shouting the right kind of things can't be good, though," Poole added.

"I agree. Some people respond well to shouting coaches if it's done the right way, but I never did." As Hart finished speaking, the coach of the team opposing Martinez shouted at his team.

"Seriously? You couldn't stop one kid who doesn't even dribble that well? I didn't teach you that!"

"Well, there you go," Hart said. "Some kids will like that, but others will shut down when they hear it."

Poole looked over at the sidelines. "Yeah, that other coach just shook his head. He's not impressed with the other guy."

Hart shrugged. "To each his own." Rather than continuing, Hart and Poole stayed to watch the outcome of the game. Ten minutes later, the referee blew the whistle three times, signaling the end of the game, and the teams lined up to touch hands. Right after the teams separated, each coach took their team for a debrief at different ends of the sidelines. Hart and Poole couldn't hear much from Martinez, but the other coach's voice carried from even farther away.

"We came here to show people what we could do," the coach said. "We didn't come here to let other teams walk all over us." The coach was pacing in front of the players. "Now I want you to think about that while we wait for our next game. No score for the other team, no exceptions, got it?"

"Yes, coach!" the players shouted, but any illusion that the players' energy was excitement disappeared when Hart saw their posture—shoulders slumped and trudging away from the bench.

"Did they get beat that badly?" she asked.

Another adult turned to her. "No, they won, 2-1. The coach wanted to end the tournament undefeated with no goals scored against him. It's one of his goals."

Poole's eyes widened. "His team won, and he's like that?"

The other adult rolled her eyes. "Yeah, that's one of his things, too." She shook her head. "I mean, the guy's a smart and competent coach, but you've got to get used to him. My son is the goalie, and he'll get an earful, I'm sure." Hart, Poole and the parent looked over and saw the coach speaking forcefully with the goalie, identified by his gloves and vest. The goalie nodded as the coach spoke, but his shoulders were as slumped as the other players'. When the coach finished, the goalie ambled toward his mother. When he was halfway to them, Martinez intercepted him and placed his hand on the boy's shoulders. He spoke to the boy for less than a minute, and the boy nodded as he had with his coach, but when he and

Martinez parted, his shoulders had risen again. He turned to his mother with a smile.

"What did that other coach say to you?"

Her son turned and looked at Martinez. "He told me I was an outstanding goalie, and that his kids had a tough time getting anything through. He said I should be proud of what I was doing and to keep it up."

This surprised his mother. "Oh. I didn't know coaches talked like that to players from other teams."

"Mr. Martinez does," her son said. "Everybody likes him, plus his team has gotten really good this year. He talks to other players and coaches like that all the time."

"Yes, you did a good job," Poole said. "What little I saw was impressive. You keep it up." Poole and Hart left the mother and son and continued their walk. "How somebody coaches can make all the difference, can't it?"

Before Hart could answer, the other coach's voice shattered the silence again.

"You don't have to talk to my players after games," the man was saying. "I'm working on building a winning tradition here, and I need to be the one to tell them how they do, not you." The coach was agitated, but Martinez was smiling.

"I'd never undermine you, Al," Martinez said. "And I'm sure they listen much more to you than to me."

"So why did you talk to my goalie?"

"Because he did a great job. I had another parent counting. He blocked over fifteen shots on goal, plus those two penalty kicks. That kid was incredible today."

"Fifteen?"

"Yes. *At least*. That's what my assistant coach said. Mind you, that's probably because your biggest defender couldn't play today, but still, to give up only one goal and to block both penalty kicks, he was your savior today."

"I had no idea."

Martinez raised his hands in surrender. "Because you have to focus on the entire game—my assistant only focused on the goal and right around the box. I just wanted your goalie to know how hard we had to work today because of him."

"Well, I …" the other coach stammered, "I still think I should be the one to tell him things and give him instruction."

"I agree. And I told him that if he focused on what you taught him, he'd continue being an excellent goalie." Martinez smiled again. "And that's true, Al—few coaches know more about the goal position than you do. I told the kid something that maybe he hadn't heard a lot, you know?" Martinez' tone was more a question than a statement and the other coach looked up.

"Yeah. I, uh, I guess that's something." He looked in the distance. "Hey, I have to go see my wife."

"Okay, Al. But you remember, we're getting better and better—you watch out for us." Martinez was still smiling.

The other coach smiled for the first time. "Guess that's fair." He continued his walk, and Hart saw Martinez letting out a long breath.

CHAPTER THREE

Hart and Novak arrived at 11:30 at Heaven's Home Restaurant, a common lunchtime spot for them. They entered to the smiles of the proprietor, Ruth Williams, and took the seats she showed them. "What's happening with Sheryl these days?" asked Hart, referring to Novak's wife. "We haven't talked for a few days."

"Same old, same old. There's some weird stuff happening between her boss and the board, but that doesn't affect Sheryl." Novak frowned, then smiled. "I'm smelling something extra good."

Hart laughed. "Smells like Hoppin' John."

"Not something you like?"

"No, and Ruth knows that. So if one of us is getting some, it's you. Hoppin' John is just a waste of good rice to me."

Ruth Williams emerged on cue from the kitchen with a tray. "You both look good," she said. "I've got a few special things for you." As she set the tray onto a stand, she eyed first Hart, then Novak. "Let's see: Hoppin' John for Danny along with a side of ribs." She set the plate and bowl in front of Novak, who was salivating. "And for Little Ms. Stephanie, Mustard Greens with smoked turkey."

"And the cornbread?" Hart asked.

Williams smiled. "Of course." She placed the cornbread between Hart and Novak before sitting down herself with a bowl of Hoppin' John.

"Lester outdid himself with this batch." She shook her head at Hart. "Shame you don't like it, child."

Hart ignored her and took out her fork to start on her greens. "To each her own, Ms. Williams."

The three ate in silence for a few minutes until Williams asked, "So what's been happening with you this week? I've been hearing about child abductions—are they happening here?"

"We hope not," Hart replied. "But with the publicity about cases in the East and Midwest, everyone's sensitized."

"That's right," Novak agreed. "Our captain reminded us that most child abductors are non-custodial parents, but when parents see these horrific stories, they get scared. I get it."

"It is scary," Williams agreed. "When you're a parent, nothing shakes you more than having your children harmed. Seeing your child is like watching your heart run outside your body. When they're harmed, you don't know what to do."

"I'd never downplay that, Ms. Williams," said Novak. "Until I have kids or decide not to, I won't have anything I can say about other parents. That's a hard enough job without people judging you for what you do."

Hart swallowed a piece of cornbread and nodded. "I agree. Parenting is a job that scares me to death. My parents are good people and did a great job with my brother and me, but I have friends from Philly whose parents were a nightmare. Some of them spent more time with my family than theirs because they dreaded going home."

"I can't argue with you on that, Stephanie," said Williams, one of the few people who referred to Hart by her full first name. "Even Lester and I think it's by the grace of God that Harold didn't turn out bad."

Novak laughed. "That was never an issue, Ms. Williams. Harold has been a good young man since he was a boy, and you know it."

"I still worry, day in and day out. That never ends." Williams laughed. "Only until I die—and for several weeks thereafter."

Both Hart and Novak joined in the laughter. "Well, we saw some of those problem parents at the soccer tournament this weekend," Hart said.

"I'm not so sure about that, Steve. I mean there were—" he paused "—okay, some *problem* parents at the tournament, but people parent in all kinds of ways."

"What was wrong with them?" Williams asked.

Novak shrugged. "Well, not so much wrong, as high-strung."

Hart tilted her head. "High-strung might do it, but others were almost out of control." Hart put down her fork. "One of the coaches—who is also a parent—was shouting at his team as if they had committed a mortal sin. Turns out, his team had won the game."

Williams frowned. "Then why was he shouting?"

"He wanted to go undefeated with no goals scored against his team, or at least that's what another parent told us."

"Isn't that unrealistic?" Williams asked.

"It is, though Steve told me his team is exceptional. They won the tournament championship for their age group. I can't say if they had any other goals scored against them by any other team."

Williams frowned. "Well, the coach ought to be happy with his team for that."

"Maybe he is," Hart said. "Another parent confronted him on his behavior, and he seemed to relax afterwards."

"You mentioned that Saturday. What happened?"

"This other coach—the one whose team scored the goal against the first coach—told him how impressed he was and that he should be proud of them. The crazy coach got it."

"I'll tell you what," Novak began, "seeing those coaches and parents, I still doubt I'm ready for kids, though Sheryl raised the issue again a week ago."

Williams slapped the table. "It's time for more Novaks in this neighborhood!" She smiled. "How serious is Sheryl?"

Novak held up his hands. "Wait a minute. I didn't say we were serious, just that she mentioned it again. We're just talking about it. With her job at the library, she has a great relationship with kids and isn't sure she wants to have her own. We're taking it slow."

"After what I saw on Saturday, I'm taking it even slower," Hart said. "Kids are fine, but they still give me the willies. I had pleasant interactions with the kids at Operation ID last Friday, but I didn't have to raise them to be nice."

Novak nodded. "I agree. And I'm glad that other coach handled the situation so well. The last thing we wanted to do was to have to intervene with a coach going off on a player or another parent."

"Right." Hart nodded. "Yeah, I'm definitely not ready for kids, to say nothing of still being unmarried."

"Then don't rush it," Williams said. "When it's right for you, it will be right."

At muster on Tuesday, there was something different in the moods of Sergeant Boyd and Captain Shoemaker, who surprised them by attending muster again. The captain and sergeant engaged in little banter with the officers, even those they had known for over a decade. By the time Boyd strode to the podium, the room was silent.

Boyd scanned the faces of the officers before speaking. "Today's different, people. We—the captain and I—wanted to inform you of a situation in Indiana near the Illinois border. Captain?"

Andrew Shoemaker's energy seemed low as he joined Boyd. "Not much to tell you, people. We've talked about watching out both for pedophiles and for potential child abductors." Shoemaker held up his hand. "Now, we haven't had one, but we've been monitoring several serial child abductors and we heard last night about a case in Indiana." He turned toward the screen, which had changed to a map of Northwest Indiana, from Michigan City to East Chicago. Shoemaker stood by the map. "This man has two trademarks, including taking kids into bunkers, caves and storm cellars. He sometimes bites his victims, but that's not consistent." Shoemaker faced the group again before continuing. "Well, somewhere around here," he pointed to an area east of Gary, Indiana, "is where his latest victim was found. She's alive, but barely. I won't shock you by detailing her injuries, but they're horrific. She's eleven years old and in critical condition, and authorities there think she may have been underground, alone, for a week or more since the perp left the area. She's malnourished, was beaten, and has lots of infections from animal bites. As I said, it's horrific."

Shoemaker was silent again and before he could speak, Carson Poole raised his hand. "You didn't tell us this for our general information, Shoe."

Shoemaker shook his head. "I didn't, Carson—you're right. The reason I'm telling you this is that this particular perp and all other victims were farther east from this victim, in Ohio and other parts of Indiana. But there were other reports of someone trying to abduct girls in Iowa, near Des Moines, in a vehicle that matched the description given by other victims—an old F-150, white, with a pressed-in driver's side door. They haven't recovered the vehicle, but it's possible this perp is moving west, and who knows if he might end up in Port Angel."

"Why here, Cap?" asked Marin.

"This guy has always operated in medium-size cities, places like Dayton, Toledo, and Gary, but he skipped Indianapolis," said Boyd. "Something about medium-size cities, maybe it's big, but not too big, small, but not too small."

"Which means a city of a quarter million people like Port Angel might be a target?"

Shoemaker nodded. "That's the current thinking. With the truck abandoned, the perp is either walking in Iowa, or he bought another vehicle. There's no evidence to connect any car or truck sales to this truck. It's not a dead end, but we can't do much with what we've got."

Boyd returned to the podium. "The victims they've found before have sometimes had bite marks or been beaten, but few have been sexually assaulted."

"Small consolation," Hart said.

"Agreed," Boyd said. "These kids have been through enough even without a sexual assault, and what they've gone through might still constitute sexual assault regardless of whether it's also rape."

"We're worried about this guy coming here?" Marin asked. "How are we supposed to handle that?"

Shoemaker sighed. "The best way we know how—by being vigilant, engaging the community, and being ready for another Operation ID once the public hears of this little girl. It shouldn't take more than a day or so before it hits and you see interest peak again, and I for one, am happy to hold more of these events if it gives us valuable tools to recover missing kids."

"We all are, Shoe." Boyd returned his attention to the other officers. "And that goes for all of us. We'll send you copies of the info on the perp. Even though we have nothing specific we can follow up on, this has become a national priority. The FBI will share everything it gets." Boyd paused. "We could discuss other minor things this morning, but I don't want to. I just want you to do what you can to protect our kids. Dismissed."

Chapter Four

Spool had just left work when he picked up the newspaper. He didn't read them often because of the big words in some of them, but something compelled him to pick up this one. He bought the paper from a vendor and walked back to his new-old truck. The headlines never changed: something stupid from politicians in Washington, or in the state capital. *Geez, are people in every state capital in America a bunch of idiots?*

He flipped the paper up and glanced at the article below the fold. "Abducted Child Clinging to Life," and the complete story about that girl in Indiana. Spool sighed as he climbed into his truck. He threw the paper in the passenger seat. *Why couldn't she understand what I was trying to do?* Still, Spool felt bad about what happened. That wasn't the way he wanted to get to know her. Maybe he'd do better in Port Angel. He remembered the other girls he had before the last. They weren't happy when he met them. *Didn't they deserve better? Didn't they deserve me?*

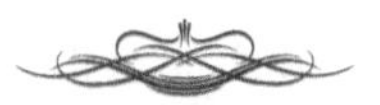

Hart finished making the last few punches in the pliable leather for the wallet. She knew Boyd would like it since he commented so much about the one she made for Novak's last birthday. Boyd hinted about it without mercy until Hart said she'd consider it, knowing all along she'd make one for him. She had the television on for background noise and had strapped on her sewing palm when the news report distracted her.

"Another tragedy today reported from outside Gary, Indiana. A young girl discovered yesterday has died of exposure and her injuries. We believe her to be the latest victim of a serial child abductor who remains on the loose, and police have few clues to go on. WRBL reporter Sandy Morris joins us from Gary. Sandy."

Hart put down her work and watched the report. The girl who had been in critical condition: she's the one who died. *Eleven years old. What was I doing at eleven—deciding if I still wanted to play with dolls or not?* Her telephone interrupted her.

"Hello."

"Steve, Danny here. There's a news report on and—"

"I have it on now, Danny. That's the same girl, isn't it?"

"I'm sure of it. Sheryl knew nothing about the case, and it hit her hard."

Hart sighed. "She's not the only one. I can barely remember being eleven, but I wasn't worrying about being raped and killed by a monster. This shouldn't happen to anybody, Danny."

"I agree," Novak said. Hart sensed the strain in her friend's voice. "This just brings into focus how important our work is. I hope to God this guy doesn't come to Port Angel."

"It's got me down, too." Hart paused. "Hey, go on back to Sheryl, Danny. We'll talk tomorrow."

"I will. You gonna be okay?"

"Sure. I've got ways to cope. I'll see you tomorrow." Hart hung up the phone and looked at the leatherwork, knowing the distraction wouldn't be enough. She took off the palm and placed her leatherworking materials in a container to start again the following day. Hart glanced at her athletic bag by the door, searching her memory for the dojo schedule. Remembering the dojo should be open until 9:00 p.m., she put on her shoes, grabbed her bag and walked to her car.

Twenty-five minutes later, she parked by Sunrise Kenpo Academy in the Uptown North neighborhood and climbed the stairs to the second floor. Mitchell Street, the Sensei, was teaching an advanced class in forms and escape techniques in the main room of the dojo. Hart removed her shoes and bowed before entering the room.

Street locked eyes with her and frowned, then called up one of his advanced students to continue the class. He waited for Hart and caught her before she entered the equipment room, which contained a universal weight machine, a bike, two heavy bags and a speed bag. "This is a surprise. I thought you weren't coming in until Saturday's workout."

"Yeah, about that. Look, Mitch, do you mind if I go crazy on the heavy bag tonight? I promise to pay if I break it."

Street frowned again. "That bad?"

"That bad."

"Uh huh." Street nodded. "Then it must be these child abductions and the fear that they might start in Port Angel."

Hart nodded. "No one ever said you weren't a good cop."

Street leaned against the wall. "Lee and I didn't have any kids, but I understand as much as I can about kids being abducted and treated like this. That's why I was never comfortable in juvenile when I was a detective." He looked up. "You want somebody to spar with?"

Hart shook her head. "No. I just don't want anyone to judge me if I lose it tonight."

Street pushed off the wall and laughed out loud. "Not me. I'm the last person to judge you." Street stepped aside and gestured toward the heavy bag. "Have at it."

Spool lifted the hood of his Dodge Ram, looking at the belts and alternator, anything to appear natural. He didn't know what or who he was looking for, but felt that middle school was the proper level. They were more likely to understand what he was trying to do, even though none of them had yet.

I should tighten that belt. The last thing he wanted was for people to hear noise from his alternator or from a belt slipping as he drove. Lying under the radar was part of the plan. As he weighed his options, the school bell sounded and kids ran for their buses.

Spool grew confused and overwhelmed as he watched the kids. How to pick someone out when there were so many of them? He scratched his head and saw that one of the school buses didn't line up in front of the school, but was off to the side. Several kids walked toward that bus, including a girl of about thirteen, not too old, but old enough. She might be just right. Spool closed the hood of his truck and kicked the engine over. The buses left in a long line, and the bus he was trailing left last, turning left out of the parking lot. Spool noted the number and followed at a discreet distance. The bus turned onto Central Avenue at the second intersection, then continued for several blocks before turning left on Twelfth. Spool was surprised that there were no bus stops for so long, and before he figured out why, the bus flipped on its turn signal, entering the parking lot of Spencer Elementary School. That made no sense to him, but Spool stayed in his car and parked across the street, raising the hood of his truck again. The girl he had been watching and three boys got off the bus and stood at the curb along with a teacher or aide. Fifteen minutes later, the school bell sounded and screaming elementary kids left the school. A little girl ran up to the thirteen-year-old and took her hand, and they walked to another bus. Spool didn't know what this meant, only that he needed to follow the older girl again.

With her little sister in tow, this could be two for the price of one.

CHAPTER FIVE

Andrew Shoemaker liked his office the way it was: formal with a large desk and conference table, yet informal with its scarred leather sofa and his disheveled desk surface. He sat in the overstuffed chair while Lt. Samuel Perkins reclined on the sofa.

"I've known you a long time, Shoe," said Perkins. "You're not a poker player."

Shoemaker smiled. "That obvious?"

"To me, and to anyone who looks at you. You want to talk about it?"

Shoemaker shook his head and looked away. "You already know." Shoemaker stood and walked to the window, which looked out on the parking lot and neighborhood beyond. "I don't want to live through that again."

Perkins sighed. "You aren't the only one who remembers, Shoe. I had just gotten into plain clothes at that time, working robbery. Her kidnapping brought us all together to work on it, for all the good it did."

Shoemaker's shoulders slumped. "My thoughts exactly." He faced his long-time friend. "You may not remember, but I served on that task force—a young lieutenant in my second year in the command spot."

"I remember."

Shoemaker was surprised, but continued. "We thought we almost had the kidnapper—that we were so close," Shoemaker squeezed his right hand into a fist. "But no. We were too far behind him and that young woman died."

"You aren't remembering the complete story, Shoe, especially the fact that she likely died long before we received the first note, before her family and roommate even realized she was missing."

Shoemaker turned to Perkins. "Are you telling me you wouldn't feel the way I do? Feel that maybe if you were faster, you might have stopped it?" He shook his head again. "And autopsies aren't perfect with estimating time of death, you know."

"As someone who's taught forensics, I agree." Perkins stood and leaned on the corner of Shoemaker's desk. "And yes, I would feel the same way you do. You were in the middle of everything, and the task force members all felt they had failed, so—"

"We did fail, Perk. We failed when it mattered most."

Perkins smiled, suppressing the desire to laugh. "Sorry, Shoe, but being melodramatic won't make a difference either. Nobody failed that young woman, except the man who kidnapped her and left her for dead not knowing she was diabetic. We did everything we could to get to her in time." Perkins stopped, taking a breath. "I'm as sorry as I can be about that, and I feel that every day." He held up his hand. "I know it isn't the same as it is for you and the other task force members, but—" Perkins stopped and frowned.

Shoemaker looked up. "What?"

Perkins shook his head, smiling again. "The task force. I just realized that—"

"I'm the only one left? Yeah, I already knew that."

Perkins nodded again. "That tells me a lot, Shoe. One thing on your mind is what happens if a serial abductor comes to Port Angel. My guess is somebody will look for the members of the original task force, and everybody's going to be looking for you."

Shoemaker shook his head. "That's only part of it, Perk. I remember what that case took out of me—almost everything I had as a cop. I doubt I could go through that again."

"Here's hoping you don't have to, Shoe. But we can hope all we want, but we'll do what we have to if it happens again, won't we?"

"Damn right."

Spool thought he did well tracking the girls. He followed them on the bus and saw where they got off. They weren't paying attention to anything around them other than getting home, less than a block away from the bus stop on Countess Avenue. Once he scribbled the address, he drove away so we wouldn't draw attention to himself. He drove back to his rental house and then to a corner store for a sandwich. He returned to the girls' house at 6:30.

Driving by, he realized he should have been more careful. The younger girl was outside the house with her father, practicing soccer. A small goal stood in the corner of the front yard; the father was dribbling a ball, trying to get the girl to take it from him. She might be too young, Spool thought, but if he wanted the older girl, he'd have to take this one, too.

The father and daughter were enjoying their time together. *Why can't I have that?* Spool thought. Maybe soon.

"Girls, you don't have all morning," Martinez said. He stood near the front door, holding lunch boxes and checking his watch at the same time.

"Lacey, c'mon," Alicia said. "Don't you want to see Julia on the bus? If we don't go now, you'll have to wait for your own bus in an hour!"

"I'm coming!" Lacey grabbed her bookbag and raced through the dining room to her father and sister. She smiled as she grabbed her lunch box. "What did you make me?"

Martinez smiled. "I'm not telling—it's a surprise."

Lacey pouted. "I don't like surprises."

"Yes, you do, Bug," Alicia said. "And do you think it'll be something bad? Let's go."

"Fine!" Alicia and Lacey kissed their father, then launched themselves out the front door. Martinez watched them and smiled as they approached the end of the street. He watched until they went around the curve and were lost behind the trees, then turned back into the house.

CHAPTER SIX

Patty Stevens worked as a secretary for a box factory in the Uptown North section of Port Angel. She and Martinez had a solid schedule for taking care of their girls. Patty left for work, arriving before 7:00 a.m., and Alejandro got the girls up for school before leaving for his job, which started at 8:30. Patty arrived home before Alicia and Lacey got off the bus from Spencer Elementary, so neither girl had to be home alone, and they always had adult supervision.

Patty produced five reports for her bosses, entered payroll data before sending it to the payroll company, and made several calls to offices in other states to schedule deliveries. She was looking forward to a quiet evening at home.

She changed her clothes and grabbed a soda from the refrigerator before sitting at the kitchen table to look at the mail. A few bills, junk mail, and a new lingerie catalog. She paged through the catalog, then remembered they were saving for their vacation, and that Alex was right: there was nothing in there she had to have. She flipped on the television to pass the time as she waited for the girls and got caught up in a talk show. When the show broke for a commercial, she realized it was after four o'clock; the girls were usually home by 3:30.

Puzzled, Patty called Martinez at work, something she did rarely. He picked up after the third ring.

"Hey, Patty. What's up?"

"I'm not sure. I got home forty-five minutes ago, and the girls aren't here."

"Even now?" Martinez' voice rose. "It's after four o'clock. Did you call their schools?"

"Not yet. I thought I'd call you first. Was everything all right this morning?"

"Same as always. Look, can you call the schools from home? I don't have the numbers here. I'm sure it's nothing, but I'll be home as soon as I can."

"Okay." Stevens hung up the phone and looked at the refrigerator, searching for the telephone numbers for Spencer Elementary and Eastern Middle. Since Spencer closed later, she checked that number first, then picked up the kitchen phone. But before she could dial, she heard the double dial tone that told her she had a voicemail. Stevens logged into the voicemail and entered her passcode. In five seconds, a robotic voice began.

"This is a call from Eastern Middle School for the parents of Alicia Stevens. We note that Alicia is not present in school today. When she returns, please remember to bring a note explaining her absence to the central office at the school. If you have questions, you may call the office during normal school hours, 7:00 a.m. to 3:00 p.m., Monday through Friday." The voice asked if the parents wanted to leave a message, but Stevens was too stunned to remember what it said. She dialed the number again to be sure of what she heard the first time, but every word caused her to slump more against the kitchen counter. Before she could hang up the phone, she heard another double dial tone: another message. Stevens pressed in the passcode.

"This is a call from Spencer Elementary School for the parents of Lacey Stevens. We note that Lacey is not present in school today. When she returns, please remember to bring a note explaining her absence to the central office at the school. If you have questions, you may call the office during normal school hours, 8:00 a.m. to 4:00 p.m., Monday through

Friday." Stevens dialed Spencer's number and reached the principal, who was preparing to leave.

"Spencer Elementary."

Stevens caught her breath first. "Hello, I'm ..." she began, then started to cry. "This is Patricia Stevens and my daughter Lacey wasn't in school today, and—"

"And you got one of our robo-calls?" the principal said. "You don't have to worry about that. Just send a note explaining her absence so we can document it."

"I understand that. But we sent Lacey to school today. Her father saw her and her sister walking toward the bus this morning."

"Today?"

"Yes. We don't understand what could have happened. Was Lacey really not there today?"

"And she's not home with you now? Could she be with her father?"

"He's at work. Our other daughter was absent too, and we sent them both to school."

"Okay. Let me sit down." Through the phone, Stevens heard the principal take a deep breath. "When did you send them to the bus stop? I'm checking the records now to make sure we're accurate, but if we made the call, she must have been absent. But that's not what worries me. If she wasn't in school today and she's not home with you, where is she?"

"And where is Alicia?" Stevens said. She stood more upright, saying, "I need to call my husband."

"I still want to check the records," the principal began.

"I can call on my cell while you're checking that." Stevens didn't wait for the principal to respond before pressing her speed dial for Martinez. He answered on the first ring.

"Patty. What did you find?"

Stevens caught her breath. "Honey, we have a problem."

"Nine-one-one, what's your emergency?"

Stevens held back tears. "It's my girls—they're missing. I mean, they didn't get to school." Stevens paused. "I'm sorry. I just can't think straight."

"That understandable, ma'am. I have your address as 1622 Countess Avenue, Port Angel. Is that correct?"

"Yes."

"We can get someone out to speak with you, ma'am, but why don't you tell me what happened?"

"Well, it's my daughters. They never got home from school. I mean, the schools said they never got there. But we sent both of them this morning, and now—"

"I'm with you, ma'am," the operator said. "Can you give me your name please, and more information, and we'll do what we can."

Stevens started again, but the more she tried to talk, the more she sobbed. "I'm sorry," she said. "I don't know what to do. They're my babies and I have to find them!"

"Is there anyone else there with you, ma'am? I realize this is hard on you."

"My husband is on the way."

"Good. Tell me when he gets there. Now, please tell me your name and the names of your daughters."

"Uh, I'm Patricia Stevens. My daughters are Alicia and Lacey. Um, Alicia is thirteen and Lacey is eight."

"Okay. And they're not home, but did you also say they didn't get to school? I want to be sure of what you told me."

"Yes. I just got home and had calls from both schools saying they didn't go to school today. But we sent them both to the bus stop."

"Right," the operator said. "What else can you tell me: what schools do your daughters attend?"

"Well, our daughter, I mean Alicia, attends Eastern Middle School, and—"

Martinez flung the door open and rushed to his wife, who started crying again and handed the phone to Martinez

"Ma'am? Are you still there?"

"Hello?"

"Hello. Are you Mr. Stevens?"

"Martinez. But I'm the girls' stepfather."

"Can you tell me anything else? What schools do they attend? Your wife said one daughter attends Eastern Middle School, and—"

"Lacey attends Spencer Elementary. I saw them leave the house at seven this morning and walk toward the bus stop. I didn't see them get on the bus, but then I never do. Alicia, the thirteen-year-old, is very responsible, so we never worried about them." Martinez' eyes filled with tears and he cleared his throat. "We got calls from their schools earlier today, but they came to our home phone, so we didn't know the girls were missing until my wife got home."

"Could they be at another home, maybe a neighbor or other friend?"

"I don't think so, but hold on." Martinez covered the receiver. "Babe, can you call the neighbors to see if they saw the girls today?"

"But why would they go somewhere else and not go to school?"

"Patty, work with me, here. The lady on the line asked me—we should check it out."

"Okay." Stevens took Martinez' cell phone and started making calls.

Martinez took his hand off the receiver. "Sorry. My wife is going to make the calls, but it makes no sense. It's odd enough that they might go somewhere after school instead of home, but why didn't they get to school in the first place?" Martinez looked at his wife on the phone and moved farther from her, turning away. "Can you call the hospitals just to make sure? I mean, if the girls were hurt, a hospital would have called, wouldn't they?"

"I'm sure they would have, sir, but that's a good idea."

The 911 operator entered the call information into the department-wide database, and a special ping notified Kat Neely at the ninth precinct. As she read the notice and transcript, Neely looked up and saw Danny Novak standing near her desk with his eyebrows raised. Neely silenced her microphone. "Two missing kids."

"What happened?"

"Two girls didn't show up for school, but the parents only found out when they got one of those robo-calls from the school."

"I don't like the sound of that."

"Neither do I. They're still on the line with the center, but we're getting the call. As far as I can tell, the father is on the line now, and his wife is calling friends of the girls, but he's not optimistic."

"Should we get rolling now?"

Neely shook her head. "The center hasn't released the call yet, but I think we ought to kick this upstairs now."

"Perk is here."

"Can you get him? I need to be ready for the transfer."

"I'll get him, but I don't know how to tell him—this may be his worst nightmare."

CHAPTER SEVEN

Samuel Perkins saw Novak standing in his doorway. He frowned when he saw Novak's expression. "You must have something for me, Danny. Come on in."

Novak entered the room, looked at the paper in his hand, then back up at Perkins. He extended his arm, gave the older man the paper and waited. Perkins took the paper, read it, consulted Novak's eyes, then read it again.

"You think it's started here?"

"Can't tell you, sir. It's possible. Kat and I felt we needed to tell you about it."

Perkins sat back in his chair, then sat erect again. "We can't waste time here, Danny." Perkins picked up the phone and dialed. "Paul," he said, referring to the shift supervisor. "I need you in my office: something big. Right." He hung up the phone and turned back to Novak. "I'll call Shoe, plus we need to get people out to the family now. Go out there with Andrews, Danny. We'll send out the detectives later depending on what Andrews says." He searched Novak's face. "You up for that?"

"Sure. It's a little out of my line, but I'm ready."

"I was hoping you'd say that." Perkins picked up the phone again "I'll call Shoe now. If Andrews comes in while I'm on the phone, fill him in."

Perkins continued the call to Andrew Shoemaker and answered the few questions he could. Paul Andrews appeared in the doorway and Perkins waved him in as he finished his call with Shoemaker.

"Did Danny fill you in?"

"Not completely, but something about a child abduction?"

Perkins shook his head. "Not sure it's that yet, Paul, but we're taking it seriously even though they were just reported missing minutes ago. You and Novak need to go there first and check in with the parents. As I told Danny, I want you to assess what we need, then bring in the detectives as necessary."

"Got it," said Andrews, an eighteen-year veteran with a strong reputation. He looked at Novak. "Let's go in two cars, Danny."

Perkins stood. "There's a good chance Captain Shoemaker will meet you there. He wants to be involved in this from the beginning."

Novak frowned. "Isn't that odd, bringing out the big guns so early?"

"Not for Shoe," Perkins said. "I'll fill you in on that some other time, but the captain will be there from jump, and while he rarely gets in the way of uniforms and detectives, he'll have a hard time backing off this one. Be patient with him."

Novak and Andrews looked at each other, confused, but nodded and left for their cars. As they left the office, Perkins deflated again, and wondered how to keep Shoemaker focused and undamaged if the worst were to happen.

Novak and Andrews arrived at the Stevens and Martinez home twelve minutes later after conferring once more with Kat Neely. Martinez was out of the house and walking toward the cruisers before they stopped.

"Have you found them? Our girls?"

Novak saw the stress in the man's posture. "Not yet, sir. We're here to get more information and to start the process."

"Shouldn't you be out looking for them, instead of being here?"

"We have to know where to look first, sir—that's why we're here. I'm Sergeant Andrews, and this is Officer Novak. We're in the first group that you'll meet with before we involve other officers and detectives." Novak looked behind Martinez to the house. "May we come inside and speak with you?"

Martinez shook himself. "Oh. Sure. Come on in." He led the way through the front door and pointed to a woman. "This is my wife, Patty Stevens. Honey, these—"

"Have you found our girls?" Stevens interrupted. Not seeing the answer with either Novak or Andrews, Stevens slumped. "What are we going to do?"

"Ma'am, we're Sergeant Paul Andrews, and Officer Danny Novak. We'd like to review the information you gave us and ask more questions so we can focus our search. It won't help to start looking with no plan in mind."

"And the sooner we can start that, the better," Novak added.

"Please have a seat," Martinez said.

It took only five minutes to confirm everything Kat Neely had given them from the original report. Novak wrote as quickly as he could while Andrews questioned the parents. Andrews had a composed manner that kept the stressed parents calm.

"You've said neither girl would ever do something like this, or never has in the past," Andrews said. "Do they have any friends they spend time with from school, sports, or other people we can call?"

"We've called many of those people already," Martinez said

"Can one of those parents come over and be with you now?"

"What do you mean?" Stevens asked.

"This is stressful for the two of you," Novak continued. "It might help if another parent who understands could be here to support you."

Martinez pressed his hand on his wife's shoulder. "That's a good idea. Why don't we call Marian?"

"Okay." Novak could barely hear Stevens' voice.

Andrews stood. "Mr. Stevens, can—"

"Martinez."

"Sorry. Martinez. Can you show me where you last saw the girls? You said you watched them walk toward the bus stop. I'd like to walk in that direction to see what we might find."

"Sure. I already walked that way after I got home, but I didn't know what to look for."

Martinez led Andrews out the door and down the street. Novak turned back to Stevens. "Now, ma'am, you said you've called lots of the girls' friends. What about other people whose kids use the same bus stop?"

"There aren't any."

Novak frowned. "There are no other kids in this neighborhood who use that bus?"

"Not that one," said Stevens. "It's the middle-school bus. There are no other middle-school students in this block."

"But your younger daughter is in elementary school."

"Right. She goes to the middle school and catches a bus from there to her elementary school. We do that so Alicia can travel back and forth with Lacey. Parents can request that if they have kids who attend different school levels so they don't have to wait for two different buses with their kids."

"I wasn't aware of that."

"It's made it easier on us since we both work." Stevens paused. "Until now." She looked at Novak. "I mean, if Lacey had to wait for her own bus, she wouldn't be missing along with Alicia."

"We can't be sure of that, ma'am," Novak said. "We need to focus on finding your girls as soon as we can. That's why Sergeant Andrews went with your husband to walk the street and the neighborhood. They may find something that will help us."

Novak put on a brave face, and Stevens kept avoiding his eyes until she looked at Novak square in the face, shocking him. "You think something terrible has happened, don't you?"

Novak sighed. "I don't know what's happened, and I won't make any assumptions about what kids will do or won't do. But nothing is off the table, either difficult things or innocent things." Novak smiled. "Our job is to prepare for the worst and hope for the best."

Stevens chuckled as she wiped her forehead. "My father always says that." She looked up. "I should call them. They should know what happened."

"Why don't you do that now?"

Stevens picked up her cell and called her parents. Novak left the room to give her privacy. He waited alone, thinking, before he called his wife.

"Hey, Sheryl. Listen, I'm at the home of a family, and their girls are missing."

Novak heard the intake of Sheryl's breath. "Did somebody take them?"

"We're not sure. Paul Andrews is here with me and is talking to the father. The mother is calling her parents for support." Novak looked at Stevens, who was trying hard to hold it together as she spoke on the phone. "Anyway, I just wanted to call you. This just hits you in the gut."

"Me too. Call when you're on the way home. Should I hold dinner?"

"Don't bother. Food will be the last thing on my mind when I get home."

"I hear you," Sheryl said. "I love you."

"Love you, too." Novak hung up the phone.

"Were you talking to your kids?" Stevens asked.

"Me? Uh, no. I was talking to my wife, to let her know why I hadn't come home yet."

"You aren't on duty?"

"Officially, I should have left two hours ago."

Stevens' face fell. "Sorry."

"You have nothing to be sorry for, ma'am. This is what—"

Andrews and Martinez reentered the house, looking grim. "Nothing outside to go on, Danny." Andrews gestured toward the outside with his arm. "There's a hundred and fifty feet, more or less, between the edge of the hedge and trees and the bus stop. That's not much space for something to happen, but there also isn't anywhere else they could have gone in between the house and the bus stop except for other houses. Can you contact those families?"

"Sure. You gonna make the call?"

Andrews looked at Martinez, who moved closer to his wife.

"Already did. Shoe should be here shortly. Perk is forming the team, and they'll be here soon, too."

Stevens looked at her husband and back to the officers. "What's going on?"

Andrews and Novak shared a glance, and Novak was ready to speak as Martinez sat next to his wife.

"They're going to call in an official notice that the girls may have been abducted," Martinez said. "I don't remember all the stuff Sergeant Andrews said, but there's a whole procedure they're going to follow. This means there will be a lot of people here really soon."

Stevens leaned against her husband. "And that's a good thing, right?"

"We certainly hope so," Novak said.

CHAPTER EIGHT

ndrew Shoemaker arrived at the Martinez and Stevens home thirty minutes later. He stopped the car three houses away and stretched his frame out of the car. He looked skyward, then at the police vehicles, noting one officer who was part of the door-to-door canvas of the neighborhood. Police were questioning people in houses near both of the girls' schools at the same time and would report to the command center once it was established. He also received a report that neither Lacey nor Alicia had ridden their buses on that day after a quick call to the school district transportation center.

Shoemaker waved to two officers before approaching the front door. Paul Andrews opened the front door.

"Captain."

"Paul." Shoemaker inclined his head toward the house. "How is it going so far?"

Andrews shook his head. "It's been tough, Captain. The mom is just barely holding it together. Her, uh, mother came over to help."

Shoemaker frowned. "Something tells me she isn't making things better."

"I didn't say that, Captain. But the first thing she did was lay into the father—stepfather, I guess—for not walking the girls all the way to the bus stop. Her rant took ten minutes, and it pushed the mood in the wrong direction. It's calmer now, but I'm guessing she'll lay into you when you go in."

Shoemaker shrugged. "I've got big shoulders, Paul."

"You'll need them."

Andrews opened the door, leading Shoemaker to Alejandro Martinez and Patty Stevens and to an older woman sitting with Stevens. Before Andrews could speak, Shoemaker offered his hand to Patty Stevens. "I'm Captain Andrew Shoemaker, commander of the ninth precinct."

"Thank you for coming over, Captain," Martinez said. "This is my wife Patty and my mother-in-law Clarise. The last few hours have been difficult."

Patty Stevens just nodded as her mother's face shifted from neutral to a scowl. "Have you found them yet? Why are you here when the girls are out there somewhere? Or should I tell my husband that the police in this city don't care about missing children?"

Shoemaker ignored the dig. "May I sit?"

"What?"

"May I sit?" Shoemaker repeated. "I'd like to speak with you."

Patty Stevens stood. "I'm sorry. Where are my manners? Please sit down. May I get you something to drink?"

"Not at all, ma'am," Shoemaker said. "And I'm fine." He smiled. "I'm here to tell you what is being done and what our next steps will be. We don't want there to be any secrets between us."

"Go on," Clarise Jones commanded.

"My officers are conducting a house-to-house canvas of this neighborhood—every house and every other structure, such as garages and sheds. They're doing the same thing in the neighborhoods around their schools: Spencer and Eastern, right?" Martinez and Stevens nodded.

"We need to issue an Amber Alert, but I want to explain what that means to you."

"What do you mean?" Martinez asked. "Doesn't that mean that you tell the media that the girls are missing? Is there something else to it?"

"That's the basic idea. But we also issue pictures of the girls, and make sure we contact agencies that need to know about their disappearance. That includes any other important relatives, do you see?"

"I'm here," Jones said. "And my husband knows, too. Who else do you need to contact?"

Novak cleared his throat. "The birth father, for one. We've tried to call him and have a unit going to his home now."

"Him? Why?" Jones asked.

"Because he is their birth father," Novak replied. "And since there's no restraining order on file or any other legal action against him, there's still the possibility that he may know something about the girls, or that he has them."

Clarise Jones snarled at Shoemaker. "I don't like him being contacted. He was never a great father."

"*Mom*," said Stevens.

Jones looked at her daughter, then at Martinez, then back to Novak and Shoemaker. "I have a right to my opinion."

"Yes," Shoemaker said. "You do. What we want to do is ensure that Ms. Stevens and Mr. Martinez know what's going on and have a contact they can call." Shoemaker ignored Clarise Jones's frown as he continued. "We'll determine the primary contact tomorrow, but in the meantime, here's my personal number that you can call." Shoemaker took two business cards from his shirt pocket and gave them to Patty Stevens, who passed one to her husband.

"Another thing I wanted to tell you," Shoemaker continued, "is that once the Amber Alert goes out, there will be a lot of attention paid to your daughters, not just by the police, but by the media and curious onlookers."

"What do you mean?" Martinez asked.

"Media outlets are an important way for people outside law enforcement to know what's happened and to help us. This is an important partnership we have with the media. We couldn't run an Amber Alert without them. So expect to have reporters calling you and asking for statements or for interviews." Shoemaker paused and lowered his voice. "It's your choice whether to speak with the media or not. They're going to expect it, but you decide what you are comfortable with."

"Might it get our girls back faster?" Stevens asked.

"It might," Shoemaker said. "Your speaking with the media might encourage people to come forward if they have information about the girls or think they do. It's our job to investigate what those people give us to see if it helps."

Martinez looked at his wife and winced before facing Shoemaker again. "But it's possible it will help us, right?

"Yes."

Martinez looked at Stevens again. "I think we should do it, Babe."

"What do you think, Mom?"

"Oh, now you ... never mind," Jones said. "If the captain and Alex think it's a good idea, I guess I agree."

Patty Stevens turned to Shoemaker. "I guess we should talk to them."

Shoemaker stood. "I'm not in charge of media contacts or what they follow up on, but when the Amber Alert goes out, I'll tell our communications people that you're open to talking with them. You can still refuse to talk to anybody. And if you want advice about that, we can consult with Sergeant Andrews—he's one of our department's media experts."

"What do you mean?" Martinez asked.

"Not much. Except I don't trust all people in the media. Sergeant Andrews can try to keep the wolves at bay."

"Could that happen?" Martinez asked. "When two kids are missing? What kind of people are they?"

Shoemaker shook his head. "Mr. Martinez, there are all kinds of people in the world, good and bad. I'm sorry to say that's one reason I have a job." He managed a smile. "Now if you'll excuse me, I'll head back to the precinct and get more people working to get your girls back. Every minute counts."

Chapter Nine

Officer Stephanie Hart rang the doorbell of 1640 Countess Ave, a house at the end of the block, and the farthest from the Martinez and Stevens home. She checked her notes and looked up as the homeowner opened the door, frowning.

"Yes?"

"Good evening, ma'am. I'm Officer Stephanie Hart, and I'm—"

"You're with the rest of the noise and light show down the street, I suppose?"

"Yes, ma'am." Hart turned to point toward the Martinez and Stevens home. "We're investigating a case of two missing children. Perhaps you've heard about it."

The woman's face softened and her lips formed into a giant "O." "I'm sorry. I didn't know." She opened the door wider. "Would you like to come in?"

"Thank you."

The door led into the entrance way through which Hart could see the living room and kitchen. Everything seemed to be in place. *No young children here,* she reflected.

"Would you like to sit?" the woman asked. "I'm Nadine Delaplaine."

"No, Ms. Delaplaine," said Hart, who wrote the woman's name in her notebook. "I'm here to ask whether you know the two girls." Hart took out her phone and opened it to a picture of both girls; she showed it to Delaplaine. "They're Alicia and Lacey Stevens. They live at number 1622."

Delaplaine took the phone and studied the girls' faces. "They're pretty." She returned the phone to Hart. "But I don't know them. I mean, I may have seen them once or twice, but I come into and leave the neighborhood through this corner, so I don't even drive by that part of the street often."

"I understand, ma'am. We're also asking residents for permission to search their homes, just in case." Hart noticed Delaplaine's eyes widen, but the woman said nothing. "We'd like to look into every garage and shed in the neighborhood. We want to see if the girls ran away and hid somewhere close by—we're not assuming you did anything to them. That's standard procedure."

Delaplaine listened and nodded. "Where do you want to start?" She led Hart upstairs to the bedrooms, to the rooms on the first floor and to the small basement. Afterwards, she led Hart to the garage and small garden shed, the only other building on the property.

Delaplaine had her arms crossed when Hart had finished her search. "That's all I need for now, Mrs. Delaplaine. Thank you for your cooperation."

"That's it? That's all you're going to do?"

"In your home, yes. Yours is the fifth house I've gone to and I have a few more before I finish my part of the initial search."

Delaplaine shuddered. "I'm sorry. I didn't mean to get angry at you." She stood straighter and dropped her arms. "I get frustrated when bad things happen."

Hart smiled. "I understand and thank you again."

"Uh ..."

"Yes?"

"Would the family like someone to stay with them? This must be a tough time for the family, especially for the mother."

"Her mother is at the house, so I don't know if they need or want anyone else to come by at the moment. But I'll pass your name along."

Delaplaine smiled. "I'd like that. I want to be helpful."

"Done." Hart left but was surprised by the offer given that minutes ago she didn't acknowledge knowing the family, then she walked to the next house on her list.

Hart and Novak met by their cruisers outside the Martinez and Stevens home twenty minutes later. Hart glanced at the house, then back to Novak. "How are they holding it together? This has got to be tough."

Novak shook his head. "They're both pretty broken up and worried, though I'm not sure having the grandmother here is such a good idea."

"What do you mean?"

"Just a feeling. I could sense the tension between her and the husband, and it didn't get any better when we discussed calling in the birth father."

"That's standard procedure."

"Right. And like I told the grandmother, there is no restraining order, and it's always possible the birth father has the girls."

"Where is he?"

"He's been out of town. He works in shipping for Platts Corporation and traveled with one of their truckers to troubleshoot a problem. Captain's not considering him a person of interest at this point. The guy even gave us permission to search his apartment."

"Did they find anything there?"

Novak smirked at his friend. "Steve, would they tell a lowly patrolman something like that? Nope. My job is to stay here until either the lieutenant or captain, or a sergeant for that matter, tell me to go."

Hart looked around and shivered. "It's cold here."

Novak looked at Hart, then around the house. "It's not, Steve. This is one of those times when the job gets to you."

Hart frowned, peering closer at Novak. "You have a story to tell me?"

"Me?"

"You. Out with it."

"Okay." Novak leaned closer. "When I told Perk about the girls, his entire mood changed. It shocked me."

"Perk?"

Novak nodded. "Yeah. And *nothing* shakes that man. He implied that Shoe had some connections to child abductions in the past, too. Andrews filled me in."

"So you do have a story."

Novak pushed off the cruiser and paced. "The story is more the captain's than mine. According to Andrews, the last time they had a significant child abduction in the city occurred when the captain was a lieutenant, and it didn't end well. Shoe takes the whole thing personally. I saw his face when he was talking to the family a while ago, and I've never seen him so, I don't know, broken?"

"Must have been huge."

"Sounds like it was, and it may have involved Perk, too."

"Are they going to let us in?"

"We'll see." Novak stopped pacing and turned again to Hart. "Anything from your house-to-house?"

Hart flipped out her notebook, flicking through each page, each interaction. "To be honest, no. One woman said something about Ms. Stevens being 'flighty.' That was her word, by the way. Another couple talked about the girls being normal, maybe more respectful than others, but I heard nothing unusual about them." Hart closed her notebook. "The people I talked to either had much older kids or younger. The older girl, Alicia, was the only one from the neighborhood who attended middle school. Is that what you found out too?"

Novak nodded. "That's what the parents said when we got here, what they told Andrews. He walked the whole route to the bus stop with the father." Novak turned and pointed down the street. "There's quite a distance between the edge of the growth over there and the bus stop. The father told us he watched them until they were around the trees, then returned to the house like he always does. Andrews can reconstruct the exact timing for the detectives and search team."

"Between when the father lost sight of them and when the bus would have arrived?"

"Right," said Novak. "That's the time window, and it may be as little as five minutes."

Hart shivered again, then shook herself, embarrassed. "Five minutes. Five minutes until their lives are changed forever."

"I only hope their forever lasts a lot longer."

* * *

Alicia looked up when she heard Lacey pull against the rope holding her to the wall.

"I'm over here, Bug."

"I want to go home!" Lacey cried.

"Shh. Me too, but I don't know how we do that. Let me try to get to you." Alicia wiggled her bottom toward her sister, which was made more difficult because her right arm and right leg were tied to the wall. "Try to come to me, Lacey. Come toward the sound of my voice."

"I'm scared, Alicia!"

Me too, Alicia thought. "I'm scared too, but I'm also mad." She chuckled. "This is the first day I wish I was in school all day."

"What?"

"Never mind, Bug. Keep wriggling." With her last shift, Alicia's left arm bumped into Lacey's right side. "Is that you?"

Lacey used her arm to grab at her sister's left arm and squeezed. "Where are we?"

"I don't know. I've been trying to see, but I'm sure we're in a basement, one without any windows." She stroked her sister's arm. "Do you remember what happened?"

"Um, was it that man?"

"The man whose dog was missing? Yeah, I think that's who it was." Alicia grew angrier. "I remember bending under the truck to find the dog and the next thing, I felt a cloth over my mouth."

"Me too. I didn't see anything."

"It happened so fast, and the next thing I know, I'm waking up in a basement."

Lacey turned from side to side. "I still can't see."

"You will in a minute when your eyes adjust." Alicia squeezed Lacey's arm again. "I was worried about you, Bug." Alicia suppressed her tears. "I knew you were here, but I didn't know if you were okay, so I got real quiet and tried to hear if you were breathing. I was really happy when you talked to me."

The girls were silent, holding each other as best they could. Lacey spoke again. "What are we going to do?"

Alicia sighed. "I don't know. I don't know where we are, or how long we've been here, or even if people are looking for us."

"Won't Mom and Dad look for us?"

"Of course, but do they even know we're gone yet? What if they don't even know we're missing?" She smiled. "I bet Dad's already called in the national guard."

"What does that mean?"

"Nothing. It just means they're going to look for us really hard, and that's what matters. And we have to be strong, too. Can you do that?"

"But I'm scared!"

Alicia gripped Lacey again. "I'm scared too. But once Mom and Dad know we're gone, they'll try really hard to find us. We have to be brave, okay?"

Lacey whimpered and leaned hard against her older sister. "Okay."

But who's going to help me *be brave?*

CHAPTER TEN

Hart arrived at Spencer Elementary at the same time as Detectives Thomas Fair and Sharon Shore. When they entered the outer office and asked to speak with the principal, the front office worker stood.

"Detectives Thomas Fair and Sharon Shore, and Officer Stephanie Hart," Shore said. "We're here to meet with Ms. Leander."

The worker, whose nametag was lying face down on her desk, picked up the phone. "I saw the alert last night. Is this about Lacey Stevens?"

Fair pointed to the desk plate. "Yes, ma'am. And you are?"

The woman looked down. "Oh, Cindy Lewis. This isn't my desk. Mrs. Crenshaw is out sick today."

"Thank you. And yes, we're continuing the investigation into their disappearance—both of the girls. We'd like to start with the principal."

"Right," Lewis said. "I was only thinking of Lacey since she goes to school here. Ms. Leander told us you would be here. Who else would you like to meet with?"

Shore opened her notebook. "Besides the principal, we want to speak with her teacher and the school counselor, and any other people who might know her well, such as specials teachers."

Lewis wrote as Shore was speaking. "Her teacher won't be a problem. Nor will our school counselor." She furrowed her eyebrows. "I'm not sure if the specials teachers know her very well."

"We can ask the principal that, ma'am," Hart said. "Not to worry."

"Okay. Let me call the principal." Lewis punched in two numbers and chatted with the principal while Fair, Hart and Shore shared a glance. Hart wondered how the detectives were making out at Eastern Middle. Before any of them could say a word, Sarah Leander left her office. She held out her hand to the officers.

"I'm Ms. Leander. Where would you like to talk?"

"Anywhere you're comfortable, ma'am," Shore said. "We'll start with you, then speak with the other people once we get finished."

Leander's face was grim. "Fine. Let's go to the conference room." She turned and walked back toward her office, going past it to a room with a conference table and ten chairs arranged around it. She took a seat in the middle of the table and gestured toward the open seats.

Shore took the seat at the end of the table and turned toward Leander. Hart and Fair sat and completed the small U shape.

Shore smiled. "Ms. Leander, I'm sure you're familiar with all of your students in some way, but we also understand if you don't know every one of them as their teachers do. We wanted to get your impressions of Lacey and learn anything we can from you before speaking to her teachers. We're sure they will have the most information."

"I'm sure you're right, Detective." Leander was in her late thirties, with an open face and precise manner. "Lacey's teacher Ms. Crane has worked with her all year and knows her well."

"What can you tell us about her?" Shore asked. "And before you ask, Ms. Leander, this is a preliminary interview about Lacey herself to see what we can learn about her and her family dynamics. We may return for a second round if we develop more questions."

Leander listened to Shore then sat back. "What I can tell you is that Lacey is a smart young lady who enjoys sports, soccer in particular." Leander smiled. "The only time anyone has ever had an issue with her is when she wanted to wear her soccer cleats in school so she wouldn't have to change later for practice. Other than that, she is a model student."

"Would you bring out her records?" Hart asked.

Leander nodded. "Do you want those now, or can it wait?"

"Now is better."

Leander rose. "Give me a minute." She left the conference room, returning three minutes later with a manila folder. She opened it and paged through it. "There may be items I should screen before giving this to you." She looked up. "I'm required to hold certain court records back."

"We understand," Fair said.

Leander finished paging through the file. "But not in this case." She handed it to Shore. "Here you go."

Shore handed the file to Fair, then she turned back to Leander. "Anything in the file spark your memory?"

"Not really," Leander replied. "As far as I can tell, her parents attend parent–teacher conferences after every report period. Her attendance is excellent except for a few bouts with severe colds or something else, and her grades are good. She has no disciplinary referrals." She looked quickly at all three officers. "For students, it's the lack of information in the file we look for."

The officers spoke with the principal for another ten minutes, and once they had heard all she had to say, asked to speak with Lacey's teacher. Leander rose. "Let me get her and I'll take charge of her class while she's here—unless you need me here at the same time."

"No need, Ms. Leander," Fair said. "We can always ask you questions afterwards if necessary."

"Right."

Hart reached for the file as Leander left the conference room. "May I see the file?"

Fair handed it to her. "There's not much in there. As the principal said, it's the lack of bad things that's most important for these kids."

Hart frowned. "How much trouble could they be in at eight years old?"

"I wish that were it, Steve," Shore said. "What we don't want to find in the file is conflict between the parents, or some other person, that sort of thing. That often leads to the kids acting out in school. It isn't the kids who are at fault, it's just tough for them to handle adult problems when they're eight."

"That's what we hope not to see as well," said Fair. He pointed to the file. "This file is a nice clean one."

Hart nodded. "I remember Lacey. She came to Operation ID with her sister and father, and she was so excited to get an ID. She was even wearing her soccer shin guards for the picture."

"She sounds like a nice kid," Fair said, and looked at his colleagues.

Betty Crane, Lacey's teacher, appeared in the doorway waiting for an invitation to enter. Fair rose and smiled at her. "Good morning. I'm Detective Fair." He indicated Shore and Hart. "This is Detective Shore, and this is Officer Hart. Please take a seat."

Crane sat, nervous, and Hart smiled at her. "Detectives Shore and Fair are easygoing, Ms. Crane. You can relax." Crane laughed nervously and waited.

"Thanks for coming, Ms. Crane," Fair continued. "We are conducting this first investigation to learn more about Lacey Stevens. The more we learn about her, the faster we can get her back to her parents."

"You don't suspect anyone at the school, do you?"

Shore shook her head. "No, but this is standard procedure. For example, what if Lacey is close to another child in school in your class or someone else's? She may have chosen to visit that person's house yesterday and got lost."

Crane nodded, frowning. "I suppose that makes sense." She raised her chin, pointing at Lacey's file. "Everything you need to know is in that file. Lacey is an excellent student, very energetic and easy to work with. I can't think of any children who don't get along with her."

"Would you say the same thing regarding the teachers?" Hart asked. "How about her specials teachers, gym, music, those?"

Crane shrugged. "Same thing. Lacey is a very enthusiastic learner. She's also very athletic, so the gym teachers just think the world of her. I'm in the classroom with the art teacher, and Lacey's as engaged as anyone else. I can't say if she has any talent for art or music, but there are no red flags."

"Is everything good at home?" asked Fair.

"I'd say so. I've met her parents at every parent–teacher conference so far, and they're supportive and very involved. In fact, only about half of our parents come every time. Lacey's always do. I wish all parents were like hers." Crane caught herself. "I don't mean that she's perfect—she's just a kid. She can get annoyed by a boy teasing her, things like that. But I can always count on Lacey to be pleasant, work hard, and have a smile on her face when she goes home."

Shore sighed. "If only that was enough to keep her safe."

The officers met again at their cruisers before leaving Spencer Elementary. Fair was shaking his head. "Nothing in this situation encourages me, I gotta tell you."

"I agree," Shore said. "We have little—if anything—to go on." She looked up. "We need to focus more on the family, maybe enemies, or conflicts in the past. What do we know about the birth father?"

Hart opened her notebook. "Danny told me they located him in Clearview. He's been there for a while. Mr. Stevens doesn't spend a lot of time with the girls. He seems to have moved on."

"What kind of guy is he?" Fair asked.

"That I can't tell you. I can only tell you he was way out of town and not involved in this. We have to look elsewhere."

Shore looked back at the school. "And something tells me that won't be here."

"Like the Middle School for the older girl?" asked Fair.

Shore shrugged. "I see no reason Lacey would have been targeted. She may have been in the wrong place at the wrong time."

"I wonder if both of them were," Hart said. She looked up at frowns on both Shore's and Fair's faces. "I don't know that, you understand, but don't you think something would have come up with the parents or with Lacey if anything was going on that would lead to this?"

Fair stroked his chin. "Not saying you're wrong, Steve. But if that's the case, we have nothing to go on, unless a neighbor saw something yesterday morning. That's not what's happened."

"Nothing at all?" Hart sighed. "Then you're right, that's not good." She shook her head. "I guess I'm just worried about this little girl. She had such a big smile on her face and was so excited to get her ID." Hart turned to Fair and Shore. "Have either of you ever been involved in something like this, a child abduction?"

"Twice," Shore said. "They're never easy and sometimes very messy. It takes a lot out of you even when you're on the outside looking in like I was."

Fair agreed. "So if this is your first one, don't be surprised if you get kicked in the gut a few times. We all go through that and if you feel that way, tell someone."

Hart looked again at Fair. "I take it that advice comes from personal experience." She held up her hand. "And I won't ask you how you got that experience, Thomas, but I promise to take it."

Samuel Perkins consulted officers outside the Martinez and Stevens home before ringing the doorbell. Alejandro Martinez answered. Perkins hadn't met the man before, but he was showing the normal signs of stress: he had bags under his eyes, his hair was unkempt, and there was a general edginess about him like he was ready to pounce on someone or something. Still, he gave Perkins a genuine smile and welcomed him.

Perkins looked at Patty Stevens and her mother. "I'm Lieutenant Samuel Perkins of the ninth precinct. Captain Shoemaker, my boss, is hard at work with the FBI and other agencies trying to find your daughters." Perkins looked around, then indicated a chair. "May I have a seat?"

"Please," said Patty. "We ... we were going to have coffee. Would you care for some?"

Perkins smiled. "Coffee would be nice. I take mine black." He turned back to Martinez and Jones. The older woman was as Andrew Shoemaker had described her: she looked combative and protective of ... what? Was it her granddaughters—her daughter? Perkins could also sense the distance between her and Martinez.

"We have officers continuing our door-to-door canvas near the schools and we've interviewed several teachers and the principals at both schools."

Martinez sighed. "And nothing?"

"No. I could tell you that it's still early, and that's true, but we have little to go on right now." Perkins heard a whimper from the kitchen. "But because of that, we've issued the Amber Alert and will keep searching more and more areas. One thing we wanted from you was articles of clothing we could give to the search-and-rescue dogs—dirty, not clean."

Martinez shot from his chair. "Do you think that will help? I can get you something from each of the girls."

"It's just one tool, Mr. Martinez. The challenge is where to have the dogs begin their search. We'll start here and take them near the place where you last saw them. If they went somewhere on foot, that may be helpful."

"But it won't be helpful if they were taken away in a car," Martinez said, glancing at his wife.

"That's right," said Perkins. "We can't trust the dogs alone to find them. What they may help us do is eliminate areas where we shouldn't look."

"I guess that's something." Martinez turned toward the stairs, then to his wife. "I'm going to get the lieutenant some clothing from the girls." He didn't wait for Patty to acknowledge him.

Perkins turned toward the kitchen and saw Stevens looking out the window. She shook herself and grabbed two mugs of coffee, placing one in front of Perkins and one by her husband's seat. She looked up at her mother. "Mom, did you want some, too?"

"No. Thanks." Jones sat back, looking exhausted. "I'll be drinking a lot of it today. I shouldn't drink too much too early." She looked at Perkins as he sipped his coffee. "You don't seem very encouraged by anything that's happening."

Perkins looked over the rim of his mug, keeping his eyes neutral, then glanced at Patty before he spoke. "I want to stay focused on finding the girls, Ms. Jones. I have a cop's brain. It doesn't relax until things happen I can point to. We aren't there yet."

Martinez returned with a shirt of Alicia's and a pair of Lacey's soccer shorts. "I have one in each hand. Should I keep them separated?"

"We should. Give me a minute." Perkins conferred with the officer at the front door and returned in a minute with two bags. He placed each article of clothing in a different bag and labeled them. He gave the bags to the officer along with instructions before returning to Martinez, Steven and Jones. "Sorry for the interruption." Perkins sat and picked up his coffee. "That gave my coffee a chance to cool down a little, too."

"Sorry."

Perkins smiled. "I'm just a wuss, Ms. Stevens. Don't sweat it."

Martinez took his wife's hand, and she looked at him. Rather than look at her, Martinez addressed Perkins. "We appreciate the police response, Lieutenant. I mean, the Amber Alert, your captain and now you here. It means a lot that you did this for the girls."

Jones was nodding as Martinez spoke. *Maybe they agree on something,* Perkins thought.

"But, and I don't want this to seem ungrateful, but is this what you always do when kids go missing? I would have figured that some missing kids are runaways." Perkins conferred again with both Stevens and Jones silently. "We don't think our girls did that, but I've heard that kids often go missing like that, maybe running away after arguing with their parents. That didn't happen with us."

Perkins put down his coffee and took a deep breath, measuring his words. "This response is different, to be honest. And it's proportional to what we believe the risk *might* be."

Martinez nodded. "I was afraid of that."

"Afraid of what?" Stevens asked. "What are you not telling me?"

"Is this because of the girl from Indiana?" Martinez asked.

Stevens frowned. "What girl from Indiana?"

Jones rolled her eyes and scoffed. "What? Seriously, Patty, did I raise an idiot for a daughter? Don't you know anything?"

Stevens released her husband's hand. "What girl from Indiana? Why won't somebody tell me?"

Martinez looked down. "There was a girl in Indiana. A serial abductor took her, I guess you'd call him." He faced his wife. "She was beaten, and she died, honey. And they think he's coming west."

Stevens' hand flew to her mouth. "Oh, my God." She started rocking back and forth. "Oh, my God." Stevens turned to her husband. "Why didn't anybody tell me?"

"It was on the news reports, babe."

"And it's the reason we moved Operation ID up this year," Perkins said. "Not because of her death, but because of heightened concerns about child safety."

"And you see what all your concern has done," Jones said with a scowl. "Nothing."

Stevens stood up. "We have to find them. I don't know what I'd do if they're really gone, I—"

Martinez took her by the arms. "Patty, we can't do anything if we're not together. We have to keep it together, please." Martinez was crying silent tears. "I promise you, we will get them." He turned to Perkins. "You're going to do that, aren't you?"

"We—I—will do whatever it takes to bring them back. When this is all over, we may talk about my experience with missing children. This is my job, but it's also a calling for many of us. We will do what it takes." Perkins softened his voice. "Your husband is right, Ms. Stevens. Staying as calm and focused as you can will help you and help us."

"I'm not sure if I can do that."

Martinez smiled. "You can, Patty, because you've always worked hard for the girls. You've never let them down before, and you won't start now. I won't, either."

Perkins stood. "Thank you for the coffee. We'll keep officers here at all times and you can always call us for more information or if you want either the captain or me to come back." He pointed toward the front door. "I need to get back out there and see what I can do to keep my promise to you."

CHAPTER ELEVEN

"We have a lot to talk about today, people," said Sergeant Paul Andrews as he convened the afternoon muster. Andrews waited until more of the officers sat before starting, noticing that many of the officers were on edge, expectant. "Either Captain Shoemaker or Lieutenant Perkins will be here today. The missing kids you've seen on the news are occupying much of their time."

Patrick Weiss raised his hand. "Before we look at anything else, Paul, what's the status, and what can we do?"

"Just getting to that, Pat. I'm going to give you a brief report and we'll hear from the people who've met with the parents, people in the neighborhood, and teachers at the girls' schools." Andrews paused. "The first thing I have to tell you is we have no strong leads yet. That's our biggest concern."

"You aren't the only ones," said Ben Gore, a seventeen-year veteran of the force. "And that makes this all the more difficult." He looked at Andrews. "I'm not telling you anything you aren't aware of."

Andrews nodded. "But it's helpful to tell those of you who have less experience with missing children and with child abductions."

"We have to ask, Sergeant," began Susan Elliott, "do we suspect the man who killed the girl in Indiana took these kids?"

Samuel Perkins' voice boomed from the door to the muster room. "We aren't sure, Elliott," he said. "But I want us to go on the assumption that it is. That gives us a sense of urgency, but I'm not saying we don't already have it." Perkins walked to the podium. "Shoe will be here soon. How far have you gotten, Paul?"

"Just starting, Lieutenant," said Andrews. He looked at the assembled officers. "Everybody gets it."

"Okay then." Andrews saw Perkins' eyes as he composed himself. "We've activated the Amber Alert, and Captain Shoemaker has been on the phone with the FBI and Center for Missing and Exploited Children. We've also activated our model procedure, so if you don't know it, familiarize yourselves with it now. Much of it is common sense, but some details are worth looking at again."

Susan Elliott raised her hand. "Can you fill us in on the basics of the timing, and things we need to be looking for, sir?"

Perkins looked back at Andrews. "Paul, why don't you tell them about the family?"

Andrews gave the officers a summary of his interviews with the parents. "They're handling it as best they can. They've called in support from friends and the maternal grandmother. It's no surprise that the longer it goes on, the more difficult it's going to be."

"Search-and-rescue dogs are being deployed as well near the house, but we don't have those results yet," Perkins said. "This has all happened quickly since the parents called."

"Family seems average," Andrews continued. "There are no major family arguments, the girls are well behaved and the older one has always been responsible for her sister in the morning and after school. The father had no reason to worry when they moved out of his sight on the way to the bus stop." Weiss's hand rose. "Pat."

Weiss looked around the room. "I hate to ask this, Sergeant, but might one of the parents be involved? It wouldn't be the first time."

"Lieutenant?" Andrews deferred to his superior.

Perkins exhaled. "We're not going on that assumption, regarding either these parents or the birth father, who was out of town with plenty of witnesses all day. We made more checks on the mother and stepfather, and their activities yesterday were as they always were. Any involvement would have had to be through a third party."

"And if I had to trust my gut," came Novak's voice, "I would say neither of them is involved."

"But no door has been closed yet," Perkins said. "And the parents aren't going anywhere now."

Andrews saw no further questions and returned to the podium. "Regarding the media, the alert went out at 1900 hours. I've been in personal contact with the radio and TV stations, and they've been supportive with their scrolling notices during news programs. I think we'll have great cooperation from them."

KPAR-TV's News Director, Rod Welch, watched Jackie Moore breeze into his office. Moore was the best known of the on-air personalities at the station. Welch knew that Moore was looking to work in a larger market, perhaps even a top ten. Welch didn't mind; Moore's presence had increased ad revenues by over thirty-five percent in the three years since she'd arrived in the city. She was also smart and a good producer, a rarity among many on-air broadcasters. He smiled as Moore sat in front of his desk.

"You're going to like this," Moore said.

"Like what?"

Moore smiled. "What would you say if I got the first exclusive interview with the Martinez and Stevens family?"

"The ones with the missing girls?" Moore nodded with a smile. "I thought they were quarantined."

"Maybe to some," Moore said. "But I got a call through to them."

Welch sat forward and took out a notepad. "What's the angle—on-air appeal?"

"Yep. I spun it as their opportunity to impress upon the people that they want their help in finding their girls."

"And no resistance from the parents?"

"Not if you push the right buttons." Welch continued looking at Moore, who relented. "Okay, it was the grandmother—the girls' maternal grandmother. She pushed it with her daughter, and they outvoted the stepfather."

"What was his opinion?"

Moore shrugged. "I didn't get into it, but I suspect it was just too raw for him, or he didn't want to turn the search into a circus."

"Will it be a circus, Jackie? We don't want our reputation hurt by this."

Moore stood up with another smile. "Rod, you can trust me: KPAR will come out of this smelling like a rose."

Welch sat back, folding his hands across his belly. "And your career won't suffer either, I imagine."

"Well, that I can't say," Moore said. "But don't be shocked if you get a call about my contract."

The television camera panned the front of the house, focusing for a short time on the soccer goal and a bicycle. "The parents inside this house hope their young daughters will be playing soccer and riding this bicycle soon. But for now, they're two very concerned parents," a voiceover said.

The camera opened on Jackie Moore in the Martinez and Stevens living room. "This is Jackie Moore, KPAR-TV, in the home of Patty Stevens and Alejandro Martinez, parents of two girls who've been missing since yesterday—Lacey, eight, and Alicia, thirteen." Moore turned to Patty Stevens. "Mrs. Stevens, I know this is a hard time for you. How are you holding up?"

Patty Stevens fidgeted in her seat on the couch. "It's been tough, you know. They're both so young, and every parent worries about their kids, but you're never really prepared if something happens."

"I see," said Moore. "Now, the Amber Alert gave details on what the girls were wearing when they left for school, but can you add any more details, Mr. Martinez?"

"I remember that Alicia was wearing a blue jacket, her favorite jacket," said Martinez. "Lacey had on a pair of warm-ups since we had a soccer game last night, and—"

Moore interrupted him. "Let's look at a picture of the girls together. They took this picture less than a year ago." Moore turned and talked to the camera. "We want these girls found as quickly as possible, and KPAR-TV is a partner with law enforcement in helping to find the girls. We will offer a reward for accurate information passed to us and to the authorities for the safe return of Alicia and Lacey. Contact us at 541 555-7871."

Moore turned back to Stevens and Martinez. "Now, we're also concerned because of the reports of a girl in another state—Indiana—who was abducted and passed away earlier this week. What message do you have to give to the people of Port Angel about Lacey and Alicia?"

The camera aimed squarely at Patty Stevens, who started to cry. Martinez held her shoulder and looked into the camera himself. "We'd like our girls back. Please, if anyone can help us, please call. Please bring our girls back."

Martinez looked back to Moore, who turned to the camera. "Thank you. This is Jackie Moore, KPAR-TV, urging you—our viewing public—to help bring back these girls." She gave a brief nod to the camera, and the light faded. She turned to Martinez and Stevens.

"You did a magnificent job, both of you."

"Now that wasn't so bad, was it?" asked Clarise Jones. "And you were so worried, Alex."

"It's fine, Clarise," said Martinez, who focused on his wife. "I guess anything that helps bring the girls back is a good thing."

Moore stood. "I agree, Mr. Martinez, and KPAR-TV will do everything it can to help you." She smiled. "We're in your corner."

Chapter Twelve

"Jackie, you spent time with the parents of Lacey and Alicia Stevens this evening. What's the status of the case and how are the parents doing?"

The newscaster turned to Jackie Moore, who looked somber. "The family is holding it together, but it's been challenging, Chad. But I think it's important that KPAR-TV will continue to help in this fight to bring the girls home. Here's a part of my interview with the parents today."

"This is Jackie Moore, KPAR-TV, in the home of Patty Stevens and Alejandro Martinez, parents of two girls who've been missing since yesterday, Lacey, eight, and Alicia, thirteen." Moore turned to Patty Stevens. "Mrs. Stevens, I know this is a hard time for you. How are you holding up?"

"It's been tough, you know. They're both so young, and every parent worries about their kids, but you're never really prepared if something happens."

"I see. Now, the Amber Alert gave details on what the girls were wearing when they left for school, but can you add any more details, Mr. Martinez?"

"I remember that Alicia was wearing a blue jacket, her favorite jacket."

"Let's look at a picture of the girls together. This picture was taken less than a year ago. We want these girls found as quickly as possible, and KPAR-TV is a partner with law enforcement in helping to find the girls.

We will offer a reward for accurate information passed on to us and to the authorities for the safe return of Alicia and Lacey. Contact us at 541 555-7871."

"What message do you have to give to the people of Port Angel about Lacey and Alicia?"

"We'd like our girls back. Please, if anyone can help us, please call. Please bring our girls back."

"Chad, we're urging our viewing public on KPAR-TV to help us in the search for these missing girls. you. Together, we're making a difference."

"Thank you, Jackie. Now, in the world of sports today ..."

Novak turned off the TV. "That's not how I remember the interview."

Sheryl was in the kitchen with Stephanie Hart, cutting vegetables. "What do you mean?" asked Sheryl. "Did she make something up?"

"Hardly." Novak shook his head. "I guess they have to edit things, but I remember it lasting longer than fifteen or twenty seconds."

"Ha!" Hart said. "We've seen how they do that in the media, Danny. It's nothing to get concerned about."

"That may be true. But it still seems dishonest to me."

Hart put down her knife. "I think Moore was more interested in promoting her station than in getting the girls back."

"My thought exactly," Sheryl said. "If she said 'KPAR-TV' one more time, I was going to scream." She frowned. "How are the parents doing?"

Novak sat back on the couch. "They're hurting, like you'd assume. The mother seems lost, and the father is trying to hold it together by being logical and calm with our people, but you can tell he's torn up inside."

"He's the stepfather, right?"

"Right," Hart said. "He's also Lacey's soccer coach. She really looks up to him. She called him 'Dad,' as I recall, not, I don't know, Alejandro, or Mr. Martinez."

Sheryl chuckled. "Wouldn't it be odd calling the person who's living in your house as your parent 'Mr. Martinez'?"

"Probably." Hart looked to her friend. There was an odd look in his eyes. "What's up, Danny?"

"What?" said Novak, surprised. "Oh, I was thinking about missing kids."

"I didn't think you ever had a case like this before."

"I haven't. We've dealt with kids who wander off and are found an hour later only a few blocks away. No, I was thinking about years ago when I was growing up."

Hart and Shery Novak looked at each other, and Sheryl lowered her knife. "Do you have a story for us?"

Novak sat back. "Not a story, a bunch of them. Back in the day, two kids I knew ran away and, unlike most, stayed away. Both families disintegrated before my eyes." Novak shook his head. "I didn't understand it. One family had to come together to grieve about the missing kid and a year later, they're getting a divorce, and in the other case, the remaining child was sent to live with a relative because the parents couldn't take care of him. It was tragic."

Sheryl took off her apron and crossed near her husband to lean on the kitchen counter. "I see this all the time, not missing or abducted kids, but families that are torn up when something like this happens. I've seen families get closer after a child gets killed, then everything falls apart not long after. And it's not just the parents who take it hard. Little kids change from bright and active to sullen and withdrawn overnight. And the hard part for me is that I only get to see them when they come to our library or a school-based program. I'm never able to help them."

"We can only do what we can do," said Hart. "I haven't met the mother in this case, but the father is in it for the long haul. Besides Operation ID, I also saw him at the soccer tournament. He's a natural parent and mentor, and Lacey and Alicia could do much worse than have him as a father figure."

"That may be true," said Novak. "But it doesn't help us find the girls."

Hart scoffed and pointed to the television with her knife. "Well, all we have to do is call Jackie Moore at KPAR-TV—she'll take care of everything."

Novak laughed. "You don't like her, do you?"

"Something about that woman gives me the willies."

"Everything gives you the willies," Sheryl Novak said as she returned to the kitchen counter. "Like certain vegetables."

Hart looked at the mounds of chopped carrots, celery, onion and broccoli and sighed. "What are you making here, anyway?"

"Something you might like, but that's more likely if you don't know what's in it."

"What?"

"Steve," Sheryl continued, "you don't have the widest diet."

Novak laughed from the living room, while Hart frowned at Sheryl. "What do you mean? I eat salads and vegetables all the time!"

"Right," said Sheryl. "Sugar snap peas, peas, green beans, edamame: do you see a trend here?"

"They're green! And it's hard to make a few collard greens, since you can't buy a tiny package of ham hocks!" She laughed. "I just thought of Jackie Moore eating collard greens for Sunday dinner."

"Oh yeah," Novak said. "I can't imagine her doing that. I'm more likely to have collards on Sunday than she ever was."

Hart agreed. "Yeah. I can't imagine little miss bougie on the homestead."

Alicia and Lacey were awake but groggy when they looked up and saw the man's shadow. "I've been wondering when you would awake up again," the man said. "Listen, are there certain foods you like to eat? I mean, I've gotten you food before, but maybe you wanted something new?"

"If you're going to get me anything, I want ice cream," Alicia said. "But I really just want to go home." She looked down at Lacey, who nodded. "So does my sister."

The man sighed. "Nah. You'll adjust and be happy here with me." He stood and moved away from the girls toward the only door. "And when that happens, you'll get all the ice cream you want." The door closed with a loud thud.

The interview room at the ninth precinct was more crowded than usual. It contained Patty Stevens, Alejandro Martinez, Thomas Fair and Sharon Shore. Detectives Siem Porter and David Moody were in the observation room along with Stephanie Hart and O. C. Boyd. It was standing room only.

Fair started the questioning with a caveat. "Ms. Stevens and Mr. Martinez, we're not interrogating you here. We're conducting this interview so we can record it. It's always possible that something you say will trigger a memory that may help us find your girls. Please don't worry." Fair glanced at Shore, then back to Stevens and Martinez. "But I want you to understand that some people prefer to have an attorney present when they're in this room to protect their rights. You were offered an attorney, is that right?"

"Right," Martinez said. "But we, that is Patty and I don't think we need one." He looked to his wife, who nodded. "You can tell him what you think, too, Patty."

"We don't need a lawyer," Stevens said. "We just want the girls back."

"So you are declining having a lawyer present?"

"Yes."

"That's fine," said Fair. "Keep in mind that if you want an attorney later, we will stop the interview and have you call one, okay?"

"We understand," Martinez said.

"Good," said Fair. "Let's get started."

Shore leaned forward. "Tell us about your morning routine again—when the two of you get up, how the girls get up and out of the house, things like that." Shore smiled. "You've told us this before, and we're not trying to trip you up, but we wanted to ask you this now that the shock of the girls going missing has passed."

Martinez looked at his wife, then to Shore. "Patty gets up first, at five, and is usually out of the door, about what time?"

Stevens frowned. "I leave between six and six fifteen for work."

"By that time, the girls and I are up."

Fair interrupted, "When do you get up, Mr. Martinez, and how about the girls?"

"I get up at five and wake the girls at six." He turned to Stevens. "Patty sees them before she leaves for work, but I make sure they get breakfast and make their lunches, either in the morning or the night before."

"Now don't take this the wrong way, but I'd like the exact time—as best you can remember—on the morning the girls disappeared." He raised his hand. "I want this to be as exact as possible."

Martinez leaned on the table. "Okay. I got up at five thirty when my alarm sounded, but the girls didn't get up the first time I called them. They didn't get up and moving until sometime around ten after six—it was right before Patty left, I remember."

"Right." Stevens' voice was quiet. "I went to their room to say goodbye, and they were still sleeping." She looked at Martinez with a look of guilt. "I guess I yelled at them." Her eyes filled with tears. "I'm sorry."

"Patty, you didn't yell at them. You said something like 'girls, it's time to get up. It's way after six,' or something like that. You didn't scare them into running away."

Fair turned again to Martinez. "So the girls were a little late that morning, is that right?"

"A little," Martinez agreed. "But not by that much. They left the house on time. It was cutting it close, and I had to yell for them to leave the house on time. Most days, they leave the house between six forty and six forty-five. It was almost six forty-five when I called to them. They came scrambling with their backpacks and I gave them their lunches, kissed them and they left the house." Martinez cleared his throat. "I think it was six forty-five on the nose."

In the observation room, Boyd was stroking his chin.

Moody spoke to him. "Something bugging you, O. C.?"

"Hm," Boyd mused. "It's the mother, something about her."

"She seems a little immature," Hart said.

"That's it," Boyd agreed as he turned to face Hart. "I hope the girls learned some strong survival skills, but with that mother, I'm not optimistic."

"You never know," Porter said. "This kind of trauma often leaves many parents lost."

"Right," Hart said.

Moody laughed. "We don't see you as the motherly type, Hart."

Hart rolled her eyes. "I might surprise you with what I can do, Dave."

"Well, what I hope is that these two girls show us what *they* can do," Boyd said. "That would make me really happy."

Chapter Thirteen

Hart, Moody, Porter and Boyd reconvened in the squad room after the interview. As far as they could see, Fair and Shore had learned nothing new from the parents, and the parents were still distraught when they left the station to return home.

"This is only the beginning," Moody said. "And it could get a lot worse."

"I agree," said Boyd. "The only good thing is the father seems to be holding it together."

"Stepfather," Hart said.

"What?"

"Stepfather," Hart repeated. "He's the stepfather, remember? The birth father's been out of town."

Porter turned back to the interview rooms. "Stepfather and backbone of the family, it seems."

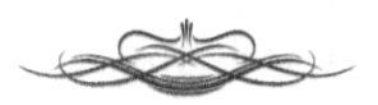

Danny Novak escorted Martinez and Stevens to their home that afternoon and was scheduled to stay until the change of shift at 5:00 p.m. Ten minutes after they arrived home, Clarise Jones rang the bell. Martinez answered.

"Hello, Clarise."

"Alex," said Jones. She looked behind him. "Where's Patty?"

"She's here." Martinez stepped aside. "Why don't you come in?"

Jones smirked. "Thought you'd never ask." She walked into the house and saw Novak. "Oh. I didn't know anyone else would be here."

"It's standard procedure in cases like this, ma'am," Novak said. "Someone will be outside while you're sleeping as well. I have this daytime assignment. Is there anything I can do for you?"

Jones sighed. "I have to watch my tongue. No. I need nothing right now."

Martinez returned a few minutes later with Stevens, who reached for her mother. Where is Brian?" Martinez asked. "I thought he might be with you."

"Brian will get here when he has time," Jones snapped. "He has some things to finish up, but he's called every night, hasn't he?"

"He has," said Martinez, who looked uncomfortable in his own house. "What can I get you, Clarise?"

"Nothing. I'll just sit with you and find out what's happening from this officer."

Novak sat on a kitchen chair and told Jones what was going on with the investigation. Jones sniffed several times, showing little interest in Novak until Martinez stood.

"Patty, you remember I have to go to the office today, but not for long—the final project report?"

"Oh," said Stevens, "I forgot." She looked at her mother. "Now is a good time since Mom is here."

Martinez stood. "That's what I thought. It's better than having you stay alone." He turned to Jones. "Thanks for being here, Clarise."

Martinez grabbed his jacket and Novak stopped him. "We can have someone take you there, Mr. Martinez."

"No need," said Martinez. He picked up his keys. "It might clear my head." He turned once again to look at his wife, nodded to Novak and left.

"I don't understand how two little girls could have just disappeared so easily," said Jones. "It makes no sense to me."

"Nor do we, ma'am," Novak said. "But I can tell you that every officer in the city and several FBI Special Agents are making calls and investigating, following every lead we get. I'm hoping the police tip line together with the one from KPAR-TV will pay off soon." The doorbell interrupted Novak and three pairs of eyes turned to the door. "I'll get that." Novak strode to the door and opened it, and was surprised to see Jackie Moore at the door. She was smiling and carrying a microphone by her side.

"I hope I'm not intruding."

Novak turned to Stevens. "It's Ms. Moore, the reporter."

"Oh," said Stevens, who rose from the couch. She walked to the door. "Ms. Moore. What can we do for you?"

"Well, we wanted to speak with you again, Ms. Stevens. Is your husband here?"

"No, he had to go to work to take care of something. He'll be back soon, though. I don't understand."

"That's okay, ma'am," said Moore. "We just have a few more questions that we think will help you."

"I suppose that would be all right," said Stevens. "Won't you come in?"

Moore stepped aside and gestured toward the TV camera set up on the front lawn. "We could also do it outside. Your choice."

Stevens frowned. "I don't understand," she said as Moore backed out of the house. Patty followed, and Moore turned her attention to the camera.

"This is Jackie Moore, KPAR-TV news at the home of Patty Stevens and Alejandro Martinez, parents of the two girls missing since Thursday." She shifted her attention back to Stevens. "Ms. Stevens, we've learned that there is more to your background—actually your husband's background—than you led us to believe, and we hope you've told the police everything."

Stevens stared. "What? We've told the police everything. Who do you think—"

"Then you've told the police that your husband was arrested twenty years ago because of a gang rape in his home city of Chicago? You told us nothing about that."

Stevens' mouth opened, but no sounds came out at first. "I don't ..."

"Our interest is getting the girls back, Ms. Stevens. Your husband's arrest may not be important, but we feel—"

Stevens regained her full voice. "Get away from me! Get off my property—you have no right to be here!" At this, Jones emerged from the house to console her daughter. Stevens kept advancing toward Moore, who backed away toward her cameras, saying nothing, though Novak was sure her smile never faded.

Andrew Shoemaker sat in his office waiting to watch the television news. Novak had called him as soon as Moore left the Martinez and Stevens house to warn him of what was coming. Shoemaker thought he was ready for the report, but it turned out he wasn't.

"You have more information about the missing girls tonight, Jackie?"

"Not about the girls, Rod," Moore said. "This is about the stepfather, Alejandro Martinez."

Shoemaker noticed that Moore used a slight Spanish accent when she said *Martinez*. He was sure she hadn't done so before.

"This is interesting, Jackie. What can you tell us about Mr. Martinez?"

"I returned to the home today to ask then, but only Ms. Stevens was there. My report is brief as you'll see."

The screen faded and came up on the worn face of Patty Stevens.

"Ms. Stevens, we've learned that there is more to your background—actually your husband's background—than you led us to believe, and we hope you've told the police everything."

"What? We've told the police everything. Who do you think—"

"Then you've told the police that your husband was arrested twenty years ago because of a gang rape in his home city of Chicago? You told us nothing about that."

"I don't—"

"Our interest is getting the girls back, Ms. Stevens. Your husband's arrest may not be important, but we feel—"

"Get away from me! Get off my property—you have no right to be here!"

The camera showed Moore retreating behind her cameras and the television van before fading again.

Rod turned to Moore in the studio. "This is quite the bombshell, Jackie. What can you tell us about Alejandro Martinez' police record?"

"Rod, our sources tell us that Martinez was a person of interest in a gang rape of a young girl in Pullman on the south side of Chicago. Now, no final action was taken against him. But Mr. Martinez has never told his wife about this, and with her having two daughters, that causes me some concern."

"You and me both, Jackie. I look forward to hearing what the police have to say. Let's hope it doesn't impact getting the girls back safely."

Shoemaker looked at the screen and resisted the urge to throw the television into the wall. He sat back in his chair, then looked up to see Samuel Perkins. "I don't know what makes me angrier, Perk—Martinez not telling us about his arrest or the fact that Jackie Moore discovered it first."

Perkins entered the office and leaned against the back of the overstuffed chair. "A bit of both, most likely."

"You're right. And I'm not happy in either case." Shoemaker rose. "But what I need to do now is see what we've found out about the Martinez case in Chicago."

"Who's on it?"

"Fair and Shore. They should have something for us soon, though if it's a juvenile record that will be tougher."

"Then how did Jackie Moore get it?"

Shoemaker frowned. "Now *that* is an excellent question."

Chapter Fourteen

When Martinez arrived two hours later, Novak sprang up when he opened the door. His wife and mother-in-law were sitting on the couch, and Danny Novak on a kitchen chair. Novak rose when he entered. Martinez looked back and forth among the faces and frowned.

"Did something break about the girls?" He looked at Stevens' face and grew frightened. "Is it something bad?"

Jones blurted. "It's something bad all aright. But the something bad is about you!"

Martinez frowned. "Me? What are you talking about?" Stevens was crying again and looking into space, and Jones rose from the couch and approached Martinez. Novak stood close by to prevent a physical altercation.

"You know exactly what we're talking about, you rapist!"

"Are you out of your mind? You're calling me a rapist?" He shook his head. "Woman, you are *insane!*"

"Am I? I'm not the one who was arrested for rape in Chicago."

Martinez looked to Stevens, who refused to meet his eyes. "Babe, you don't believe this, do you?"

"Well, *I* certainly do," Jones said. "And if you think you're going to rape my granddaughters, you've got another thing coming."

"I've never raped anybody," said Martinez. "That whole incident is more than half my life ago, and I didn't do anything wrong." He turned again to Stevens. "Patty, you *know* me. I would never—"

"Oh, we know you now, all right," Jones said. "And you will not rape my granddaughters!" Martinez started moving toward Stevens, but Jones blocked his way. "Oh no you don't! You need to leave her alone—leave us alone and go back to the hole you came from." Jones pushed Martinez, and he fell back.

Novak intercepted her. "We can't get physical here, ma'am."

"That man is a rapist."

"We don't know that, ma'am. All we know is what one reporter told us a few minutes ago." He looked to Martinez then back to Jones. "That's something the police will look into. That's why I called my captain."

Martinez collapsed into a kitchen chair. Novak looked at Jones, held the stare, and Jones returned to her daughter, whispering in her ear.

Martinez looked up again at Novak. "What happened?"

Before answering, Novak looked again to Stevens and Jones, who weren't paying him and Martinez any attention. Novak ushered him toward the front door for privacy. "Jackie Moore came by not long after you left for work. She said you had been holding information back from the police, and that included being arrested because of a gang rape in Chicago. It's going to be on the news tonight, we're sure." He looked back to Stevens and Jones. "I discouraged them from watching it, but it's bound to be on the news tomorrow."

Martinez gave a nervous laugh. "Well, thank you for that warning, for all the good it's going to do." He sighed. "I've spent so many years running away from my past—from anything to do with my family in Chicago." He looked at Novak. "I was so sure I'd outrun it." His eyes watered. "I had a great wife, two wonderful daughters, a fulfilling job—the American Dream, right?" Novak nodded. "Not much of a dream now, is it?"

"You want to talk about it?"

Martinez rubbed his eyes. "No, except to say I wasn't arrested. They brought me in for questioning, then released me. I'll ... tell people more when I have to."

Novak looked again to Steven and Jones. "You might try that sooner rather than later."

"Wait," Martinez said. "It just occurred to me—that happened when I was young. I was thirteen—no, twelve, so I was a juvenile. There shouldn't be a public record of it, either. How did Jackie Moore find out about it?"

"Got me," Novak said. "But now everybody who watches TV news in Port Angel knows it." He faced Martinez again. "Get ready for a storm."

Hart and Novak met at muster the following morning. Novak looked the worse for wear, given he was still working into the night beforehand. Hart couldn't resist. "You don't look good."

"Thanks, friend. I've had a rough time, what with dealing with normal stuff, working extra hours, and spending time at the Martinez and Stevens house last night."

"Whoa. I didn't realize you were there last night. So you were—"

Novak nodded. "I was there for the whole sordid thing, including when Martinez came home."

"How did *that* go?"

Novak sighed. "Patty Stevens refused to sleep with her husband, and he refused to leave the house, so Stevens went to her parents' home last night. Martinez left for work this morning, according to Elliott. I shudder to think what will happen tonight."

"What's the deal with this arrest charge Jackie Moore was talking about?"

"According to—"

"Let's get started, people," O. C. Boyd said. "We have a lot to cover today, including another of those burglaries that have plagued this precinct and the twelfth. Fair and Shore will get us up to speed on the missing girls."

"And the Martinez arrest in Chicago?" Mike Canady asked. "Is there any truth to it?"

Boyd looked to Fair and Shore, then stepped back from the podium. "May as well lead with that."

"Got it," Fair said. "We made several calls and got into hot water almost immediately."

"Why?" Hart asked.

"That's what surprised us, Steve," said Shore. "The incident in question happened when Martinez was a juvenile, and there is almost no record of it since he was never under arrest."

"No?" Canady asked. "But that woman said he was arrested for rape."

"Do you believe everything you see on TV, Canuck?" Boyd asked. "I thought I raised you better than that." A few officers chuckled. "What did you find out, Dinah?" Boyd used Shore's nickname.

"After going through far too many hoops for a routine call, we were told that his brother was involved in a gang rape, but when it happened, Martinez left the house, going to a neighbor's house because he was scared and didn't want to be involved. The police brought him in as a person of interest."

"So what happened?"

Fair and Shore shared a glance. "We have a guess."

"What's the guess?"

"We believe when this happened, the police brought everybody in for questioning, even people at the fringes. They released Martinez after questioning him with no further follow-up."

"So it's unlikely he did anything wrong."

"The person we talked to wouldn't tell us anything else and was ticked that we called in the first place."

"Then how did Jackie Moore find out about it?" Canady asked.

"And what are the Chicago police trying to hide?"

"Those are two excellent questions," Fair said. "Dinah and I kicked it to the captain to make the next calls."

Boyd steepled his fingers and held them to his lips. "What else?"

"Dinah and I have been looking into the family." Fair looked at the officers and spotted Novak. "We should talk to Novak too, but we were trying to learn more about the family dynamics."

"Right," Shore agreed. "Nothing out of the ordinary. The house is owned by Stevens. Turns out she wanted to get away from the birth father. Her parents made the down payment so Stevens and the girls had somewhere to go, though both husband and wife now pay the mortgage."

"When did Martinez come into the picture?" Boyd asked.

"About six years ago," Shore said. "They met when Martinez was playing soccer in an adult league that started their games after youth practices. Stevens and Martinez caught each other's eyes and started from there."

"What about his current record—anything?"

Fair shook his head. "Clean as a whistle. People in the neighborhood say that they weren't happy with Stevens before Martinez moved in. She—"

"Wait," Hart said. "What does that mean?"

"Nothing terrible, Steve," Fair replied. "They were the typical things neighbors complain about, like the lawn not being mowed regularly, or not having candy at Halloween, but taking her kids around anyway."

Canady shook his head. "Do people get so riled about shit like that?"

Fair laughed. "Move into a neighborhood with a homeowners' association and find out, Mike. Anyway, they say that when Martinez came in, he made it a point to talk to people in the neighborhood, and was the first one over to help a neighbor when a tree fell on their property. They see him as a good neighbor."

"One of them also told us that the girls just seem better since he joined the family," Shore added.

"Meaning what?" asked Novak.

"That's out of my depth, Danny." Shore looked to Fair for help. "My sense? It was things like the girls not getting to school on time, or not playing with the other neighborhood kids, stuff like that."

"They're more of a nice, regular family now," Fair added. "Neither Dinah nor I heard much, but the neighbors respect him."

"I wonder if they still feel that way after Jackie Moore's report," said Hart. "Their opinion could change in a heartbeat."

"Hold on, Steve," said Boyd. "Let's not assume this guy is as good as some people think until we get more information."

"Fair." Hart frowned. "But that begs the question—what about Martinez' brother? Was he charged those years ago?"

"He's a bad actor," Fair said. "He was charged in that gang rape, and the judge sent him to juvenile hall." Fair laughed. "The guy we talked to was happy to tell us about the brother, even his juvie record. The older Martinez brother went to juvenile hall for this offense, and two years later did something similar and ended up in Joliet."

"Thomas and I worked on a timeline," Shore added. "And we think it was during the older brother's time in Joliet that Martinez joined the Navy. We doubt he's been in Chicago since that time, except for leaves. He settled in Port Angel after his discharge."

"Guilt by association?" Canady asked.

"With the brother?" Shore shrugged. "That might be the case."

"Huh," Hart said. "I wonder if Jackie Moore is going to tell us all about Martinez' brother." The other officers looked at her and sighed, knowing she was right.

CHAPTER FIFTEEN

Spool opened the door and Alicia and Lacey turned their heads to face him. The girls moved closer together. Spool remained in the shadows carrying a tray with two sandwiches on it and two cans of soda.

"This is all I had," he said. "I'll get you something better when this is over." He was leaving when Alicia spoke.

"Would you please let us go? My sister is afraid."

He stayed in profile rather than looking at the girls head-on. "Why would you want to do that? I told you I'd get better food for you." He realized his voice was rising, and he calmed himself. *This is how it started before. I have to change this time or we won't be happy.* Before he could speak, he heard Lacey crying.

"Please, mister. Let us go. We didn't do anything."

"Is that what you think? That you did something awful?" He tsked to himself. "What kind of parents could you have that make you think you always do something bad? I'm not that way."

"You're not my father," Alicia said.

"You're right. You're not my daughter. We're just going to be together. It'll be great, you'll see." He looked to the corner and the bucket he had placed there as a toilet. "But you'll need to use the toilet. Let me bring that over here, and I can change how you're tied. How would that be?"

"Please, mister," Lacey whimpered.

"I'll take care of that right now." He brought over the bucket and pointed to the toilet seat on top. "It's kind of fancy, I mean it's got stuff in it so it shouldn't smell so bad. Use it like a regular toilet—there's paper for you here, too." He slipped to a dark corner and took out more rope, tying both girls to rings embedded in the wall, then untied the original ropes so the girls could stay together, yet not move too far from one corner of the room.

He rose, pleased with himself. "This will be better, you'll see." For the first time, he looked squarely at Alicia, whose eyes burned, then went blank as she looked away. "Yep. We're going to be great together."

Stevens arrived home at noon, accompanied by her mother. She walked into the house, still snuffling and ignoring her mother's constant chatter. "Mom, what is it you want?"

"What?"

"I said, what do you want?"

Jones scrunched up her face. "What do you mean? I'm here to support you and help get the girls back. Why are you asking this?"

Stevens sat on the couch, surprising herself with how hard she sat. "Because you haven't shut up since we got up this morning, and it's getting old."

"What? Can't you carry on a decent conversation? Did Alex hurt you so much that you're afraid to talk anymore?"

"Mom!" Jones opened her mouth and Stevens raised her finger. "No. More. Words." She sighed. "Whatever words I need to say to Alex are mine to say and no one else's."

"I'm just trying to be supportive."

"But you're not, Mom. Your talking, talking, talking is just confusing me more and giving me a headache."

"I can get you something for that."

"But you won't shut up, will you? Don't bother, Mom, I—"

The doorbell rang, and Stevens walked to the front door to answer it. She opened the door, and before her were Nadine Delaplaine and two other women. "Hello?"

"Hello, Ms. Stevens," Delaplaine said. "We wanted to stop by and give you any help you might need." Delaplaine looked behind her and saw Jones. "You're not from the neighborhood." Stevens turned to look at her mother and Delaplaine walked past her, leading the other two women.

"Yes, I'm Mrs. Jones, Patty's mother."

"And we're so sorry about what happened and know this must be so difficult for you." She stopped and looked around the house. "I, uh, don't suppose your husband is here, is he?"

Stevens shook her head. "No, Alex isn't here right now."

"Maybe for good," Jones said.

"Mom."

Delaplaine nodded. "Well, that may be for the best, but we wanted to focus on you." She approached Stevens again, placing her hand on her shoulder. "We're all mothers here, and we know what it's like."

"Amen," said another woman.

"Somebody understands. *Finally*," Jones said. "I've been trying to tell her all day and all night that having Alex leave was for the best." She waved to the living room. "Won't you sit down? I'll make us tea." She flashed a stern look at Stevens, who shrank, then started into the living room to be swallowed up by the other mothers.

Hart and Novak returned to the precinct toward the end of their shifts; Novak needed to get back to the Martinez and Stevens home and relieve Paul Andrews. They met with Don Brown, who was completing training paperwork for the newest cadets.

Brown liked any excuse to stop paperwork, and he stopped Novak and Hart when they walked past his office. "Hey, can one of you fill me in about the family? This thing is still confusing to me. What have you learned?"

Hart shrugged. "There isn't much to tell, Brownie. Typical blended family." Hart laughed. "I guess blended families are typical nowadays, but there's not much about the family that *isn't* typical. They have two daughters who seem nice, no money problems we can find, they're well regarded in the neighborhood, and—"

"Until this info about Martinez came up."

"True," Novak agreed. "But we're skeptical about that information. What most concerns us is how Jackie Moore found information we had a devil of a time finding out about ourselves."

"Exactly," Hart said. "That woman has connections I don't understand, and I see myself as pretty smart."

"You are," Brown said. He made a money gesture with his hand. "But you don't have the deep pockets of KPAR-TV."

"True." Hart flicked her eyes toward the captain's office on the second floor. "How's the captain taking it?"

Brown smiled and pointed beyond Hart. "You can always ask him yourself."

Hart looked up and saw Andrew Shoemaker approach. He stopped and let out a deep breath. "I know what you're going to ask me, so before you ask, let me give you the story." He turned to face Brown. "I was at central today, and to say that the deputy chief was unhappy would be a gross understatement. He was furious that there was information on Martinez floating around that we didn't have, and—"

"Did you tell them about the juvenile record?" Hart asked. "That should count for something."

Shoemaker rolled his eyes, something Hart had never seen him do. "When your bosses are pissed at you, Hart, logic doesn't do you a damn bit of good. Oh, they acknowledged the challenge, but said we still should have dug harder ourselves."

"What did the FBI say?" Brown asked.

"That's a good point, Brownie," Shoemaker said. "The FBI told the deputy chief they didn't have the information either, and when the brass heard that, they realized their mistake, and tried to backtrack." Shoemaker laughed. "So I took a page out of the Stephanie Hart book."

"Whoa. What?"

Shoemaker smiled. "O. C. told me when you were probationary and didn't like something he told you, like a correction, you gave him a blank look with the tiniest smirk, and he backed off."

Brown and Novak laughed.

"What? Are you saying I do that?"

"You're the master at that, Steve," Novak said. "Sheryl says it too." He turned to Shoemaker. "Did it work?"

"It did. They followed with something about continued vigilance and wanting us to get ahead of the news. I agreed."

"You gonna keep Moody and Porter on that?"

"Yes. They're better at the stuff here and putting other evidence together, that's what Perk says. Fair and Shore can do any necessary follow-up with the schools."

"Good decision," Brown said.

"I want them to go beyond the police and official records to find out what they can about Martinez, like family background, schools, and his time in the Navy. If there's something bad in this guy's background that we don't know, I want it before Jackie Moore can get to it."

Spool sat for lunch next to another finish carpenter working on the school project. He hadn't been listening to the lunch table conversation and flinched when he heard his name. "Spool? What do you think? Haven't you been listening?"

Spool shook himself. *I guess not.* "What are we talking about?"

"Those missing girls, man," one man said. "Everybody's watching that woman on TV, Jackie Moore, and she thinks the stepfather of those girls is the one who took them and did who knows what with them. What do you think?"

Spool frowned and took another bite of his sandwich. "Hard to say. It sounds like he's a bad guy if what's on TV is true, you know?"

"Isn't everything you see on TV true?" asked another man. The people at the lunch table laughed. Spool laughed too, and thought more about the conversation and the girls.

Shortly after 5:30, Martinez arrived home and saw the police sergeant outside his front door.

"Afternoon, sir," Paul Andrews said.

Martinez turned and saw Andrews, but his presence didn't register. "Hello?"

Andrews smiled. "I'm here in case you need me, sir. In fact, I think it would be best if I went into the house with you."

Martinez slumped. "I won't do anything to my wife."

Andrews shook his head. "I didn't think you would. But it's gotten tense in there and there are three other women from the neighborhood inside along with your wife and her mother." Andrews pressed his lips together. "And from what little I could hear of their conversation, they don't want to see you."

"But I did nothing wrong! I left a bad situation and reported it to the police. I've never committed any crime. Why doesn't anybody believe me?"

"I don't have the answer for you, sir, but you're walking into a hornet's nest."

"But I live here!"

"I know that, sir. And I should also tell you that things are likely to get worse before they get better. So, I'm going in there with you, and I'll do my best to keep things at a proper level." He pointed at the door. "But don't expect much of a welcome."

CHAPTER SIXTEEN

Novak arrived at the Martinez and Stevens home and saw Paul Andrews standing outside. Neighbors walked by the house, some slowing their pace and turning toward the house. Listened would be more accurate; the shouting assaulted Novak from the curb, though the words were indistinct.

Andrews waved to Novak. "You're just in time." He pointed to the house. "They've been going at it for twenty minutes—it's been Stevens and Martinez with a dash of Jones thrown in for good measure."

"You're outside."

Andrews shrugged. "They asked me for privacy. So far, it's only been verbal with no slaps or anything else. But now that you're here, let's ring the bell and let them know of the changing of the guard." Andrews was set to ring the bell when the door flew open and Stevens threw an enormous pile of clothing out the door.

"Out!" she screamed. "I want you out! Don't you understand English?"

The officers listened for Martinez' response, but heard only a muffled reaction.

"Honey, come back inside." Jones's voice was more soothing than either Andrews or Novak remembered. "Come back inside, he's leaving. Don't air our dirty laundry to the entire world."

Too late for that, thought Novak. He looked to Andrews, who only smiled.

"All on you now, kid."

"Thanks."

The officers looked up to see Martinez framed in the doorway carrying two suitcases and a suit bag. He stopped at the pile of clothing on the doorstep and sagged. He looked up at the officers. "Can you?"

"Absolutely," Novak said. "Where's your car?"

Martinez pointed with his head. "Over there, the Camry." He hesitated, then looked to Andrews. "Would you ask Patty for a trash bag or something for these clothes? I don't want, I don't need—"

"Of course, sir. Give me a minute."

Novak picked up the pile of clothing, surprised by its weight, and followed Martinez to his car. He stood and waited as Martinez opened the trunk and placed the suitcases inside, then Novak placed the loose clothes into the trunk. They both looked up and saw Andrews standing in the doorway talking to Stevens. Andrews nodded his head several times, pointed toward Novak and Martinez, then turned and walked away.

Andrews was carrying three black trash bags and an empty duffel when he got to the car. "She gave me these trash bags, then remembered this was yours from when you were in the Navy."

"I guess she didn't want that around anymore, either," said Martinez, who took the bags and closed the trunk.

"Aren't you putting your clothes in the bags?" asked Novak.

Martinez looked back to the house, then shook his head. "I just need to get out of here."

Novak looked at Martinez again and realized for the first time that he was an almost immaculate man, well put together with nice creases in his pants. He inclined his head toward Andrews, who frowned, then looked at Martinez.

"Mr. Martinez, Officer Novak has to stay here with your family. Why don't we take some time and get your duffel packed a little better?" He smiled. "Navy men don't throw things into their duffels, right? You've got to have a system."

For the first time, Martinez laughed. "I've heard that too many times." He looked to Andrews. "I'd appreciate the help."

Andrews touched the brim of his cover. "Happy to do that, sir."

"Where are you headed?" Novak asked. "You don't have any family in Port Angel, as I recall."

"To a hotel for tonight. A friend from work has offered me a bed for a few days, though I don't want to wear out my welcome."

Novak pointed to the house. "Do you have more back at the house?"

"Lots. Soccer equipment, two tents, I mean, my entire life has been here for over five years. I own things in every room of that house. What's in the car was only from our bedroom."

"You let us know when you want the rest," Andrews said. "We can help you with that."

Martinez sighed. "Sure. But to be honest, the only things I want from that house right now are Lacey and Alicia." He turned toward the car, then again to Andrews. "I'd like to go now."

Novak watched Andrews and Martinez drive away and sighed himself. *This went downhill too fast.* He noticed no one around him until he turned and saw two women approaching him with what looked like angry faces.

"Is he gone for good?"

Novak frowned, but turned toward the departing cars. "Mr. Martinez?"

"Yes. Is he gone for good?"

"No, but he's certainly gone for now."

The woman seemed to grow taller. "Why can't you keep him away? We don't want rapists in our neighborhood. Isn't there a registry so families would know where those people live?"

"Wait a minute," Novak said. "First, I ..." Novak hesitated, wondering what he could reveal. "Hold it. First, we have to be sure of our information before taking legal action against someone. This is a family dispute for now, between Mr. Martinez and Ms. Stevens. We're only here because of the girls."

"Are you people blind? Don't you care about us?" said the other woman. "You have a rapist right here, and you let him drive away in his own car?"

"And what about the girls?" asked the first woman. "Where did he take them?"

Novak tried to defuse the mood, but the women were prepared.

"Why don't we talk instead of throwing out accusations." He held up his hand. "Wait, please. I know you're concerned about the girls, we're all concerned. But we won't make any progress if we just repeat what we see on TV. Do you believe everything on TV?"

"How can you say that? Didn't you watch the report?"

Novak sighed. "I watched the report. And I've interviewed Mr. Martinez and Ms. Stevens and other people in this neighborhood. Our detectives are interviewing people in the other neighborhoods and we've made calls to Chicago to learn exactly what happened over twenty years ago." He stopped, trying to remind himself of how to speak with angry citizens. "And if I thought Mr. Martinez was a threat to anybody in this city, if my bosses believed he was a threat, he wouldn't be walking the streets." He pointed down the street where the cars had gone. "He's going away. And did you see the look on his face?" The women shook their heads. "I did. And I think he is a very sad and broken man." He pointed toward the house. "I'm going to be here for a few hours, and another officer will relieve me at nine thirty tonight. Ms. Stevens will not be alone, so there's no—"

"You're right. She *won't* be alone," said the first woman. "We'll be here with her too, and we're going to have our eyes open in case he comes back!"

"Ma'am, do what you wish, so long as it doesn't break the law. And the law doesn't tell a man he can't go to his own house when he wants to. If he does, an officer will be here. If he makes trouble, we'll handle it. Please don't insert yourselves in the middle of this."

The first woman ignored Novak and turned toward the house. "Well, I'm going to help my neighbor handle this terrible situation. Is that all right with you?"

Novak nodded. "If it's fine with Ms. Stevens, it's fine with me." Novak walked by the women as they approached the Stevens and Martinez house. They rang the bell, and Clarise Jones answered.

"Good evening, Nadine. Are you here to see Patty?"

"Yes. We're here to offer our support. This officer," she pointed to Novak, "seems to think *I'm* the one who needs to calm down."

Jones glared at Novak, arms firmly across her chest. "I assume it's all right to invite people into our own home."

Novak noticed the "own home" remark by Jones and ignored it. "It is, Mrs. Jones. I'm here to keep you all safe."

Jones turned back to the visiting woman and shut the door.

And it doesn't take a rocket scientist to know that you're making the situation a hell of a lot worse.

Alicia felt the warmth of her sister's head on her chest as they sat on the small pad. Lacey had whined about the food, about being cold and everything in the last few ... was it hours?

"I don't want to use a bucket to pee!"

"Bug, that's all we have unless you want to go in your pants."

"But it's ... I just don't want to."

Alicia took her hand again. "Neither do I, Lacey, but what else are we going to do?"

Alicia was thankful that Lacey had wolfed her sandwich. She was still wary of eating. But she also figured if he wanted to hurt them, he didn't need to use poison, so she ate her sandwich, too.

The hardest thing about being away from their parents was not knowing what time it was. What *was* going on outside? Were people searching for them? And how would they find them before something terrible happened? She looked down at Lacey again and smiled. *It was a great idea to get our IDs, wasn't it, Bug?*

CHAPTER SEVENTEEN

Martinez arrived at work early the following morning and ran into his boss. Martinez liked his boss. Bill Cook had started as an IT consultant as well and rose through the ranks to supervise several teams. He was fair, an excellent manager, and left people alone to work out their own problems. Martinez entered the office to find a somber Cook.

"Hey, Alex. Have a seat."

Martinez sighed. "Maybe I should stand. Is something wrong?"

Cook sighed. "Yes, and no." He looked at Martinez and tried to smile.

"Bill, what is it?"

"It's the news from that reporter. I got a call from my boss's boss who asked me why we didn't know this about your background."

"Bill, I didn't do—"

Cook held up his hand. "I told them that, Alex." Cook grew angry. "I told them we ran the same background check we do on everyone that included your time in the Navy, any charges pending and convictions in the past—everything. They still want to know why we were in the dark."

"Because…" Martinez threw up his hands. "What's the use? I do nothing wrong, never get arrested or charged, and people call me a rapist. I thought better of this company than that."

Cook stood and walked around the desk. "Alex, wait. Sit. Please." Martinez sat, and Cook sat on the edge of his desk. "They want us to run a background check by another vendor. In the meantime, they want you suspended—with pay—until this is resolved." Cook smiled. "I insisted on the 'with pay' part, and so did Alan, my boss. He knows you're a good guy, too."

"Thank you for that." Martinez shook his head. "I hoped work would help me feel better. I need something to do. Now what do I do?"

"You go home. You go home to your wife and wait for your girls to come back."

Martinez was silent, looking to Cook, then at the floor. "I can't do that, Bill. Patty threw me out."

Cook had met the girls several times and knew how close the family was. "But why? You need to support each other right now."

"Right. The way this company—minus you and Alan, of course—supported me?"

"But that was only on TV!"

"Right. And people always believe what they see on TV, even if they say they don't." Martinez rose. "Bill, I don't hold this against you, and I'm grateful that you're going to pay me. How long will I be suspended?"

Cook turned to look at his desk, picking up a paper. "This company says they can learn more about a person in three days than any other company can. Bank on maybe five work days. We have to give corporate time to evaluate anything they find."

"Five days with nothing to do, huh? Any suggestions?"

Patty Stevens scowled as her mother approached her. She stroked her daughter's hair, saying, "It's for the best, honey. And your neighbors are just trying to help you."

Stevens shook her head away from her mother. "Mom, I don't like other people knowing my business."

"They're trying to help, and—"

Stevens sat up in bed and threw off the covers. "I don't want their help, Mom, and to be honest, I don't want yours, either."

Jones frowned. "Honey, you're upset right now." She reached for Stevens, but she pushed her hand away.

"Not now, Mom." Stevens got out of bed. "You should go home now."

"Patty, you shouldn't be alone, and—"

Stevens grew angry. "Mom. I am almost thirty-seven years old. I know when I need to be alone."

Jones was silent, then looked down, hurt. "I'm just thinking of you. If you want me to go, I will."

Stevens stared at her, struggling with what to do. "Mom, I appreciate the support and know you're trying to be helpful, but I have to decide what to do and how. Having you and all the neighborhood biddies telling me to have Alex arrested and call the police is more than I can take right now."

"Do you trust him right now?" asked Jones. "You're the one who told him to leave."

"I was thinking about the girls."

Jones smiled. "That's what a mother is supposed to do, Patty. The point is when you thought of the girls, you didn't think of Alex, at least not in a good way." Jones looked at the bedroom door. "I'll go home now, but please think about what I said. You've already made your decision: the girls come first, and that's the way it's supposed to be."

Jones looked around the bedroom to see what else she might have left, then started for the door. "Mom."

"What?"

Stevens looked down at the floor and sighed. "You can stay—in the girls' room. I guess we can get along for another day."

"Only if you want me to."

"It's okay," Stevens said. "But let me make my own decisions, okay?"

Jones looked offended. "I always do that. You're their mother; you make the decisions, honey." She smiled and turned back to the door.

As Jones went through the doorway and down the hall, Stevens let out a breath. *But Alex has helped me make every important decision for the last five years. What do I do now?*

CHAPTER EIGHTEEN

A well-dressed woman entered the precinct building after muster. Kat Neely kept her face blank and watched her approach. The had a healthy smile plastered on her face.

"Good morning," she said. "I'm Jackie Moore with KPAR-TV news. I'm here to speak with Captain Andrew Shoemaker."

Neely hesitated for two seconds before nodding. "Is he expecting you?"

"We didn't have an appointment," said Moore. "But I imagine he's expecting me."

"I'll tell him you're here." Neely indicated the chairs in the lobby. "You can have a seat there if you'd like."

Moore looked around the room, glanced at the furniture, then turned back to Neely. "I'll stand if it's all right."

Suit yourself. "I'll call him." Neely touched a button on the switchboard and waited.

"Shoemaker."

"Captain, Kat Neely here."

"Yes, Kat?"

Neely glanced at Moore. "Jackie Moore to see you, sir. She's in the lobby." Neely heard the intake of breath.

"Tell her I'll be there in a few minutes."

"Pleasure." Neely ended the call and looked up at Moore. "Captain Shoemaker will be here in a minute, Ms. Moore."

"Thank you."

Five minutes later, Shoemaker walked down the hallway from the interview rooms to approach the front desk. Moore was as he pictured her from television: a woman of average size, but tremendous charisma. She was shorter and slimmer than he expected. He approached her with a measured smile.

"Ms. Moore."

Moore took his offered hand. "Good morning, Captain. Something tells me you would like to talk to me."

Andrew kept a straight face. "That may be true, but what I don't understand is why you want to talk to me."

Moore's eyebrows furrowed. "Looking for a quid pro quo?"

"No," said Shoemaker. "But I've been around long enough to understand that some people always do." Before Moore could respond, Shoemaker pointed to the hallway. "Shall we?"

Shoemaker led the way to his office, walking past uniformed officers and detectives, all of whom would know of Jackie Moore. Shoemaker greeted no one, which was unusual for him, and he ignored their raised eyebrows as he passed them.

When they arrived at his office, Samuel Perkins was standing in the doorway. "This is Lieutenant Samuel Perkins, who leads the detectives in this precinct. Sam, Jackie Moore."

"Ms. Moore," said Perkins. He didn't offer his hand; neither did Moore, though she studied his face.

"I asked Lieutenant Perkins to join us. We're a command staff of two other than our patrol sergeants. Why don't we go sit in my office?"

The group entered Shoemaker's office and sat at the conference table. Shoemaker had debated whether to use the couches and overstuffed chairs, but preferred the formality of the table. He directed Moore to a seat, and Shoemaker and Perkins took their usual chairs.

"May we get you anything, Ms. Moore, water, coffee?"

Moore shook her head. "No, Captain. I'm fine." Moore sat straight but appeared comfortable.

"Well, thank you for coming in, Ms. Moore," Shoemaker said. "We've had questions and concerns since this case began." He looked to Perkins. "It's shocking to realize how little time has passed since the parents reported the girls missing."

"It is a tragedy, Captain."

Perkins cleared his throat. "And it's equally of concern that less than twenty-four hours after everything hit, you're spreading information about Mr. Martinez that we feel is very misleading."

"In what way?" Moore interrupted. "They took him into custody Chicago, and—"

"Not arrested, as you said, Ms. Moore," Shoemaker said.

Moore waved her hand. "Semantics."

"It's not semantics. 'Custody' or bringing someone in for questioning is not the same in the public's mind as 'arrested,' and you know it," Perkins said. "That simple choice of words on your part makes an enormous difference to public opinion."

"I could always say that my editors insisted on the choice of word."

"We wouldn't believe you," Shoemaker said. "You're important enough that you can say what you want to say on the air." Shoemaker paused. "We want the truth, and that truth is most likely to be here in Port Angel."

"Or if it has anything to do with the serial abductor of the girl in Indiana, it may be broader," Perkins offered. "I doubt it's related to a twenty-year-old incident involving Alejandro Martinez."

"Then why are you worried about that, or about him?" Moore asked. "You should spend your time finding the girls. I'm not telling you to look in Chicago or at Martinez or anything else."

Perkins laughed. "Ha. You're the reason we have to split our investigation, and until you either broadcast a retraction or we find information to discredit you, we'll be wasting our time with a multi-front investigation."

"If we don't," Shoemaker added, "the public will think we don't care about their safety."

Moore smiled. "I think you've got your work cut out for you."

"And you could make it easier by not painting Mr. Martinez as a rapist," Shoemaker said. "This ignores the fact of your access to sealed records from twenty years ago that should have been expunged. Care to tell us how you got access to those records?"

Moore smiled. "I wouldn't. And it's your job to figure out what's going on and how to get those two missing girls back." She cocked her head. "You saw the tip line we started at KPAR-TV to help you, didn't you? Would we do that if we weren't trying to help?"

Perkins shook his head. "I think your idea of help differs greatly from ours, Ms. Moore. We're happy to receive tips through our own line or through your station's. What we want less of is the tarring and feathering of a citizen without any real evidence."

Moore leaned forward. "Oh really? And did you investigate Martinez, or did you just take his word for it? Did you talk to people to see if he could have taken the girls somewhere before he went to work?" Shoemaker opened his mouth, but Moore stopped him. "And if you had, we wouldn't be having this conversation." She stood. "No, you're embarrassed because we got the scoop on the police department, and now you're getting pressure from your superiors and the public to do your jobs." She took her purse and started for the door. "And now you want me to do your job for you, or reveal my sources?" She shook her head. "I think you have a lot to learn about journalists. I'll see myself out."

Stephanie Hart and O.C. Boyd saw Moore as she exited Shoemaker's office with a smile on her face. They looked up at Perkins and Shoemaker standing in the doorway and crossed over to them.

"What did 'Jackie Moore, KPAR-TV' want with you, Shoe?" Boyd asked. "I'm guessing she didn't come to apologize or share information with you."

Perkins smiled despite himself. "Very perceptive, O. C. No, I suspect Moore was here trying to find out what we knew about the case that she could use."

Shoemaker laughed. "You got that impression, too? I was going to mention that, but thought I was being paranoid."

"Not your style, Shoe. Moore didn't come here because she heard we wanted to talk to her, but in hopes we might leak something."

"Does that mean she has nothing else she can use to get a scoop, like more about Martinez?" Hart asked. "Last I heard, there wasn't much more to know."

"That's our sense too, Hart," Shoemaker said.

"What could you say, Shoe?" asked Boyd. "That there's nothing else to say?"

Shoemaker shook his head. "Not sure." He turned to Perkins. "But I wonder if we ought to investigate this differently? I don't mean we stop the investigation in Chicago or we did anything wrong. But what about shifting our work here?"

Perkins turned. "What do you mean?"

"I mean let's go back over the evidence and testimony we've got and try to make something else of it, put it together in different ways."

"You think that will help?" Hart asked. "We've got people looking at this from all angles."

"I don't know." Shoemaker looked down the hallway. "But the last thing I want is for Jackie Moore to come up with something else we don't have."

CHAPTER NINETEEN

Hart and Boyd were still speaking with Perkins and Shoemaker when Novak walked by and saw their faces.

"You folks don't look too good." He smiled. "You want to talk about it?"

Hart gave him a smirk. "We just heard from 'Jackie Moore, KPAR-TV.'"

"She was here?"

"In the flesh." Perkins looked down the hallway. "And as pretty as she is, I think she's a barracuda."

"Oh yeah," Hart said. "I could swear she was smiling when she left your office, Captain."

Shoemaker shrugged. "That doesn't surprise me. That's what we can expect from her and people like her." He turned to Novak. "Well, we talked about what we can do about it. Danny, we decided to look at this information a little differently and—"

"Shoe, let's go in your office, and put our five heads together." Perkins looked at Novak and Hart. "Unless you two have something special happening on patrol, that is."

"Nothing special today, sir," Hart said. Novak nodded his agreement.

Perkins turned back to Shoemaker. "Let's head into your office. We can call in one of the detective teams, too."

Shoemaker turned and gestured. "A good idea. Would you get Thomas and Dinah?"

Perkins nodded, left, then returned shortly with Fair and Shore. They joined the other officers in the captain's office and sat at the conference table.

Shoemaker filled Fair and Shore in on his conversation with Jackie Moore. Shore shook her head. "That woman is not helping this investigation, no matter what she says."

"I agree," Novak said. "Have you heard that Martinez isn't living at home anymore?"

Shoemaker sighed. "I suspected that might be the case, but I wasn't sure."

Hart frowned. "Because of what Jackie Moore reported on the news?"

"It was a valid point to raise, Hart." Shoemaker raised his hand, noting Hart was ready to pounce. "Valid and someone should have known it."

Boyd shook his head. "Shoe, I have to take exception. If all they have are juvenile records—and I know we're not sure of that yet—her access to those is illegal. Somebody in Chicago is responsible for that."

Fair snorted. "From what little I know about Chicago or any city of that size, there's always somebody who'd divulge confidential records for a price. Let's not waste time trying to find the leak."

"As much as I want the leak, I have to agree with Thomas," Shoemaker said. "Moody and Porter have to investigate, but their focus is on Martinez, not on the leak. We don't have time for that, nor is it our job." He smiled. "After we find the girls, I might deploy a few more resources."

"FBI?" Boyd asked.

"I could do that now," Shoemaker said. "Let me check with the Senior Special Agent in Charge."

Hart turned to Novak. "Danny, can you tell us more about the Martinez and Stevens family? Was there an altercation last night?

"Was there?" Novak shivered. "There was, and it wasn't pretty." He looked to Shoemaker. "Did you get the report from Paul Andrews, sir?"

"I got it, but tell me what you know."

"I arrived at the house right before four o'clock to relieve Sergeant Andrews," Novak said. "I could hear the shouting from inside the house.

They had asked Andrews to stay outside, so they had some privacy, but he was listening to the shouts—he couldn't miss them. Less than a minute later, Stevens appeared and threw a pile of clothes out of the house—she was shouting for Martinez to get out. He came out a few minutes later with two bags. That's when Andrews went inside to check on things. He exited with a duffel bag and a few other things."

"Where did he go?" Boyd asked.

"He said he was going to a hotel last night, then to stay with a work friend. Nothing specific."

Shore paged through her notebook. "We can check up on him through his work."

"Do it," Perkins said. "I'd like to know more about his work—probe as much as you can."

"Got it."

"What about the mother?" Hart asked. "If we're going to dig deeper on Martinez, why not on her, too?" She looked around the table. "Hey, who knows what dirt we might find, or do we want Jackie Moore to reveal that first, too?"

Perkins was nodding as he was listening. "Hart has a point. I'm not sure we're going to find much in either parent's background, but we can't afford to ignore Stevens."

"We're on that, too, unless you want somebody else—"

"No," Perkins said. "You and Thomas keep on the local angle until we get something more definitive from Moody and Porter, which I hope will be soon."

"Something else we need to do is circle back to people we've already interviewed," Hart said. "They may have something else to share now that some time has passed."

"You have any specific ideas, Hart?" asked Shoemaker.

Hart's lips pressed together. "Well, I remember our talk at Spencer, and what we learned about Lacey and her parents."

"I don't think we learned much at all," said Shore "Everybody likes Lacey, her family is normal, there's nothing unusual about her." She looked around the table. "Nothing earth-shattering there, or did I miss something?"

Hart shrugged. "I'm not sure, but we didn't ask the teachers about how Martinez related to Lacey, how it might be different from the mother."

Shore smiled. "How would you ask that question without giving away what we're looking for?"

Hart raised her hand in surrender. "Hey, I'm not the detective." She smiled. "But I'd ask the teachers or the principal how they thought the parents—individually—related to Lacey. I'd ask what was similar and what was different, things like that."

Perkins laughed. "She's got you there, Dinah. Those are decent questions. When you go there again, take Hart with you."

"Something else," Novak began. "Did Alicia go to that same school?"

"Spencer?" asked Fair. "We didn't ask. We assume so. Moody and Porter visited the middle school. We'll ask them."

"I think you should—" Novak stopped, and Hart leaned forward.

"I know that look," Hart said. "What have you got?"

Novak smiled. "Nothing for sure. But it occurs to me that at Spencer, Lacey has always been with this family, I mean, with Martinez and Stevens as her parents. Alicia has always had the same family at Eastern Middle School, but—"

"How was Alicia at Spencer *before* Martinez became her stepfather?" asked Perkins. "That's a good question." He sighed. "I don't know if it's going to help us so much with the current case, but it may be valuable background on Martinez." He looked to Fair and Shore. That's something else you ought to probe. Have any of you watched Martinez or Stevens interact with their kids?"

"I have," Hart said. "I took Lacey's picture at Operation ID at Spencer. She was with Martinez and Alicia."

"Get any vibes?"

Hart sat back. "That's hard to say. I mean ..." She paused. "The problem is I saw them at Operation ID and later at the soccer tournament. It's hard to separate one interaction from the other."

"Never mind that," Perkins said. "What did you see?"

"Well, at Operation ID, Lacey was all smiles and very excited about getting her ID. Alicia as I recall was more the cynical teenager, but something happened—I don't remember what it was—when she said something nice or even sweet to her sister." Hart frowned. "No, that's not it. I asked her about getting her ID taken and she was very polite and smiled at me. That's not what I expected from a sullen teenager." Hart sat forward again. "I remember Alicia standing next to Martinez while I took the picture." She shook her head. "But I was so focused on Lacey that I wasn't looking at either Martinez or Alicia. I didn't sense any tension among any of them."

"Wait," said Shore, who leaned toward Hart. "Steve, did you notice any kind of powerful connection between Martinez and Alicia? Were they standing close, maybe holding hands?"

"I don't remember, but I doubt it."

"Was Alicia on her cell phone?" Boyd asked. "I see that all the time, kids on cell phones wearing earbuds."

Hart frowned. "I don't think so, I—"

"She doesn't have one," Novak said. "I just remembered that. Andrews asked that when we first met the parents, so she wasn't on her phone."

Shore turned again to Hart. "You said you saw them again at the soccer tournament?"

"I did," said Hart. "But not the entire family. Martinez is Lacey's soccer coach, but I only noticed him a bit during the actual game. I remember what happened later much better."

"The coach who was out of control?"

"That's the one. Martinez is the one who got him to chill."

"That guy? That was Martinez?" asked Novak. Hart nodded. "I remember you telling me after it happened."

"Care to fill us in?" asked Shoemaker. Hart described the incident she and Carson Poole saw, along with her conclusions. Shoemaker looked around the room as she finished. "We're getting bits and pieces of information, little of which we can use." He turned to Perkins. "Perk, are you good with getting the detectives to the right places?"

"Yep." Perkins looked to Shore and Fair. "And if you see Moody or Porter in the precinct, have them come see me. We want to get the Chicago part of this probe completed as soon as possible."

"Yes, sir," said both detectives.

Perkins turned his attention to Novak. "Danny, whose sector is the Martinez and Stevens house in?"

"Elliott's," said Boyd. "But she only took over that sector five weeks ago. Before that, it was Canady's."

Shoemaker nodded. "Let's speak with both of them and see what they know about the neighborhood and family dynamics."

"That's a long shot, don't you think?" Boyd asked.

"It may be." Shoemaker sighed again. "But there's no telling what we may find. And if we don't ask them and don't find the girls, is that a chance you want to take?"

The room was silent.

Novak, Boyd and Hart, along with Shore and Fair, left the office and returned to the muster room, where they ran into Dave Moody.

"Dave," Boyd said. "You got a minute?"

Moody smiled the cockeyed smile he always had. "I got nothing but time, O.C. What's up?"

"You finished the background on Martinez in Chicago?"

Moody shook his head. "We finished it, though I can't say we have everything we need."

"What do you mean?" asked Novak. "Couldn't you even get the info that Jackie Moore got?"

"Eventually," said Siem Porter. "And that took the FBI calling their field office in Chicago and putting more pressure on the locals. It was a shit show from the beginning."

Novak surveyed the muster room. "We can always sit, you know."

"Wait, have you already told the lieutenant what you're going to tell us?" asked Hart. "You don't want to do it twice."

"Not yet," said Perkins, appearing in the doorway. "But I bet they were on the way."

"We were, sir." Moody smiled. "Siem was parking the car. You want to stay here or head to your office?"

Perkins answered by sitting and turning to Hart. "Get Captain Shoemaker, Hart. Let's make this one big happy party."

"Yes, sir." Hart left and returned two minutes later with Shoemaker.

"Are we having our private meetings in the muster room now, Perk?"

Shoemaker waved his hands and smiled. "I guess we can share the wealth." He turned to Moody and Porter, who had laid out their notes while waiting for Shoemaker. "You have things to tell us."

Moody and Porter looked at each other, then back to Shoemaker. "We wish we had more, Captain."

"Fine," Shoemaker said. "What do you have?"

"Oh, not nothing, that's for sure," said Moody. "Except there wasn't much to learn."

"Start from the beginning, Dave." Perkins indicated the assembled officers and detectives. "We've got most of the precinct brain trust here."

"Okay." Moody glanced again at his notes. "After extensive arm twisting from us and the FBI offices in Port Angel and Chicago, we've learned that Martinez' brother is a very bad actor." Seeing Shoemaker's face change, Moody continued quickly. "It's relevant, Cap—let me finish." Shoemaker gave him a "go on" gesture. "Anyway, Martinez is the younger of two brothers. His grandparents emigrated from Mexico about fifty years ago on both sides. The grandparents and parents are naturalized, but his siblings and cousins and so on are native-born American. I only mention that for background."

"This brother—Diego—was trouble from the start," Porter said. "He's five years older than Alejandro, and they're as different as night and day. Where Alejandro excelled in school, Diego went looking for trouble and found it everywhere he went."

"Drugs?" Hart asked.

Moody shook his head. "Gangs mostly, and basic hustling. He enjoyed bullying people, extorting money and being a big shot. And part of being a big shot is getting what you want from women." He glanced at Hart, then back to Shoemaker. "Anyway, Diego had already been in trouble for skipping school, and some nasty fights on the south side of Chicago when their parents were out of the house overnight on a Friday. Both boys were home, but Alejandro was sick and was watching TV—nothing special. Diego went out and picked up this young girl of fifteen or sixteen, then called over a bunch of his buddies for a gang rape."

Porter looked around. "It's as bad as it sounds. Before the other guys arrived, Alejandro came downstairs and heard the sounds of sex, and told his brother he should take it somewhere else."

"He was that tough with his older brother?" Hart asked. "How old was he then?"

"Twelve. Well, a few days from turning thirteen," Moody replied. "Diego and Alejandro were never close as brothers, and Alejandro told Diego like it is. For whatever reason, Diego never fought back much, just ignored Alejandro."

"How about this time?" Perkins asked. "What happened next?"

"This is the first time Diego told Alejandro to fuck off, and that if he didn't want to watch the fun, he needed to be the one to leave, not Diego or his buddies."

Moody held up his hand. "Wait, didn't somebody say that one of the other guys had arrived by that time, Siem?"

"Right, right. Alejandro left the house right after the second guy arrived. But he walked to a friend's house down the block. He got concerned when he saw more of his brother's friends show up and he heard screaming." Porter looked up. "Alejandro's the one who called the cops on his brother."

"That took guts," Novak said. "Given his brother's background and his friends, I mean."

"That's how we see it," said Moody. "He called the cops, and when they arrived, he came out after most of the guys were in custody and the ambulance drove off. When he told them he lived in the house, they took him in, too."

"Wait," Shoemaker said. "How long was he in custody?"

"Not long," Moody said. "We didn't see the record, but we learned second or third hand from the FBI that once they realized who he was, they asked him questions about what he knew and why he called. After that, they let him sit for a while, and once they had enough to confirm his story, they let him go."

"How long do you think?" asked Perkins.

"Couldn't say, Perk." Moody consulted with Porter. "Maybe a couple of hours. They told us he definitely wasn't kept overnight."

Shoemaker shook his head. "So how did he become the 'arrested rapist' in Chicago? Never mind. What else did you discover either about Martinez or his brother?"

"The brother was still a juvenile himself at that time, Captain," Moody said. "They sent him to juvenile hall for this, which doesn't offer much in the way of rehabilitation."

"Typical," Perkins said. "Those places house pre-criminals predominantly."

"Anything else?" Shoemaker asked.

"He stayed in juvie for three years, then got out on probation. By the time he was twenty or twenty-one, and Alejandro was sixteen, he was involved in more hustling and some theft through his gang and got charged as an accessory after the fact in a manslaughter case. They send him to Joliet, but he got off on a technicality."

"Later, he got involved in a gang war that escalated, and they convicted him in a racketeering sting," Moody said. "Back to Joliet he goes, where he got himself shanked a year or so later. He's in a halfway house now, barely making it. He reports every month to his parole offer, so we know where he is and what he's doing. I doubt he's grown from his experiences, and frankly, I don't care, but you asked."

"I did," said Shoemaker. "What about Alejandro?"

"It's weird, Captain, but even when Diego found it was Alejandro who ratted him out, he didn't retaliate. Instead, he grew to respect Alejandro even more. But Alejandro had lost all respect for his brother—what little he had for him, that is. According to that same source, the parents weren't supportive of Alejandro either, feeling that ratting out his brother was a crime worse than rape."

"Are you kidding?" Hart asked. "What about the victim?"

"You don't have to tell us that," Moody said. "The cop the FBI talked to told us that the family kept disintegrating. Alejandro left Chicago to join the Navy when he graduated high school, and they doubt he's been back."

All eyes were on Shoemaker, who sat with his arms crossed, thinking. He looked up with thinned lips. "Dave, Siem, what can we share about Martinez?"

Moody and Porter looked at each other. "That's the problem, Shoe," Moody said. "We have this only as third-hand information, and some of it is expunged or sealed records. Siem and I are confident in what we heard. Right, Siem?" Porter nodded, and Moody turned back to Shoemaker. "But we can't betray a confidence or get other officers in trouble here, you know?"

"I know," his captain said. "And I know that whatever we reveal may be viewed by some as simply a reaction to what Jackie Moore said first."

"But what *can* we say?" Novak asked.

Shoemaker chuckled as he looked at Novak. "I guess we can say that we can neither confirm nor deny the allegations made by KPAR-TV, but that we will continue to monitor the situation."

"Can we add that we don't think Martinez is an imminent threat?"

"I doubt it, Hart," Perkins said. "But we can treat him that way ourselves."

Hart sat back with an exclamation of disgust. "A lot of good *that's* going to do him."

CHAPTER TWENTY

Hart, Shore and Fair met at Spencer rather than ride together so Hart could go back on patrol after their meeting. They had visited the school before and knew where to go and who to speak to. They surprised the principal when they walked in.

"Oh, you're the officers from the other day," Sarah Leander said. She turned toward the conference room. "Shall we go to the conference room?"

"Not yet, ma'am," said Shore. "Our questions weren't for you—unless you were the principal or teaching here when Alicia was a student at Spencer."

"When was that?"

Hart took out her notebook. "She was in the fifth grade and left three years ago."

"They assigned me at the tail end of the school year and I didn't arrive until late March. I got to know few fifth graders that year, so I didn't know Alicia."

"Well. We'd like to speak to her teachers. Can you check that for us?"

"That shouldn't be a problem. Let's check the records." Leander led the officers to her office, where she logged in and searched for Alicia Stevens. She found her records, then traced back to her teachers at Spencer. Leander took out a pad and paper and looked up at Shore. "Do you want all her teachers back to first grade?"

"Let's focus on teachers she had while Martinez was her stepfather and right before," said Hart. "That would be her the last three years of elementary school, wouldn't it?"

"That's a plan," Shore said. "Can you point us to those teachers?"

Leander glanced at the records again. "Let me see—her third-grade teacher retired last year, so that wouldn't work, and her fifth-grade teacher is at Joseph Pierce Elementary now. I'll give you her name. Her fourth-grade teacher is here, though. That's Ms. Stewart. I'll call her."

Leander led the officers to the conference room where they sat and prepared questions. Five minutes later, Leander returned with Ms. Stewart, a young woman in her mid-twenties who Hart would swear was still in high school. But Stewart had the assured manner of an experienced teacher, and after introductions, she sat at the head of the table.

"Before we start, I should tell you I wasn't the teacher of record for the fourth grade when Alicia was here."

"Oh," Fair said. "We thought you were."

Stewart shook her head. "No. My name is on the record since I was grading the students along with my cooperating teacher for two report periods. Ms. Leander saw my name and focused on it rather than on Ms. Ryner, who left for an administrative job two years ago. I took over her classroom the following year, and I've been here ever since.

"Did you know Alicia Stevens?"

Stewart smiled. "I did. She was in Ms. Ryner's class when I was the student teacher. Ms. Ryner's an excellent teacher and mentor. She had me as the primary right away, so I worked with all the students during that year, and had to plan individual curricula within the first month."

"Ms. Ryner sounds like quite the taskmaster."

Stewart laughed. "I agree, she was. But she got me prepared and confident as a teacher in less than six months. Because she threw me in so early, I had more and richer experiences than my peers in college. They were always envious of me."

"I see," Shore said. "We're interested in learning more about Alicia. How did she and Mr. Martinez get along?"

Stewart frowned. "That was years ago. Why is it relevant now?"

"You never know what might be relevant, Ms. Stewart," Shore replied. "It's important for us to learn as much as we can about her family background and dynamics. We asked about Lacey a few days ago, but neglected to ask about Alicia. Can you help us?"

"Sure. I had Alicia in class when she was in the fourth grade and I was responsible at first for the rotation in social studies for this class and two others. She wasn't a good student then, and when Ms. Ryner called for a parent–teacher conference over her progress, she said it with a grimace. When I asked her what was going on, she recounted the last parent–teacher conference she had with Alicia's mother." Stewart shook her head. "Ms. Ryner said that the mother was in denial. She kept trying to put the blame on us, saying that her daughter was just fine or that she didn't need to study stupid subjects, anyway. Ms. Ryner said that meeting was a nightmare, and she wasn't looking forward to the upcoming conference, especially since it was to suggest that Alicia repeat the fourth grade."

"I'm guessing the meeting didn't go that way?" Hart asked.

Stewart laughed. "Not at all. Mr. Martinez came in with Patty Stevens and introduced himself. He emphasized that he wasn't Alicia's birth father, but he wanted to be helpful to her and her mother. Since Mrs. Stevens had no objection, Ms. Ryner and the Assistant Principal started the meeting. They didn't get two words out of their mouths before Mr. Martinez pulled out a notebook and asked if he could take notes. And that's just what he did. He listened to the teacher and asked several questions about support services. He asked how to structure things at home so that Alicia could be a better student. It was a textbook description of the engaged parent. We all left the meeting smiling, especially when he asked to meet again in six weeks to check on Alicia's progress." Stewart laughed again. "When they left the room, my Assistant Principal looked at Ms. Ryner and me and told us she could just 'eat him up.'"

Fair nodded his head. "You have a high opinion of Mr. Martinez."

"I do." Stewart sat back in her chair and her expression changed. "And we think it's terrible the way you're treating him."

Shore frowned. "Hey, wait a minute. We're not trying him in the press, that's the TV station and network doing that."

"That may be," Stewart conceded. "But you don't seem to be doing much to stop them."

Shore sighed. "What happened after the meeting?"

"Mr. Martinez began tutoring Alicia every night and helped her edit essays and other assignments for the school. I saw his critique marks on one of her essays, and they were great—they were clear enough to understand and didn't take responsibility off of the student.

"Alicia had a dramatic turnaround and we discovered she was one of the sharper students in the class. At the interim in the last report period, Mrs. Ryner told Ms. Stevens and Mr. Martinez that she recommended that Alicia move on to the fifth grade next year with her classmates. Mr. Martinez thanked us and asked how they could start the next year even better, and we discussed other interventions and activities to keep Alicia challenged and on track. The principal said that if we had more parents like Martinez, we'd all be happy and less overworked."

"This sounds impressive," Fair said. "Do you remember any interactions with her birth father during that year or the next?"

Stewart frowned. "Is he living?" Then she smiled. "That's an odd question, I'm sure, but I've never met him. So, is he living? And in Port Angel?"

"Yes to both," Shore said. "He's not involved much in the girls' lives, we've been told, so I guess it wouldn't help to ask about differences between him and Martinez."

"Wait. Not necessarily." Stewart leaned forward. "When Alicia was in the fifth grade, she attended the Daddy/Daughter Dance, one of our traditions."

"They still have those?" Hart asked. "We never had them in any of my schools in Philly."

"A lot of schools don't have them anymore, because what if you don't have a father?" asked Stewart. "Or a mother, for that matter. But it's something we've held on to here. I attended as a teacher chaperone, and she was so excited to be there. Both she and her father, uh, stepfather were excellent dancers, as I recall."

"Did she attend the dance in the fourth grade?" Fair asked.

"Oh, no," Stewart said. "I spoke with her mother the year before, and she told me that Alicia had no interest in going to the dance."

Fair, Shore and Hart paused, then Hart asked, "What about his interactions with other students?"

Stewart thought for a moment. "Mr. Martinez got involved early on with our sports programming—we always have parents volunteer with soccer and basketball for the kids. Mr. Martinez realized how few of the fathers were involved, and because of that, few of our boys took part in organized sports. He encouraged more of the other dads to get involved in the PTA and then started the intramural soccer program for the boys, since the girls had one. Before him, no one was interested in coaching the boys because they can be wild at that age."

"Again, impressive," Fair said.

Stewart nodded. "It is. Mr. Martinez became a leader in the PTA from the get-go, with his girls and other kids in the school. We're going to miss him after Lacey goes to middle school.

"Is there anything else you want us to know about Mr. Martinez?" Stewart smiled and leaned forward. "Make sure he gets a fair shake: he's earned it."

When Samuel Perkins entered the reception area, Kat Neely was standing by her desk speaking to Alejandro Martinez. She was alternately shaking her head and nodding. Neely relaxed when Perkins approached. Perkins smiled at Martinez.

"Mr. Martinez. What can I do for you?"

Martinez looked around the station. "May I talk to you in a private place?"

"My office is available. Or did you have something more formal in mind?

"Your office would be fine," said Martinez. "Things have been getting out of hand here and, well—"

"Let's head to my office." Perkins led Martinez down the hall. He motioned Martinez into his office and let him choose the chair he wanted, which was right in front of Perkins' desk. This surprised Perkins, but he sat behind his desk and smiled again. "I won't try to guess what you're going through right now, Mr. Martinez, but is there anything you'd like us to do, or want to tell us?"

Martinez looked around the office and at the desk before looking up again at Perkins. He chuckled a little. "I'm not usually so quiet. But all my energy and my ability to make decisions—everything has just left me, and—"

"Before you say anything else, Mr. Martinez," Perkins began, "did you want counsel here for any reason?"

Martinez sat back. "I guess I forgot about that." He paused for a moment before saying, "No, I'm fine."

"What about other legal representation? Have you spoken to a lawyer about your domestic situation?"

Martinez shook his head. "I can't focus on that right now. With the girls gone, how can I worry about anything else?"

"I understand. But you need to consider your legal protection." He shrugged. "Just friendly advice—don't forget yourself while you worry about the girls."

Martinez was silent before looking ap again at Perkins. "Do you have any children?"

"One. A young adult son. He's in college now."

"So you know."

"I know enough. But I've never had a pretty daughter like your two. If had, I might feel even worse. But I get it. And I know what this can do to you."

"What do you mean?"

"I mean that whatever happens, be whole when it's done. The same thing applies to your girls and to your wife, but it will be different, no matter the outcome."

"You don't sound very encouraging."

"Sorry. I don't have the best bedside manner, but then again, being a father isn't for the squeamish."

"I'll remember that."

Perkins made a gesture and Martinez began his tale.

Alicia sat leaning against the wall while her little sister slept. She couldn't figure how Lacey could sleep so easily when she was still restless. Of course, the man hadn't stroked Lacey's hair as he did hers. But that wasn't what bothered her. What she worried about was what would come next.

Danny Novak arrived alone for lunch at Heaven's Home, a restaurant he had eaten at since he was a young boy living in the neighborhood. He entered the restaurant and stood by the cash register rather than taking a seat. Ruth Williams came to join him after three minutes. "When you're standing by the cash register, that means either you've got a question about the neighborhood, or you're getting takeout."

"Takeout today, Ms. Williams. I'm buying for Sergeant Boyd and myself."

"Well, you tell Oliver Christian Boyd to come in himself sometime."

"I thought O.C. came in here a lot."

Williams leaned forward and smiled. "Not enough for Lester. They hit it off a while ago, and I think Lester is a little lonely."

"I'll pass it on."

Williams turned toward the kitchen. "Let me get a few things together for you." She left Novak at the register, returning two minutes later with glasses of water. "Let's sit while we wait."

Williams and Novak sat at a booth, sinking into the cushions. Williams smiled again. "Since you don't have questions for me, I have one for you."

"Sure. What is it?"

"What's happening with those missing girls?"

Novak recounted several of the steps being taken to locate Lacey and Alicia Stevens. Williams listened, asked a few clarifying questions, then touched Novak's hand, stopping him. "And what about the stepfather, that Mr. Martinez? Is everything okay with him?"

"That's harder."

"Why? Don't tell me you're worried about what Ms. Jackie Moore is saying about you—or about him."

"I'm not, but then again, that's not my job."

"So it's your captain that's getting all the pressure?"

"Him and the lieutenant. You know both of them, right?" Williams nodded. "Well, they're trying to use all of us to investigate, but having to look into Martinez' background makes it harder."

"You think it's a waste of time?"

Novak laughed. "That's my guess, but it's still part of our job."

"I suppose so. But so is keeping the people in every neighborhood safe. People are saying the police aren't doing that."

"Where did you hear that?"

Williams shrugged. "All around. Now, I know that isn't true, but I know a lot of you. The question is how to help all the people feel safe."

Novak sat back. "And I only wish I knew how to do that."

CHAPTER TWENTY-ONE

Perkins interrupted Martinez. "May I get you anything—water or coffee?"

Martinez shook his head. "Not for now." He laughed. "I haven't been hungry for the last few days. That might help me with my waist."

"You've left your house, I understand. Where are you staying?"

"With a friend from work. Staying in a hotel wouldn't work long term. He's a good guy, and is nice enough to let me couch surf, but he only has a one-bedroom apartment."

Perkins nodded. "A far cry from a house with a yard."

"And a family," Martinez said. "That's what matters. I don't need much for myself, but it's different when you have a family."

"I agree. Are you able to focus on work?"

"That's something else. I'm not working right now."

Perkins frowned. "I don't understand. Did something happen at work?"

"I'm being paid, if that's what you're asking." Martinez sighed. "The reports of my being a rapist and abducting children have made the front office nervous. They were angry that the situation in Chicago didn't come up during the background check."

"It wasn't supposed to."

"That's what my boss said, and his boss said the same. But they hired another firm to do the background check again, and they guarantee it will be back in only a few days. Until that's done, my company placed me on paid leave."

Perkins peered out his window. "Do they understand how long these things can take?" He saw Martinez' reaction and stopped. "I don't mean finding the girls—we want that to take place as soon as possible—but repairing a man's reputation is not a short-term task. What is it they're expecting before they let you go to work again?"

Martinez shrugged. "I don't know. My boss has been supportive and was embarrassed to tell me about the paid leave. But in the meantime, I have way too much time on my hands." He slumped in his chair again. "And the person I want to spend it with won't even talk to me."

Perkins looked at Martinez, willing him to relax. "You never told me how you met your wife. I'd like to hear about that, unless it's a sore subject for you."

"Not yet." Martinez smiled. "Patty and I have a pleasant history. I work as an IT consultant, and ... What am I telling you that for? You know everything about me by now, don't you?"

"We know a great deal, we've made several calls. I'll tell you the things I can, but I need to keep some of them private."

Martinez nodded. "I understand—that makes sense." He looked at Perkins again. "Anyway, I'm working IT, and Patty worked in a box factory—she's a secretary/office manager—still does." He stopped. "Well, even before that, I played in an adult soccer league. One night, I had a game right after Alicia's youth soccer team had a practice. I looked over and saw Patty, and she looked at me, and ..." Martinez' voice trailed. "I was shy and didn't approach her for her number." His face brightened again. "But the good thing is, my company had a contract to reconfigure the box factory's network, including secure internet. It took four days of work, including preparation. Patty was the one who set up the meetings. She seemed nice and brought me coffee a few times, even when I didn't ask for it."

"That was very nice of her."

"It was, and when the job was complete, I asked her for a date."

"And she didn't accept."

Martinez stared. "How did—?"

"It's a common story. Was she divorced by then?"

"Yes, and still frazzled. It's tough raising two young children. Remember, the girls were only two and seven then, and still figuring out what it meant to be a family without a father."

"This is informal, but do you mind if I take notes?" Perkins asked. "I may want to follow up on some things, and I don't want to forget."

"Go right ahead," Martinez said. "If it will help."

Perkins placed a pad in the center of his desk and picked up a pen. "Go on."

"Right. Anyway, I asked if I offended her, and she got embarrassed, saying that she wanted to go out, but that she had two daughters. I knew enough not to ask her to bring the girls with us, but suggested that she find a babysitter for an evening and call me when she got something arranged. We talked to each other by phone a few more times, then a week later, she got her mother to sit with the girls." He smiled. "We didn't even go anywhere fancy, just a tiny restaurant in Uptown North. We ate and talked, and then took a walk by the river. It was a perfect first date."

"How were things with her mother?"

"We didn't interact much in the early days, and I think she was torn. She never liked Rory, Patty's first husband, and while I wasn't her first choice, she thought I was better for her daughters than him."

"Which may have changed now."

"No. Clarise knows what she wants and what she doesn't. I never fit her ideal image of a husband for her daughter, unless compared to Rory."

"What drew you to your wife?"

Martinez smiled. "Patty is a very warm person—she'd give you the shirt off her back. She truly loves the girls and would do anything for them." Martinez hesitated. "Now I don't want to say anything negative about my mother-in-law, but she wasn't the best mother figure to Patty. I think she was highly critical of Patty and Rory, so Patty didn't have a good role model for a wife or mother."

"Can you give me more details?"

Martinez thought. "Neither Patty nor Clarise are good at managing money. And since Rory wasn't either, they ran to her parents for help all the time. It's not that either of them is irresponsible, but managing money and planning just isn't their thing. And since Patty didn't go beyond high school, financial planning confuses her."

Perkins waited as Martinez sat and wrestled within himself.

Martinez looked up. "It sounds like I'm criticizing Patty, but I'm not. More than anyone, she's helped me enjoy and engage in life. I've always planned well and done the right things, but to enjoy things—simple things like eating ice cream outside and watching a sunset—I didn't do that. Patty taught me. She taught the girls right from wrong, taught them to try their best, and doesn't ignore the girls so she can hang out with her girlfriends. The girls are her top priority and if I suggest something she doesn't like, she tells me straight up. But if I make a suggestion about the girls that she likes, even something we both have to work at, she puts in at least as much effort as I do. She is also kind and supportive. There was a kid at the elementary school whose family was struggling financially, and Patty is the one who held a drive to get her family some things—anonymously, since she knows how that can feel to a parent. I didn't do that, she did that." Martinez looked up again, resolute and almost angry. "Patty is a wonderful mom, a great wife and a wonderful person. And together, we've done pretty well, you know?"

"I see that." Perkins smiled. "It sounds like you're proud of her."

"I am. I'm proud of Patty, proud of both girls, and a little proud of myself to be honest." He chuckled. "If you know what it's like to be the only male in a house of women, you know what I mean."

Perkins smiled again. "You never adopted the girls, but was that ever on your mind?"

Martinez looked away. "That's a sore point. I would have adopted them in a heartbeat, but Clarise didn't think it was a good idea. That's given me fewer rights as a stepparent, but I've been more involved than Rory in the last few years anyway, and I think he'd admit that."

"Do you think Clarise—Mrs. Jones—regrets her decision?"

Martinez studied the carpet. "A week ago, I might have said yes."

"But now?"

"Huh. I think now Clarise feels vindicated. But right now, that doesn't matter. I just want the girls to be safe. That's all I care about."

"Spoken like a true father."

Chapter Twenty-Two

Hart, Fair and Shore stood outside Spencer Elementary looking up at the building. Hart frowned at Shore. "You have something on your mind, Dinah?"

Shore smiled at her nickname and looked at Hart. "I'm not sure."

Fair smiled at his partner. "I know you, Dinah. There's something that isn't working for you."

Shore shook her head again, pointing at the school "It's not that, Thomas." She looked up again. "But we've found something important about the family dynamics that we didn't know before."

"But that's not what's bothering you," Hart said.

"It's not. But I think we need to go to Eastern Middle School now."

"What questions?" Fair asked. "I read the report from Moody and Porter—they were thorough."

"I agree. But in their report, they said the guidance counselor was out that day, so they only spoke with the principal and Alicia's teachers."

"They talked to seven people," Fair said. "That should be enough."

"Right. *Then.*" Shore said. "But now I think we should talk to the guidance counselor. I want to dig deeper into the relationship between Martinez and Alicia. We can always pass what we find on to Dave and Siem, but we're already out here. Why stop now?"

"Wait a minute," Fair said. "We left that meeting—I left that meeting—believing Martinez was a good guy, and likely not the rapist the TV news is saying he is. What are you suggesting?"

"I'm not suggesting anything, Thomas."

"Due diligence?" Hart asked.

Shore nodded. "Plus, no one's spoken to the guidance counselor there and we should."

"Let's go," said Fair. "No time like the present."

Hart shrugged. "Well, I want to go, too. Let me call in to make sure it's okay."

Fair smiled. "Happy to have you."

Eastern Middle School was in the precinct's heart at Lowe and Uber streets. Fair and Shore got out of their unmarked car and looked around. Hart arrived two minutes later and parked behind them.

"Any problem getting approval?" asked Fair.

"It was O. C.," Hart said. "We have an unspoken agreement. Canuck's going to run though my sector today while I can't."

The officers entered the school office and presented their credentials. "We know other detectives were here only a short while ago, ma'am," Shore said to the school secretary, an older woman with a grandmotherly appearance. "But on that day, the guidance counselor wasn't available."

"Oh," said the secretary. "Mrs. Crandall. I remember. She was sick that day, wasn't she?" She smiled. "Mrs. Crandall's in today, though. Won't you have a seat while I get her?" She smiled and left, and Hart, Shore and Fair looked around the office.

A student sat at the edge of the office looking at her phone, ignoring the officers. She rose when the guidance counselor entered the office accompanied by the school secretary. "I'm Melanie Crandall, the head counselor here. I also work with students in Alicia Steven's area of the alphabet." She turned toward the offices. "Let's go to the conference room."

"Works for us," said Fair.

Crandall opened the door to the conference room, then turned back to Fair. "Where do you want me?"

"Sit anywhere you'd like, ma'am. This is informal."

"I know," said Crandall, taking the seat at the head of the able. "I was told by others that this wasn't stressful, but I'm still nervous." She smiled, pressing her lips together.

"I'm Detective Thomas Fair, and these are Detective Sharon Shore and Officer Stephanie Hart. We've interviewed teachers, counselors, neighbors and the family. It's been a lot of work."

"I've watched television shows about missing children and they always have a million people involved, it seems."

Fair smiled. "A million sets of hands would make our jobs easier, ma'am. We have some support from other agencies, including the FBI, but it's still a lot of work."

"How can I help you?"

"Do you know Alicia Stevens?"

"Oh yes," Stevens said. "We're a small school. I know most of our students, at least in passing."

"Did you know Alicia in more than a passing sense?" Hart asked.

Crandall nodded. "A bit." She looked up for a second to recall the situation. "As I remember, an administrative issue came up. Her birth father came to school asking for information and we had an annotation in the file not to tell him. I had to speak with Ms. Stevens to resolve it."

"What happened?" Fair asked.

"Oh, he got the information he needed. It wasn't anything important, something to do with grades or attendance. The notation was a mistake. A secretary noticed Mr. Martinez' name in the file and assumed the birth father had no parental rights. The birth father was annoyed but understanding."

"When was this?" Fair asked.

Crandall frowned. "Oh, that had to be in the sixth grade. That's when I met Alicia, and how I got to know her and her parents, her mother and stepfather, I mean. I'd never met her birth father."

"Have you ever made a home visit with them?" Hart asked.

"Yes," Crandall said. "We usually conduct those at transitional times. But in Alicia's case, she had been sick for almost a week, so I took her class assignments to her."

"How would you describe their home life?"

"I've never thought much about it." She sat back and smiled. "Well, it's a normal family—Mom, Dad, two kids with the normal amount of chaos. They're a nice family, as I recall."

Fair leaned forward. "You smiled a second ago. Was there something you remembered that made you smile?"

"Yes, and it's silly."

"What is it?"

"Well, we were sitting at the kitchen table, and Mr. Martinez came in wearing sweats on a sweltering day. It seemed something odd to wear when it was so hot. I must have looked at him oddly, because his wife started laughing and asked, 'Do you want to tell her, or should I?' Mr. Martinez looked away, and in a few minutes, Ms. Stevens told me what happened."

"Which was?" Shore asked.

"Well, Ms. Stevens admitted it was partly her fault, but Alicia was getting teased by the other students about having a little hair on her legs—it happens to all of us. Anyway, Ms. Stevens refused to let her shave them. She didn't explain why, but something about it made her uncomfortable."

Hart chuckled. "I know where this is going."

"And you'd be right," Crandall said. "Mr. Martinez felt bad for Alicia, so one day, he went into the backyard with Alicia and helped her shave her legs, by first shaving one of his so she could see how to do it. He hoped it would be their little secret." Crandall laughed again. "But when he finished shaving his leg, then making sure Alicia didn't cut herself, she burst out laughing."

"One smooth leg and one hairy leg, right?" Hart asked.

"Yes," said Crandall. "So right then, they knew they couldn't keep the secret. Ms. Stevens said she wanted to get mad at her husband, but after seeing his legs that way, she couldn't stop laughing. It's been a family joke ever since."

"Sounds like a nice family dynamic."

"They all get along well."

"How so?" Shore asked.

"Well, I glanced at their family photos in the living room while I waited for Mr. Martinez to come in. They're all very chummy."

"Chummy?"

"Yes. He and Alicia are often together in the pictures. I think he's the 'preferred parent.'"

"Is he involved with her in school here, and if so, is that the same or different from Ms. Stevens' involvement?"

"Oh, they do the same things. They've attended parent–teacher conferences from the beginning, attend school functions like assemblies, special programs, that kind of thing. The difference is, I always felt that Mr. Martinez was more engaged with Alicia than his wife. I got the sense that he's also more engaged with Lacey—is that her name?" The officers nodded. "Right. With Lacey, too. Ms. Stevens attends all the conferences, for example, but seldom asks questions, according to her teachers." She shrugged. "I guess it isn't her thing."

"What else can you tell us about Alicia, such as how she worked with other students, maybe acting-out behaviors?"

"She's about fair to middling with other students, not popular, but she has her group of friends. Oh. Would you want to interview her friends, too?"

"That might be helpful," Fair said. "But that's a more complicated procedure since they're minors. What do you think they would tell us?"

"I'm not sure. Middle schools are full of drama, but I don't remember hearing much about Alicia."

Hart noticed that Fair and Shore shared a glance.

"Anything we didn't ask you that we should know?" Fair asked.

Crandall shook her head. "I don't think so." She turned toward the door. "I looked at Alicia's student file before we came in, and there isn't much in it."

"From what the original detective told us," Shore began, "I have to agree with you. At least there was nothing in the file we felt we needed to follow up on." Shore looked to Fair and Hart, who both nodded. "I think we're finished, but here's my card. Please call us if something else comes to mind that you want to tell us."

Crandall looked at the card, then back to Shore. "I can do that." She smiled, rose, and shook the hands of all three officers as she left.

The officers left the building and met at their vehicles. "Any impressions?" Shore asked.

Hart sighed. "The leg-shaving incident is a pleasant story and Ms. Crandall saw it positively."

"I hear what you not saying, Steve," Fair said. "I don't want to throw shade on someone either, but it's not what you expect a father or stepfather to do."

"Exactly." Shore looked to her partner. "But we have a resource who can help with this."

"Marianna?" Shore nodded.

"Is she the profiler?"

"That's her," Fair said. "She's reviewed the profile of the guy from Indiana. Maybe she ought to look at Martinez."

"But he couldn't have been in Indiana when that girl was killed," Hart countered. "I agree we have to dig deeper, but are we trying to hang this guy out to dry for no reason?"

"Can't agree with you there, Steve," Fair said. "Two missing girls is reason enough for me."

CHAPTER TWENTY-THREE

Clarise Jones opened the car door and walked to the passenger side. She frowned at her daughter, who was looking down at the floor. Jones opened the door and reached for Stevens. "Patty, we're here."

Stevens looked up. "What?"

"I said we're here," Jones repeated. "At the lawyer's office."

"Okay." Stevens gathered herself and allowed Jones to lead her into the officers of Slade and Dolman, LLP.

Past the entrance was a reception desk with a smiling young woman sitting behind it. "Good morning, and welcome to Slade and Dolman. Do you have an appointment today?"

"Yes," Jones said. "Not with a particular lawyer, but ..." She glanced at her daughter. "We want to file paperwork against her husband."

"A domestic situation?"

"Yes."

"And you have an appointment, correct?"

"Right," Jones said. "We made it yesterday."

"The name?"

Jones hesitated. "My name is Clarise Jones, but the appointment is in the name of Patricia Stevens." She smiled. "One of those names should be in your book there."

The receptionist looked at the calendar, then back to her visitors. "Yes. Ms. Stevens." She turned to Stevens as she rose. "Your appointment will be with one of our senior associates, Ms. Mangino. Please have a seat." Stevens and Jones walked over to the couches in the well-appointed reception area and sat. "May I get you something while you wait?"

Jones looked at Patty, who shook her head. "Nothing for us, thank you."

"I'll be right back."

The receptionist passed through a set of double doors and disappeared. As soon as she was out of range, Stevens turned to her mother. "I don't know why I let you talk me into this, Mom. I've got better things to do than waste money on a lawyer."

"Your father and I will pay for this, Patty. We just want you to be protected."

"Protected from what?"

Jones stared at her daughter. "Are you kidding? You find out your husband was arrested at a gang rape and you're not worried about your girls?"

"But Alex doesn't live with us anymore, Mom. We even changed the locks."

Jones sniffed. "A good thing, too. Who knows what might have happened?"

Stevens stood. "I know, I know." She was pacing in the reception area. "But now that he can't get into the house, what are we worried about?"

Jones shook her head. "We're worried, or at least your father and I are worried about Alex coming back and demanding to see the girls, or claiming he has some rights to you or the house. We're here to make sure that doesn't happen."

"But the house is in your name, Dad's and mine. Alex's name doesn't appear on the deed at all, since we bought it before we got married."

"Patty, sometimes family courts give half of everything the couple owns to each person when they divorce. We can't take the—"

"Who says I'm getting divorced, Mom?" Stevens turned on her mother with scorn in her eyes. "Can I at least make *that* decision on my own?"

"Honey, of course," said Jones. She smiled. "But you need protection, too. Do you want to be struggling again if you divorce because Alex has taken half of the money?"

Stevens hesitated, then sat. She looked dejected again and looked up at her mother. "Most of the money in the bank is only there because Alex made us save more of it. It's not right for me to claim as much as he put in."

"And how are you going to take care of the girls if you split up? Have you thought about that?"

"They're not his girls, Mom," said Stevens. "Are you saying you want him to pay for them even when they aren't his girls and he doesn't live with them?"

Jones patted Stevens' hand. "The girls and their welfare have to come first, Patty, and—"

"Ms. Stevens?" The woman speaking was in her mid-thirties, wearing a light business suit. She looked at both women with a straight, open face.

Stevens and Jones rose. "I'm Patty Stevens."

The attorney approached with her hand outstretched. "I'm Elizabeth Mangino, an associate here, but please call me Liz."

Stevens took her hand, then turned to her mother. "This is my mother, Clarise Jones."

"Pleased to meet you, Ms. Jones. Won't you come back with me?"

Jones and Stevens nodded and followed Mangino to a conference room, taking seats near her. The lawyer smiled again and faced Stevens. "Now I understand this is a domestic case, so before we begin, I need to ask if you're reporting anything regarding child sexual abuse?" Stevens shook her head. "Okay," Mangino continued. "When we say domestic, we mean many things, so tell me why you came in today."

Stevens sighed. "It's my husband, and my two daughters." Stevens started crying and looked around the conference room.

Mangino reached behind her to a bookshelf and brought over a box of tissues. "Take your time."

"May I say something?" Jones asked.

Mangino glanced at Stevens, who nodded. "Go ahead."

"Well, you may have heard about the two girls who are missing. The ones the police are sure have been abducted?"

Mangino nodded and her eyebrows furrowed. "The Stevens girls."

"Right. Those are Patty's children."

Mangino reached over the table. "I know this is hard for you, Ms. Stevens. I have a little one at home too, and I can't imagine what you're going through."

"You're a mother?" Jones asked.

Mangino laughed. "Lawyers have children too."

"I'm sorry. I didn't mean to offend you."

Mangino smiled and waved away the concern. "It's no bother, Ms. Jones. We lawyers make a lot of our own problems." She faced Stevens again, who had composed herself. "I've heard some things on the news, Ms. Stevens, but what is it you want from an attorney?"

Stevens looked at her mother, then back to Mangino. "I guess I want myself and my girls to be protected, in case my husband files for divorce or I file."

"I understand. But please spell it out for me. What is it you want protection from? Is it your assets in terms of a divorce, from your husband specifically, or something else?"

"Those are the things we talked about," Jones said.

"*All* of them?"

Jones looked again to Stevens, who was looking at her tissue. "Well, we thought it was better to be ahead of the game."

Mangino cleared her throat. "I understand that, Ms. Jones, and I want to be clear about what you're asking. If what you want is a no-contact order or a restraining order that keeps your husband way from you, or the girls once they're found, that's one procedure." Mangino gestured with her hands. "Now, if what you want to do is to freeze your assets and your husband's so he can't take any more of them, or propose a legal split of assets, that's quite another thing. I can help you with both, but please tell me what you want or what you're concerned about happening *without* legal protection. That way I can give you what you want. Does that make sense?"

Stevens looked up. "Yes." She glanced at her mother. "I think that would be best."

Mangino picked up her pen again and smiled. "I'm all ears."

An hour and a half later, Stevens and Jones left the office, Clarise smiling and Patty quiet. They returned to the car and got in, Patty saying nothing and looking straight ahead. They had been driving for ten minutes when she turned and saw her mother staring at her before turning her attention back to the road.

"You didn't answer me."

"What? Were you asking me something?"

"I've asked you several things, and you haven't spoken a word since we left the lawyer's office. What is the matter with you?"

Patty's lips pressed together. "Mom, telling a lawyer I was afraid for my life and the girls' lives because of Alex and filing for a formal separation from him before eleven o'clock in the morning was too much for me."

"Hmph," Jones said. "Those were important things, Patty. You and what you own need to be protected. Don't you see that?"

"But why did we do it by telling her that Alex was a monster? He's not a bad person."

Jones shook her head. "Not a bad person? A rapist is not a bad person? Don't you care about what could happen to the girls once we have them back?"

Stevens shrank into herself. "I just want them back. Right now, I'm not worried about Alex."

"But he can't be with them once they're found!" Jones smiled. "And now we've taken care of that."

They drove in silence for a few more blocks before Patty spoke again, quieter than before. "Isn't there something bad about lying to a lawyer? I mean, we told her things that didn't happen or didn't happen the way we said."

"What do you mean? We didn't lie."

"But we didn't tell the truth either, Mom, and I think she knew it."

"The lawyer?"

"Yes. Didn't you see how she kept frowning and asking us some questions more than once?"

Jones shrugged. "I suppose so, but that's what lawyers do. They do it all the time on the television shows."

"But this is not a TV show! This is my life!" Stevens crossed her arms and hugged herself. "I'm sure that lawyer felt we were going overboard and was trying to get us to hold back on those charges against Alex. I *know* she was."

"And what of it? That's not our problem. It's Alex who has to prove he's innocent, or that he's not as bad as people think, though I doubt that. Why should we worry about that?"

Stevens sighed. "Seems to me I used to hear something about 'innocent until proven guilty,' Mom. And now we've just made that really hard for Alex. I didn't want to do that."

"Well, then it's a good thing your father and I are here to help you, isn't it?"

Marianna Lynch's smooth face belied her occupation. As principal profiler for the Port Angel Police Department, Lynch had provided police potential profiles and information on perpetrators of serial rapes, murders, robberies and serial white-collar crimes. While profiling is not a precise science, Lynch was well regarded in Port Angel and in the state for the accuracy and usefulness of her profiles.

Her office was large and bright and resembled more a professor's office than the office of a psychologist and former military officer. As always, both she and her office were disheveled when Fair, Shore and Hart entered. Lynch didn't rise. "So you're finally here to ask me about the girls, huh? I thought you'd be here, or somebody would have been here long before now." She rose and shook Fair's hand. "Been a long time, Thomas."

"It has." Fair pointed to Shore and Hart. "You know Sharon Shore, and this is Officer Stephanie Hart."

"I've heard of Hart."

Hart frowned. "Something tells me that may not be a good thing."

Lynch waved her hand. "Nothing to worry about. We run profiles of people based on their background to check new officers for areas of concern. You're good." Lynch smiled. "I remember you because you're a more recent hire." She turned to Fair. "Whereas for an older goat like Thomas, I worry about the risks the department carries by having him on the force, but I hope Detective Shore won't suffer because of it." Lynch pointed to the chairs in her office. "Let's sit."

Fair looked at Shore and Hart, then back at Lynch. "We came to see you about the girls, Marianna, but we have something else to run by you."

"Oh?"

"Yeah," said Fair. "But we don't have an official written report to share, so—"

"It's okay. Just talk."

Fair cleared his throat. "With all the focus on Mr. Martinez, the stepfather of the missing girls, the captain and lieutenant wanted us to go back and make additional checks at the elementary and middle schools. They suggested we ask different questions to probe the relationship between Martinez and the girls and see what might come up."

Lynch nodded. "A good idea."

"We thought so, too," said Shore. "And we have information about Martinez that one of the school officials believed was okay, but we wanted to run by you."

"It's more of a check-in or at least letting someone with expertise evaluate it, rather than a suggestion that the guy is a bad actor," Hart added. "And that's not our thing."

Lynch leaned forward. "Describe the interactions he had with the daughters. As stepfather, what parental rights does he have?"

"None," said Hart. "He didn't adopt the girls, but he can pick them up, things like that."

"Only the mother—or perhaps both birth parents—could let him adopt the girls," Lynch said. "How long have they been married?"

"Five years."

"Is the birth father in the picture?"

"Not much," Hart replied. "As best we can figure, he's not a terrible guy, but not great. He has little involvement in the girls' lives."

"I wonder why there was no adoption, then." Lynch frowned. "Do you think this stepfather— Martinez—would have been willing to adopt them?"

Hart nodded. "I'm sure of it. The interaction I saw among the three of them was very natural. I saw no tension between Martinez and either girl."

Lynch thought for a moment. "What more do you have for me? There's little in what you've told me so far."

"Well," Shore began, "we spoke to her teachers at the middle school. That's why we're here."

Lynch shook her head. "Before we get to that, tell me more about normal interactions that you saw." The officers looked at each other with questioning faces. "No more about that? I ask because listening to one thing with no context isn't the way I do things, since I need to get a more complete picture." She noticed Shore's expression and added, "I'll give you my professional opinion, but it won't be my best or most accurate."

Hart nodded. "I saw Martinez interacting with Lacey at their soccer tournament."

"What did you see?"

"I saw Martinez work with his team—he's Lacey's soccer coach—very positively. He didn't yell at them but was very encouraging."

"What about touch? Describe how he touched either of the girls?" Lynch leaned forward again. "Not what you think, but what you saw?"

Hart sat back and thought. "When the team finished the game and after Martinez spoke, he turned to walk with Lacey back to her mother and sister. I remember Martinez placing his hand on her shoulder for maybe two seconds, both of them laughing, then he dropped his hand." Hart looked up. "Oh, and when they came to Operation ID, he and Lacey were holding hands at the beginning. When they left with her ID, the three of them, Martinez, Lacey, and Alicia just walked together in a group. No one held hands because Lacey was gripping her new ID."

"Uh huh." Lynch looked to Fair and Shore. "Neither of you saw him interact with the girls, is that right?"

"Right," Fair said. "Hart only saw them because of those two chance encounters. By the time they called us in, it was because the girls were missing, and—"

Lynch made an inpatient gesture. "Right. I was just confirming what you'd seen." She sighed, then looked at Hart. "Tell me what brought you here."

Shore began and described the pictures in the Steven and Martinez home. She also described the leg-shaving incident that prompted their visit with Lynch. Lynch listened, leaning in, and asked clarifying questions.

"Okay. So you have a stepfather who is shaving his leg with a stepdaughter. Now I presume they were wearing clothes when this was happening?"

"That's our assumption," Shore began. "If they were naked or something, I'm sure the mother wouldn't have put up with it."

"How close to this event was the counselor? Was it the school counselor who visited the home?"

Fair frowned. "Correct. As she told us, she thought Martinez' legs were still shaved. I imagine it was recent, like within the last week." He looked to Shore and Hart. "Would you two agree?"

"I would," Hart said. "It was clearly recent enough that Martinez was embarrassed, and Ms. Stevens was still telling everyone about it."

Lynch sighed. "But we know nothing from anyone involved. We also don't know how the girl felt about the incident."

"Wait," Shore said. "The impression I got from the school counselor is that Alicia was excited because she would get teased less. The mother thought it was funny and had nothing bad to say."

"We can't say how Alicia felt," Hart countered. "As best we can determine, the parents saw it as one of those funny family stories, like the kind you tell your kids' boyfriends and girlfriends to embarrass them later."

Fair agreed. "Right. But looking at it from the outside, and knowing that abused children often cling to the abusive parent rather than to the other one, we didn't know what else to do with the information."

Lynch looked to Hart again. "But you told me that the older girl, Alicia, wasn't clinging to Martinez."

"At Operation ID? No. Lacey was holding his hand in the beginning. Alicia was just standing by him, and nothing about their stances suggested they were close, or anything. They were just there. Alicia looked bored like all girls her age, but when I asked her a question she brightened and gave me a simple, straight answer. I remember being a little surprised because I hadn't expected it."

"What's your general impression of him?"

Hart shook her head. "They were just a father with his two daughters, doing something together. Nothing when they approached told me any-thing, nothing they said or did concerned me. I just enjoyed watching how excited Lacey was to get her ID. And the hand holding—I just thought it was a kid showing her dad around the school, proud like she was with the ID card."

Lynch sat back in her chair again, looking up at the ceiling and shaking her head, then she smiled. "Well, I understand why you came to talk to me. There is also a vibe that makes us wonder about the motivations of people around young children." She paused. "As I said, I can't say anything definitive without more information or evidence. One thing is the event that prompted the leg shaving, and that was the teasing by other middle schoolers. Now we know that happens, and kids take all kinds of extreme measures to handle teasing." She stopped. "Wait, would any of you say that Martinez was the steadier of the parents, the one who is the voice of reason?"

"I've met them and spent time questioning them, and you're right on the money," Fair said. "Martinez was grieving, but asked good questions and consulted with his wife before answering. She wasn't a wallflower, but she appeared more impulsive than him. Is that relevant?"

"It might be," Lynch said. "I can't explain why the mother didn't want to teach her daughter to shave her legs, though my mother was the same way." Lynch laughed. "I think she was afraid I was growing up too soon and wouldn't be ready for teenage and adult stuff, things like making out with boys. That's true. I wasn't ready for that, and Alicia may not be either. But we also aren't ready for the teasing we experienced—all we wanted was to be able to fit in. It sounds like Martinez was trying to stop the teasing and not just spend time with the stepdaughter in the bathroom or wherever. That's not the motivation of a pedophile." She raised her hand. "And you already know I'm going to backpedal on this like crazy, so hold it. The point is, what you're telling me raises yellow flags, but it doesn't paint Martinez one way or the other. The only way to know that is for you or me to conduct more interviews. But if you're asking me if the relationship suggests he's a rapist or pedophile, that would not be my first guess."

"And as for him being the child abductor of the girls in Indiana and Ohio?"

Lynch shook her head. "Everything I've seen said that Martinez hasn't been there in a gazillion years. Plus, I'm pegging this serial abductor as someone with less formal education, and likely in a lower-level job. I can't tell you his occupation, because there's been no evidence of occupation at the crime scene. However, whether he has a lot of formal education or not, he's smart. Leaving little or no evidence is tough.

"So not likely to be Martinez?" Shore held up her hands in surrender. "You'd say that from what little you know, Martinez is less likely to be a pedophile or a direct threat to the girls?"

Lynch smiled. "You've backpedaled that well, Detective."

Hart looked at Shore and Fair. "So, what's our Plan B?"

Chapter Twenty-Four

Jackie Moore continued to smile at Andrew Shoemaker in the latter's office, but she seemed frustrated. "So, can you tell me anything about the investigation *at all*, Captain? Any clues you can share with us?"

Shoemaker paused before answering to settle his stomach. He smiled. "As I mentioned, the safety of the girls is paramount. The last thing we want to do is to reveal information that may tip off the abductor into what we're doing or looking into. That's standard police procedure."

"I see. What about the tips you've received from KPAR-TV? Have those helped you at all?"

Shoemaker's smile widened. "We appreciate the help of the public and are looking into anything we learn through your tip line or the general police tip line, which is 741-555-7171." Shoemaker turned toward the camera. "We encourage anyone with relevant information to call one of our tip lines." He turned back to Moore. "We appreciate your help."

"We always want to work with the police to keep our citizens safe, Captain," Moore said. "Now, are you saying Mr. Martinez is not a person of interest in this case?"

"To comment on a single person wouldn't be wise, Ms. Moore. We are investigating Mr. Martinez, but understand we have not felt the necessity to take him into custody or for questioning. That should tell you something."

Moore smiled and nodded. "Oh, it does."

"You know, we should be thinking happy thoughts," Alicia said.

Lacey looked up at her big sister. "Why? Is it going to make him take us back home?"

"No, but at least we'll stop thinking about bad things and think about good things again." Alicia smiled and closed her eyes. "Now close your eyes. Tell me the happiest things you can remember."

"From forever?"

"It doesn't matter. Just think about something that made you happy."

Lacey closed her eyes and sat back. Her posture changed as she opened her eyes. "I have one!"

"What is it?"

"It's when I stopped that goal at the soccer tournament."

"Against that really good team?" Lacey nodded. "I remember that. That was great for me, too."

Lacey looked up at Alicia. "What's your happy thought?"

"I already had one. It's the Daddy/Daughter Dance from fifth grade."

"That was a long time ago."

"It doesn't matter. I just remember how much fun I had—I hadn't gone before and all the other girls told me how much fun they had with their dads. I couldn't go until the fifth grade."

"I don't remember that too well."

"That's okay. I enjoyed getting dressed up and stuff." Alicia sat back on the wall again and could barely hear her sister. "What?"

"I asked if I would ever go to the Daddy/Daughter Dance?"

"You bet, Bug, you'll go for sure." Alicia held her sister's hand and kept smiling. *Will she?*

Hart was washing her hands in the ladies' room when Jackie Moore exited a stall.

"Your name is Hart, isn't it?"

"It is." Hart glanced toward the bathroom door. "I imagine you were speaking with our captain."

"Ah, yes. Captain Shoemaker. The strong, silent type."

"I've never heard him described that way, but I'd say you were right."

Moore washed her hands and reached for a towel. "So do you think you could give me a hand with this, sister to sister?"

"What do you mean?"

Moore said, "Trying to get ahead is tough for Black folk, and we need to help each other out."

Hart looked down at Moore. "I see. Well, it's nice that you noticed me. A lot of people look at me and don't consider me Black because of my White dad, but I've always been very clear about who I am and where I come from. And let me tell you, lady, you are no sister of mine. The people I back up have integrity and care for the reputations of others." Hart threw her towel in the trash, adding, "I hope you're successful."

Moore frowned and opened her mouth to speak, but Hart cut her off. "You know Ms. Moore, I wonder how much time we're wasting trying to find who leaked that information to you from Chicago, information that it's illegal for you to have."

"It's not my fault people give me things they shouldn't. I have no responsibility in that."

"And no responsibility in ruining a decent man's reputation, either." Hart approached Moore again. "Ms. Moore, Port Angel is a big market, but there are bigger ones out there. Maybe if we're lucky, you'll get a big network job and leave us the hell alone."

"We turn now to our correspondent Jackie Moore. Jackie, what is the progress on the two missing girls?"

"Thank you, Chad. And I wish I could tell you something encouraging."

"So what's happening, Jackie?"

"To be honest, Chad, not much at all. Now, you know that the KPAR-TV tip line has received dozens of tips and information that we've passed on to the Port Angel Police Department."

"That's great, Jackie! Have any of those tips paid off?"

"Well, Chad, the Port Angel Police Department isn't sharing with us, even though we have the largest reach in the city, so we don't know if they've been helpful or not."

"Now, you also reported on Mr. Martinez, the stepfather who was arrested in Chicago years ago on a related charge. Is he being investigated, and if so, what did the police find?"

"Chad, I visited with Captain Andrew Shoemaker of the department, and he told me in no uncertain terms that he didn't want us messing with his investigation. Now, I understand that we can't obstruct the police. But to refuse valuable information that comes from a citizen? I only hope their slow pace doesn't end in tragedy for these girls."

"Thank you, Jackie, and I hope so, too."

Andrew Shoemaker heard the heavy tread of Perkins long before he spoke. "You don't have to watch that trash."

Shoemaker returned the gaze. "The commissioner is watching it. That's all I need to know."

Perkins turned an overstuffed chair around and sat facing Shoemaker, who had reclined in his desk chair. "I doubt if I've ever seen spin like that before. You'd think we were out to hurt the girls ourselves. So what is the status of the investigation into Martinez?"

"Everything we've learned from Martinez himself, from Moody and Porter, and from the FBI says the same thing: Martinez was a kid, he left the house and called the police, and after questioning, they released him."

"Did we get his military records?"

Shoemaker nodded, pointing to his desk. He picked up two pieces of paper. "You can read it if you like. Honorable discharge, and several commendations. Finished after seven years as a Petty Officer, Second Class."

"Respectable."

"So the record says." Shoemaker shook his head. "And yet he's still being painted as the bad guy on TV."

"At his job, too."

"What?"

"His job," Perkins repeated. "Martinez isn't working now."

"His bosses got cold feet?"

"Something like that, but Martinez told me it was the higher-ups who were ticked that the background check didn't find the case in Illinois."

"It wasn't supposed to."

"You're telling the wrong person, Shoe. Martinez is on paid leave until the second background check comes back clean." Perkins grew more serious. "You don't think they're going to find something damning, do you?"

Shoemaker shook his head. "Moody and Porter may be odd ducks, but when they and the FBI agree on something, I doubt it. Martinez is the real deal."

Perkins placed the report back on Shoemaker's desk. "Why does that not fill me with optimism?"

Patty Stevens turned off the television and sat down hard on her couch. Her mother had returned home after Patty screamed at her, and she was alone except for Sergeant Paul Andrews, who was sitting in his police cruiser at the curb. Patty remembered life before she met Martinez and how her daughters were now so devoted to him. She held her head in her hand. *What do I do now?*

CHAPTER TWENTY-FIVE

Hart, Fair and Shore returned to the bullpen after speaking with Lynch. They had walked silently from Lynch's office, but now sat at desks and brooded. Fair looked at his colleagues. "Are we just going to mope around all day?" He turned to Hart. "Don't you have a sector to patrol?"

Hart checked her watch. "I'm not going to worry about it." She smiled and drew herself up straight in her chair. "I was riding with the big-kid detectives today."

"I hope someone approved that, Hart," said Samuel Perkins.

Hart stepped back, hands on her hips. "Lieutenant, have I ever done something without approval?"

"Do you want my honest answer?" Perkins smiled. "I know that, Hart. I was just jerkin' your chain."

Hart smiled but realized she had never seen Perkins joke with officers before. Perkins was easy enough to approach, but wasn't known for his humor.

Perkins sat at the edge of a desk. "And since you've had so much time with the detectives today, I suppose you have something of value to share with me?"

Hart, Fair and Shore looked at each other before Fair pointed to Hart. "He was talking to you, Steve."

"Right," Hart said. She opened her notebook.

"Oh good," Perkins said. "Stephanie Hart notes." He was referring to Hart's reputation for taking precise, clear notes.

Hart ignored the dig, checked her notes, then looked up. "We spoke with a teacher who knew Alicia at Spencer both before and after Martinez arrived. This teacher would say Martinez was a change for the better. She described an incident at a parent–teacher conference where Martinez turned the whole thing into a valuable and positive meeting." Hart filled Perkins in on the details of the meeting and how impressed the teacher was. "This teacher—Ms. Stewart—said that Martinez helped Alicia stay on track so she could move into the fifth grade on schedule."

"That's it, Lieutenant," Shore added. "This teacher was sold on Martinez. Plus, she knew Alicia the year later when they attended the Daddy/Daughter Dance for the first time. She didn't say it outright, but my sense from the teacher is that Alicia didn't want to go to the dance with her birth father, but felt much closer to Martinez and wanted to go."

"There just seemed to be more positive energy with Alicia with Martinez in her life," Fair added, "though we can't compare that to anything with the birth father."

"And we're confident the birth father wasn't involved in the abductions, right?"

"Correct," Fair said. "We've got more than we need to rule him out."

"We can rule Martinez out for the abductions, too, correct?"

"As far as we can tell," Shore said. "Same overwhelming evidence and testimony. What we can't do is to counter the allegations about the gang rape or whatever in Illinois, or the idea that he may have hired someone else to abduct the girls."

Perkins looked to the side as he thought. "I think that's what bothers Martinez the most." He looked again at the officers. "Martinez came to see me, and he's worried for the girls more than anything else. But the second thing he's worried about is the allegations about the case in Illinois. He's on paid leave from his job because of it."

Hart shook her head. "Shit."

"My sentiments exactly. Martinez is taking this okay given the circumstances, but with being thrown out of his house and now not being able to work, he's being kicked when he's down, which is why we asked you to investigate him."

"And because Jackie Moore won't leave that part of the story alone," Hart said.

"She's done more than that," Perkins said. "She interviewed Shoe today, and we just watched the report on television. Not only is Moore implying that we're doing nothing on the case with the girls, but she also implied we're ignoring Martinez in our investigation."

Shore threw up her hands. "What the hell have we been doing all day then? We could have used Moody and Porter, and instead they're spinning their wheels looking for non-existent information."

"You're right." Perkins indicated the door of the bullpen. "And it hasn't made the captain any happier with this investigation and with what he's comfortable releasing to the press."

"Please don't release anything else to Jackie Moore," Hart said. "I met her in the ladies' room and I wanted to deck her."

Perkins smiled. "But you didn't, right? Last thing I want is for her to sue us for unleashing our lethal weapon on her."

"I used all my Zen powers, sir, but it wasn't easy."

"It never is when dealing with the nastier elements of the public." Perkins sighed. "What more do you have?"

Shore told Perkins about their meeting at Eastern Middle School, and the leg-shaving event, which prompted their visit to Marianna Lynch.

"Wait," Perkins said. "Did the counselor think there was something odd or out of place about the incident?"

Fair looked at Shore and Hart. "I'd say it was unusual enough that she didn't just hear about it and let it go, Perk. But afterwards, she noticed that Martinez and Stevens laughed about it as a running family joke, and the counselor felt it was just one of those odd family events."

"Why did you speak with Lynch?"

"Because we didn't have the luxury not to." Hart looked at her colleagues. "I have to tell you, sir, nothing I've seen about Martinez—and I've seen him face to face more than a few times—tells me he's anything other than what he appears to be: a very well put together father and husband. And I think he's being hurt by this more than he lets on."

Perkins sighed and shook his head. "We're not supposed to take sides as investigators, Hart—something to ponder if you want to make detective." He smiled again. "Having said that, I agree with you a hundred percent, so I wonder what that says about *me* as a detective. But I suppose this was a matter of following up on something that might be controversial."

"We just needed to run it down," Fair agreed.

"What did Marianna say?"

"She listened to it all, including information from Hart about Martinez' interactions with both girls at Operation ID and at the soccer tournament. To Marianna, everything was consistent, and Martinez' actions didn't bother her. She agreed it raised a yellow flag, but no red flags."

Perkins chuckled. "Vintage Marianna, always hedging her bets." He straightened up in his seat. "But she's often quite accurate in what she says, and in this case, she only has second- or third-hand information. We can't hope for anything more from her, I think." Perkins stood and drew his mouth into a tight line. "I'm done with this."

Hart frowned. "What do you mean?"

Perkins looked at her. "I'm done with wasting time looking into Martinez' background here *or* in Chicago. Let the FBI finish unless Moody and Porter find something new. This case is about two missing girls in Port Angel—*that* should be our focus. Given that, what do we have?"

Fair and Shore reviewed the status of the investigation, recounting Lynch's discussion of the serial abductor from Ohio and Indiana. Perkins listened while tapping his fingers on his legs and then shook his head, annoyed. "Is that all?" He looked at his three officers who kept looking at each other.

"It's like you said, Lieutenant," Fair said. "We've been treading water, looking into Martinez' background, and—"

"Why don't we take a different angle?" Hart asked.

"Meaning?"

"Well, I'm only an acting junior detective," Hart said with a smile, "but we've been asking ourselves how something like this abduction could have happened, where the girls could have been—the normal things we're required to look into."

"What's your suggestion?" Shore asked.

"Well, have we asked ourselves why somebody would move to Port Angel and how—"

"What's so hard about that?" asked Shore. "We're a major city. Hell, you came here after you left the army."

"True, but I had a specific reason or ability to do it. Who can just move across the U.S. like that? I can't anymore, I have a job. It was only when one career ended that I could move here."

"Do you think this guy was in the military like you?" Fair asked. "People leave the military all the time."

Hart shook her head. "It's possible, but I doubt it. We don't have any military installations here of any size, so people aren't transferred here. Martinez came for a job like I did. Our cases are the exception, not the rule."

"So what careers let you do that?" Fair asked.

"Marianna talked about the person in Ohio and Indiana not having a lot of formal education. What jobs with that level of education let you move all over the country?"

"There are lots," Hart said. "Skilled trades, like carpentry, welding, and HVAC, plus nurses and dental hygienists. Marianna also didn't say the person couldn't be retired."

Perkins' eyebrows furrowed. "These are interesting ideas, but how can we check on that many people?"

"He used to drive an older truck," Hart said. "Anybody can do that, but I'd go for skilled trades rather than nurses. That F-150 has skilled trades written all over it."

Fair turned to Perkins. "I wonder if they looked into these occupations in Ohio and Indiana."

Perkins smiled. "And I didn't even have to tell you to do it."

Chapter Twenty-six

Shoemaker gathered his cell phone and walked to his cruiser. The last thing he wanted to do was to keep thinking about the case, but he felt compelled to visit Stevens again and offer his support. Samuel Perkins had related his conversation with the detectives and Hart before leaving for the day. The officers' creative approach and thoroughness encouraged him.

None of that made this trip any easier. Shoemaker kept having flashbacks to the last missing child case, and he'd had difficulty sleeping for the last two nights. He drove to Stevens' address, and was annoyed to see a KPAR-TV van parked in front of the house behind a police cruiser. He cursed himself, then opened the door to his cruiser and approached the door.

Jackie Moore intercepted him.

"Happy to see you here, Captain Shoemaker," Moore said, thrusting a microphone at him. "We just finished talking to Ms. Stevens and your Officer Novak. But since you're in charge of the investigation, what can you tell our viewers?"

Shoemaker smiled and took his time. "I'm here to speak with Ms. Stevens and offer our support and give her what she needs. I don't have anything more to say to you, Ms. Moore, but it's good to see you."

"The police are working hard on this, aren't they, Captain?"

"We are," Shoemaker said. "Our investigators are working throughout Port Angel, and in Illinois thanks to your—information. It's full steam ahead. My stopping here is only to speak to Mr. Stevens, then I'll be back on the case myself." Shoemaker was turning away toward the house, dismissing Moore, when he noticed Stephanie Hart stepping out of her cruiser. *Must be relieving Novak.*

"Hart."

"Captain." Hart stood by her cruiser talking on the radio as Shoemaker approached the front door and rang the bell. She put down her radio, then turned directly into the microphone held by Jackie Moore.

"Office Hart. What can you tell us about the investigation?"

"I'm afraid I can't tell you anything, Ms. Moore. All official communications come through either Captain Shoemaker or from other authorized personnel. As a patrol officer, I'm not authorized to speak with the press." Hart smiled. "Please excuse me."

Moore made a cutting gesture with her hand across her throat, handing her microphone to an associate. As Hart approached the house, Moore started in again.

"Look, I realize that you can't say much officially, but this case is important."

"It *is* important," Hart said. "Yet you're spending time spreading rumors about people like Martinez that you can't back up. Why don't you change *your* tactics?"

"Are you serious?" Moore cried. "Don't you care about pedophiles and rapists? I don't think you do!"

Hart turned on her heel, took a deep breath then walked toward Moore, stretching to her full five-foot-nine-inch height.

"Sister, when I know you better, I'll tell you what happened to me in the God-damned army. You don't want to listen to that, so please don't tell me what I care about. At least in my situation, we *had* a case and didn't crucify people in the media. And do not waste your time looking up my case. You need to back off or we will find an ordinance you've violated, you got that?"

"Hart!" Shoemaker screamed. Hart turned and saw Shoemaker watching her interaction with Jackie Moore, and he did not look happy. "I need to see you!"

Hart smiled toward Shoemaker and added syrup to her tone. "Coming, sir!"

Hart saw the smug look on Jackie Moore's face as she walked toward Shoemaker, who was himself scowling at Moore. When Hart stood in front of him, he approached her and whispered in her ear. "Well said, but be careful."

At that moment, Novak came outside to update Shoemaker and Hart on what had happened in the Stevens house during his shift. "It's been quiet, and Ms. Stevens is lost. She's grown tired of her mother controlling her, and can't make even the smallest decision. She sent her mother home earlier, but now she's sitting here and can't even engage in conversation."

Shoemaker nodded. "Should we call her a doctor? She may require medical attention."

"That wouldn't surprise me, sir," Novak said. "It could be shock."

"Do we have her mother's phone number?"

Novak and Hart exchanged glances. "I don't, sir," Novak said. "And I suspect if we ask Ms. Stevens for it, she'd balk."

"Things that tough between them?"

Novak shook himself. "That's hard to say. But Ms. Stevens told me she almost had to throw her mother out of the house to get some privacy. That's what Sergeant Andrews told me when I arrived here, too."

Shoemaker nodded. "Suggestions?"

Hart glanced toward the house, then turned back to Shoemaker and Novak and shrugged. "How about a woman-to-woman connection?"

"That might be easier and less likely to cause issues than talking to her mother." Shoemaker frowned. "Who's on after you?"

"It's Gee, sir, Marin."

"Well, let's head inside and talk to Stevens. She may be calmer now." He looked up at Novak. "Are you heading home?"

"Unless you need me."

Shoemaker shook his head and Novak left the house. When Shoemaker and Hart entered the house, Stevens jumped up and offered them coffee, tea or water. Both accepted and Hart joined Stevens in the kitchen. "I realize this is hard on you, Ms. Stevens, and no one's staying with you at the moment. Your mother was here earlier and yesterday, wasn't she?"

Stevens sighed. "She was. And she'll be back again tomorrow, and that's fine. But I was just done with her for the day." She looked at Hart and shook her head. "I love my mother and she's trying to be supportive in her own way, but it's suffocating. I am a big girl, after all."

Hart laughed. "No argument from me." She inclined her head toward Shoemaker. "Everyone's working hard on this investigation, ma'am. I've been to the schools again, we have a profiler working to help us, and teams of officers volunteered to expand the search to more streets around this neighborhood. This is my first missing child case, but people are working as hard as they can."

Stevens looked at Hart, assessing her sincerity. Her eyes fell. "I understand you are, at least in my head. But in my heart, I fear the worst and think there ought to be something else that could be done." She looked up at Hart again. "So if I seem out of it today, it's not you, or Officer Novak or your captain. I had a premonition that I may never see my girls again, and I don't know what to do, or who to turn to."

Hart wanted to ask her about calling Martinez, but held her tongue. "Will you call your mother tomorrow?"

Stevens laughed. "I won't need to. I asked her to give me a break *today*. By tomorrow, she'll think it's business as usual and will be here right after breakfast." She sighed. "And by tomorrow, I'll be ready for her. Until then, I'm going to enjoy some Clarise-Jones-free silence."

Hart smiled. "Sounds like a plan."

Hart handed off Patty Stevens to Angela Marin at 2100 hours and headed to her cruiser. Nadine Delaplaine was standing to its side, her hands balled into fists. *Seriously?*

"Good evening, Ms. Delaplaine. Something I can do for you?"

Delaplaine rolled her eyes. "Are you really asking me that? Do you know what it's like living in fear because the police don't care enough to keep you safe?"

Hart frowned and grabbed for her notebook. "Did something happen? I didn't get a call, so if—"

"No!" Delaplaine screamed. "It's that rapist! I was watching television, and they said you still haven't arrested him! He's still on the loose!"

Hart dropped her arms. "Ma'am, I can't tell you much about the investigation, but we've—"

"But I'm a citizen! You're supposed to keep me safe! I *demand* that you arrest that man now and get him off the streets!"

Hart took a deep breath. "All right, ma'am, what would we be arresting him for?"

"What do you mean? What about his background in Chicago?" Delaplaine shook her head. "Why is it I know more about this man than you do?"

"Ma'am, it's not clear to me you do, so I'm going to ask you again—what should we arrest him for?"

"My God, you are such an idiot! For rape!"

"If you mean of the woman in Chicago over twenty years ago, Mr. Martinez left the house before the rape occurred and is the one who called the police *on his own brother*." Hart hoped she wouldn't be disciplined for revealing this information, but at the moment she didn't care.

"What?"

"I said, Mr. Martinez—who was twelve years old at the time—left the house before the actual rape occurred, walked to a neighbor's house and is the one who called the police. His own brother went to jail for that offense."

"But I ... then why was he arrested?"

"He wasn't. He was taken into custody so he could give them information. Once they realized who he was, they released him. He has no other police record."

"But I don't—wait a minute, if that's the case, why did Jackie Moore say he'd been arrested?" Delaplaine had resumed her combative stance.

"That's a question you should ask Jackie Moore. We can't say misleading or inflammatory things on television. Only news people can do that."

"Wait, are you saying Jackie Moore wasn't telling the truth? Is that what you're saying?"

Hart smiled. "I'll let you draw your own conclusions, Ms. Delaplaine." She paused and brought up her notebook again. "Now if you're suggesting that Mr. Martinez raped his own daughters, I would appreciate any evidence you have so we can follow up on that."

Delaplaine deflated, then stiffened again. "You know what? No low-level police officer will tell me what to think!"

"Excuse me?"

"You think because you carry a badge and a gun you can lie to the public and ignore us when we ask you for help? It would be just like you to throw suspicion on somebody like Jackie Moore who's actually *doing* something!"

"And what did Jackie Moore do?

"She exposed a rapist and alerted the public. You've done nothing!"

Hart closed her notebook. "Ms. Delaplaine, I've already told you more than I should about Mr. Martinez' situation in Illinois, and I did that hoping to allay your fears. What I—"

"Don't tell me what to be afraid of!"

"Never. Your fears are your responsibility or your burden." Hart turned toward the Stevens house. "But do you think causing that poor woman any more fear will help her?"

"What the ... I'm only trying to help!"

"Are you?" Hart returned to the Stevens house to talk to Marin, ignoring Delaplaine. *Oh yeah—that's going to come back to bite me.*

CHAPTER TWENTY-SEVEN

TJX Technologies opened their doors at 8:00, and Moody and Porter were there at 8:10, asking to speak to Bill Cook, Alejandro Martinez' supervisor. They waited only ten minutes before Cook ushered them into his office.

Cook greeted them with a smile. "I've been wondering when someone would come back here. What would you like to know?"

"You may have watched TV reports about the missing Stevens girls, Mr. Cook," Moody began, "but—"

"I have. And yes, I've watched the reports from Jackie Moore." He leaned forward. "I know what I think about Alex, but I wonder what *you* feel about him."

Porter smiled. "Sir, it's not our job to make judgements in these cases. We want to find these young girls, and that's all we care about."

"Well, on that we can agree. But before I say anything more, I'd like your opinion of Alex Martinez."

Moody and Porter exchanged glances before Porter faced Cook again. "We can't have what we can't have, sir. We investigate leads and people and pass along what we learn to our higher-ups. They're the ones who form the actual opinions." Porter raised his hand. "I should also tell you we've said nothing negative about Mr. Martinez to you, or to anybody we've talked to, and we certainly haven't talked to Jackie Moore."

"But we need to investigate everything that comes our way," Moody added. "It doesn't matter if you think Mr. Martinez is guilty as sin or is a great guy. Our job is to ask questions that let us put the puzzle together. Forming an opinion about him before we're finished screws up that process."

Cook sat back in his seat and looked at the detectives, and then his body relaxed. "I suppose that's fair. And I probably shouldn't have been so aggressive with you, either."

"Something tells me this has been tough on you."

"Not on me—on Alex. He talks about those girls all the time, and—" Cook stopped. "Let's go to Alex's office. It's shared with three other people since they're out in the field and meeting with clients a lot."

Moody and Porter close their notebooks. "Lead the way."

Cook led them down the hallway toward several shared offices and turned into the second one on the right. "Our most senior consultants share the same space," he explained as he opened the door. "One of them should be in here in a few minutes—they arrive earlier than most of the others. We always send our most pressing problems to this team and they decide how to distribute them." He pointed toward the desk on the far right. "That's Alex's desk."

Moody and Porter approached the desk, which had several items on it but appeared organized.

"Alex is a guy who listens to problems carefully and makes excellent decisions, but that's not why I brought you here."

Moody and Porter saw the reason. The corkboard and a small side-wall of Martinez' desk were covered with pictures of his family, some with all four of them, others featuring a single member of the family: Patty Stevens, Alicia or Lacey. The detectives approached the desk, looking at the pictures. Porter took out his phone and turned to Cook. "I'd like to take a picture of this wall, sir."

Cook laughed. "The wall belongs to the company, so go ahead. But can't you just write down what's on it?"

"Believe it or not, sir," Moody began, "there are people downtown who can look at this and tell you all kinds of things about Mr. Martinez we can't figure out as regular detectives."

"What do the pictures say to you?"

Moody smiled. "They say that Mr. Martinez is a dedicated family man, but that's not my call to make."

"I understand," Cook said, "but I appreciate hearing you say it."

As Cook led them back to his office, Moody asked, "What do you know about the case in Chicago?"

"Only what Alex told me after our company ran the second background check on him, which is a total waste of time."

"His admission didn't bother you?"

Cook frowned. "No! First, he was a kid then, and second, he did the right thing. It's got to be tough turning in your own brother, but Alex did it. That's an example of the kid he was and the man he is now."

Moody continued. "On the day the girls disappeared, we were told Mr. Martinez was here. Can you verify that?"

"He was here. We didn't have any jobs in the field that day, and everybody was here. Plus, our regional office had just sent us a new contract, and we were analyzing some challenges with the contract and assigning tasks all day. It was so intense I bought everybody on the troubleshooting teams lunch, including Alex. He didn't go anywhere from the time he got in until he left for the day after his wife called, except to go to the bathroom. It was a stressful day for everyone."

Porter closed his notebook. "I suspect it's still one of those days for Mr. Martinez."

Alejandro Martinez walked into the ninth precinct headquarters and asked to speak with the detectives, or with Perkins or Shoemaker. Samuel Perkins met him in the reception area and brought him to his office, picking up Hart and Fair along the way.

"Mr. Martinez," Perkins began, "We're always happy to speak with you given the situation, but you needn't come in every day."

"I've got little else to do."

Perkins smiled and turned to Fair. "Thomas, can you give Mr. Martinez any updates?"

Fair, a little red in the face, looked to Martinez. "Actually, Mr. Martinez, what we've been looking at for the last day or so is you."

Martinez shrugged. "I'm not surprised. Jackie Moore has caused me a lot of problems, but if you didn't look into me, she would be all over the department." He sat back. "What did you find out?"

"Not much of note, Mr. Martinez, except that the teachers in your daughters' schools have a high opinion of you as a parent and for how you got more of the dads involved in the PTA."

"That's important," Martinez said. "Schools can only do part of the job."

"And not all parents, especially dads, get that, do they?" Perkins asked.

"That's how I saw it. Did you learn anything else?"

Perkins told him about expanding the search to more streets around his neighborhood and the neighborhoods around the schools, and changing their approach to their investigation of the child abductor from Indiana and Ohio. There wasn't anything to report yet, Perkins mentioned, but the police, FBI and other agencies were on the job.

Martinez sighed. "I guess I can't expect good things will just happen."

"It can be a long process," Perkins said. "But we're pushing hard on this."

Martinez smiled at Perkins, a smile that didn't reach his eyes, then looked at the officers. "I guess that's all I needed to know." He started to rise, but stopped. "Uh, you should know that Patty had me served with a restraining order so I can't talk to her about, well, anything I guess, nor can I go to the house without a police escort. I may need that in a day or two to get more of my clothes."

Perkins saw both Fair and Hart flinch. "I'm sorry to hear that, Mr. Martinez. That makes this whole situation even harder for you, to say nothing of what's happening at your job. I didn't mean to imply you couldn't come here any time you want. If you want to stop by or just visit with me or Captain Shoemaker, we'll make the time for you."

"Thank you."

"But I was wondering," Perkins began, "how did your wife find you?"

"She called my office and had a police officer there to serve me. My boss was required to tell them where I was." He sighed. "Well, I just wanted you to know that in case I need your help. Thanks."

As Martinez rose again, Hart stopped him. "I have a question for you."

"Shoot."

Hart smiled. "What can you tell me about teaching Alicia how to shave her legs?"

Martinez shook his head and chuckled. "Oh, man, that is going to follow me for the rest of my life!" He laughed again and looked at Hart. "What can I tell you?"

"We were told Ms. Stevens wouldn't allow Alicia to shave her legs, but that she was being teased."

"Yeah, kids can be so mean. Well, both Patty and I saw how it bothered Alicia, but when I heard her crying in bed one night, I'd had it. The next day, I went and bought one of those lady razors and told her I had a surprise for her."

Hart laughed. "Did you discover that you didn't need to buy 'lady razors?'"

"Only after the first packet of three, because they aren't worth the difference in price. Anyway, I had Alicia put on a swimsuit and we sat on the deck. It wasn't the same as the bathroom, but that would have been too cramped. I wet my leg with a garden hose, put on some shaving cream and showed her to wait a bit, then shaved my leg with one of my razors.

Then she did the same thing with both of hers. She got one tiny nick, but I thought that was good for a first time."

"It is," Hart said. "It took me a while to avoid any nicks at all."

Martinez smiled. "Yeah, Alicia was thrilled and couldn't stop smiling." He looked at Hart and sighed. "And I guess you found out she looked at my one smooth leg and one hairy leg and couldn't stop laughing."

"That's what I heard."

"Well, that became a running joke in the family until my leg hair grew out, and I have to tell you, I didn't like how itchy my leg was for a week afterwards, either."

Hart smiled. "The joys of young womanhood."

"Yeah," Martinez said, then he grew sad again. "I just hope the girls get to be young women."

When Jackie Moore entered Rod Welch's office, she was smiling. He looked up and noticed that the smile was genuine. "You're seldom in here for no reason."

"Who said it's for no reason?"

Welch sat back. "You've got something?"

"Soon, and it's going to be a good one."

Welch laughed. "Tell me what's happening, Jackie. Did you get a new scoop on the Martinez case?"

"What do you mean?"

"You don't expect me to believe you aren't milking this story for all its worth. Do you?"

Moore shrugged. "Well, it's important to look into every story, chasing leads, and ..." She stopped. "Okay, so maybe that wasn't my first motivation."

"Jackie, you learned from the best. And the best don't focus on truth, but on where the story could take them on their own terms. In that regard, you're already one of the best." He pointed to a chair. "Tell me what you have."

Moore shook her head. "Later, Rod." She turned and walked toward the door, but turned at the last minute. "But not too much later. I don't think I'll be around here after Father's Day."

Alicia held Lacey as she slept. *I don't know what day it is anymore, or the time.* She wondered if they were getting their breakfast and dinner at regular times, but couldn't even tell by the sunlight with the window being so far up the wall.

She looked at her legs and saw the hair growing in, and chuckled. *I'm growing a forest, like before I first started shaving.* She sat back against the concrete wall. *I don't know how much longer I can be strong.*

Chapter Twenty-Eight

Perkins felt his full weight while sitting at his desk after Martinez left. He looked up at Fair and Hart, checking their responses. "I don't like this whole situation, people. And I want something to happen." He stood. "Let's get more of us together, and we may come up with something." He turned to Fair. "Bring Dinah and Moody and Porter if you can find them."

"Got it, Perk," Fair said. Hart rose.

"Where are you going, Hart?" Perkins asked. "You got somewhere else to go?"

Hart laughed. "A little thing called patrol."

"Later. I need your input on this case."

"Fine with me." Hart sat, taking out her notebook.

Ten minutes later, Thomas Fair and Sharon Shore entered, carrying extra cups of coffee. "Dave and Siem are at Martinez' office, Perk," Shore said as she set the coffee on the table. "I left word with Kat." Before Perkins could reply, Novak stuck his head in the office. "I'd like to sit in, if that's all right."

Perkins threw up his hands. "The more the merrier." Once the officers sat again, Perkins sat at the edge of this desk. "I've seen the reports and received general impressions from most of you." He leaned forward, placing his hands on his knees. "What do we believe?"

"About Martinez?" Fair looked around the room. "To be honest, Perk, we've been wasting our time looking into his background the last few days."

Perkins nodded. "I agree. And that's going to stop now. But first, what are your impressions of Martinez?"

The officers checked each other, waiting for someone to speak, until Fair raised his hand. "I think he's innocent of anything to do with the girls' disappearance, Perk. Everything we've seen about this guy from Chicago to now shows me an intelligent, decent guy who was, *is* a loving stepfather. This whole thing with Jackie Moore and her allegations about Chicago is bullshit, and I'm tired of looking into it. God strike me down if I'm wrong."

"You're not the only one, Thomas," Novak said. "And even if we can't say that publicly, I want to pay more attention to the girls."

"About that," Perkins began, "what do we believe? Did they run away, did they get lost, or did someone abduct them?"

"They were too happy at home, sir," said Hart, shaking her head. "They had no reason to run away. Lacey wouldn't miss a single soccer practice, and Alicia was a good student who had no conflicts at school or anywhere else." She looked around the room. "There may be other reasons for a girl to leave, but I can't find anything suggesting either girl was unhappy."

"I agree," Shore said. "And as for what Thomas said earlier, one reason they were so happy was because of Martinez. And before you challenge me on why Martinez keeps coming into the station, Lieutenant, I think it's because he's worried about the girls and has nothing else to do. I doubt it's to see if we're 'on to' him yet."

"I'd thought of that," Perkins said.

Novak nodded. "So had I."

"You didn't see him come into the office," Hart said. "He just seems ... lost."

"That's it," Perkins agreed. "And Elliott told me yesterday that Stevens is lost, too."

"Tell me about it." Hart looked at Novak and smiled. "Danny can tell you the same thing Susan did, but Stevens has nothing stable in her life anymore."

"Except her mother," Novak said. "And that's not the rudder I'd want if I were her." He laughed. "She sent her mother away last night. That took guts if you've ever met her mother."

"It did," Hart agreed. "We had a pleasant evening, and I kept her focus off of worry, but it wasn't easy. She was much more relaxed with her mother gone." She looked back up to Perkins. "Just wanted you to know that, sir."

Perkins nodded. "That's not a surprise. I've spent time with Patty Stevens and I doubt she knew how much she depended on Martinez."

"Is that mutual, Perk?" Fair asked. "What little I've seen of him, he doesn't seem much better."

"That's different," Shore countered. "He's got a prominent news person accusing him of rape, and at least for now, he's lost his wife and daughters." Shore glanced at Hart. "I agree with Steve's statement about him being lost."

Perkins got up from the desk and moved behind it, sitting with a thump. He thought for a minute before looking up again at Fair and Shore. "Any new information on the child abductor from Ohio and Indiana?"

"Not enough time yet," Shore said. "But one thing we wanted to say is that even with the girl from Indiana who died, there was no clear evidence of sexual assault."

Perkins frowned. "Wait, I thought the girl in Indiana *was* sexually assaulted."

Fair shook his head. "No. There have been other cases in both states that suggest sexual assault. But when you trace this guy back and look at his methods, we find that he abducted the kids then tried to 'seduce' or," Fair chuckled, "Dinah said he was trying to 'woo' them. Anyway, we think he tried that with all the girls, and when they didn't respond the way he wanted, he released them somewhere far from where they lived."

"But since he never let the girls see him clearly, they couldn't identify him either. Also, the girls were drugged when he abducted them."

"We can't determine the drug he used because it was long gone from the girls' systems when they were found," Shore added.

"How have the survivors been doing after all of this?" Novak asked.

Fair shrugged. "Well, even after the trauma they've gone through, they're better off than the girl from Indiana."

"What about that? Why did he break the pattern?"

Fair glanced at Shore. "Who knows? Maybe she got rough with him and he retaliated. Forensics believes that the marks on her body and vagina were from him hitting her rather than sexually assaulting her. No one's saying this guy isn't bad, just that we should be careful about using the terms 'rape' or 'sexual assault.'"

"I wish that mattered to the girl from Indiana," Perkins rose again. "And I don't intend to see the Stevens girls placed in body bags for any reason."

"Something else we ought to be aware of," Hart said.

Perkins turned to Hart. "About Ohio and Indiana?"

"No, about the mood in Port Angel."

"And Jackie Moore, I assume?" Fair said. "That woman is making too much trouble for us."

Hart nodded. "She is. And last night I met up with Nadine Delaplaine again."

"Refresh my memory, Hart."

"She's a neighbor of the Stevens and Martinez family. I interviewed her on the night the girls were reported missing. She didn't even know the family then, but—"

"What?" asked Novak. "She's been over at the house twice when I was there. You'd have thought they were long-lost friends."

Hart smiled. "Quite a transformation, isn't it? Anyway, she came at me with both barrels when I left last night, demanding that I tell her what's going on and why the rapist wasn't already in jail."

"Martinez?" Perkins asked. Hart nodded. "What did you tell her?"

Hart exhaled. "Probably more than I should have, sir. I, uh, told her that in Chicago, Martinez was the one who made the call and turned in his own brother."

"And wasn't in the house at the time of the assault?" Perkins added. Hart nodded again. "Well, yes, I didn't want that released without prior approval, but it's the truth. How did she take it?"

Hart laughed, shaking her head. "At first, she was shocked, and I thought she would back off, but then she got aggressive again, spouting another conspiracy theory. In the end, I couldn't deal with her anymore, and asked her to let us do our jobs. I told Gee about the incident before I went home."

Novak broke the brief silence that followed. "I'd like to say that was the last we'll see Delaplaine, but I'd bet things with her will get worse before they get better."

Shoemaker looked up to see Samuel Perkins in his doorway. Perkins entered the office and saw Shoemaker turned away from the desk, facing the wall. "It can't be that bad, Shoe."

Shoemaker turned. "That's a matter of opinion, Perk." He sighed and stood up. "The fact is we're both showing the strain, and it's going to be with us for a long time is my guess." He smiled. "You have something good to tell me?"

Perkins sat in the overstuffed chair. "Some good, some not so good."

"You decide how to start."

Perkins updated Shoemaker on the discussions on Illinois, but before he could finish, Shoemaker waved him off. "You're right. We've wasted enough time looking into that part of Martinez' background and for my money, we needn't spend any more time on him, even here in Port Angel."

Perkins laughed. "But we're doing it anyway—no surprise to you."

"No. Anything else?" Perkins continued by telling Shoemaker about the change in approach to both Ohio and Indiana. He also reported how they were using the abductor's profile in Indiana to look for people with a similar background in Port Angel. "Any conclusions, yet?"

"No, but we've got some good leads. I've got our primary detectives on it, besides some background work from Novak and Hart."

Shoemaker nodded. "Good people, all of them."

Perkins rose. "And just an update. Last night, Hart had an encounter with one of the angry neighbors of the Stevens and Martinez family."

Shoemaker frowned. "Do I want to hear this?"

Perkins smiled and seemed about to speak when both men heard elevated voices coming from reception. The confusion ended when Shoemaker's telephone rang. "Shoemaker."

Kat Neely was on the line, and while she spoke with her usual steadiness, Shoemaker could detect both annoyance and nervousness. "Captain? There are several people here who would like to see you."

"What do they want to see me about?" Shoemaker expected the answer.

"About the missing Stevens children, sir. They'd like to see you as soon as possible."

Shoemaker took a deep breath, then smiled into the phone. "Tell them I'll be out in five minutes, Kat. And thank you." He hung up the phone and looked at Perkins. "Time to face our public."

"What public?"

"Unless I miss my guess, it's someone from the Stevens and Martinez neighborhood, maybe even the person Hart had the encounter with." As Shoemaker started out of the office, he turned again to Perkins. "Remind me to ask more about that encounter, will you?"

Perkins smiled. "Will do."

The reception area was only a one-minute walk from Shoemaker's office, and he and Perkins walked with a mission. They noticed the group—five women and one man—standing in front of Neely. Their stances were open but tense, and Shoemaker approached them with a smile. "I'm Captain Andrew Shoemaker and this is Lieutenant Samuel Perkins, commander of our investigative unit at the ninth precinct." Shoemaker stopped and waited.

Nadine Delaplaine walked forward. "Thank you, Captain. It's nice that we can speak with you at the station if we need to."

"Always."

Delaplaine looked to her colleagues, then back to Shoemaker. "Well, is it so hard to give us an update on what's happening in this investigation? How long are we supposed to live in fear in our own homes?"

Shoemaker frowned, but recovered and smiled again. "I understand your need for information on the investigation, ma'am, but can you tell me more about 'living in fear?' I don't deny it, I just want to know more about it."

The lone man in the group rolled his eyes. "Don't you have any compassion? We have a child abductor in the city, maybe even a former neighbor, and you don't know why we're living in fear?"

Delaplaine smiled at the man's comments. "It's not only women worried about this man, Captain—everyone is concerned."

"I understand that," Shoemaker replied. "And we want you to be more comfortable and safe. Now, what I can't do is reveal information about this investigation that might give any perpetrator information on what we've learned."

"That's not our problem!" Delaplaine cried. "We are citizens! Our rights are more important than worrying about a child abductor's rights. And you have someone who needs to be arrested and you've done nothing about that!" The five people with Delaplaine shouted as she spoke.

Shoemaker remained calm and faced Delaplaine again. "Ms. Delaplaine, I am happy to listen to you, and happy to tell you what I can about the investigation. What I can't do is tell you inside information that might compromise our ability to get the girls back."

"What about Martinez? You've done nothing about him! Is he in jail yet?"

Shoemaker shared a look with Perkins, but Delaplaine attacked again. "That's what I thought!" Delaplaine shook her head and looked at her group again. "We're wasting our time here. Let's talk to the commissioner or chief of police because this man is useless."

Shoemaker suppressed a shrug. "That's your right." He smiled again. "Now, if you'd like an update on things I can share with you, Lieutenant Perkins and I are happy to do that."

Delaplaine smiled again. "Why are we getting more updates from Jackie Moore than from our own police department? Who is the public servant here, her or you?"

"A good question," Perkins said. "But it may be the wrong question. You may want to ask how Jackie Moore got information that should have been expunged and not available to anyone—certainly not a civilian—on a case involving a juvenile. Who might she have paid or bribed to get that information, none of which implicates Mr. Martinez?" He looked down at Delaplaine. "We're not investigating Ms. Moore because that would be unproductive. But you have to wonder about someone with that kind of information and who draws, uh, interesting conclusions without any background and with a disregard for the facts."

"No," said Delaplaine. "No. You're just trying to distract us by throwing dirt at Jackie Moore." She shook her head. "At least she's on our side."

"We *are* on your side, Mrs. Delaplaine," Shoemaker said. "And we're happy to give you an update, but is that what you want, or did you just want to shout and make a point?" Shoemaker pointed at the camera rolling in his direction. "Cameras aren't allowed in this building without permission, and you don't have it."

"But Jackie Moore—"

"Had permission from me to film in the precinct. You do not."

Delaplaine pressed her lips together, and she grew red. "This is outrageous!" She turned on her heel and led her group away. "You haven't heard the last of this!"

She was well out of earshot when Shoemaker turned to both Perkins and Neely. "Oh, I'm sure of that."

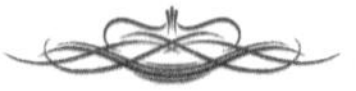

Jackie Moore spoke with her guest before the interview, trying to keep him relaxed. The man was nervous, his eyes revealing his state of mind. "You'll be just fine, Mr. Stevens," Moore said. "I won't ask you any questions you aren't comfortable with. It's all about the girls, right?"

"Sure," said Rory Stevens. "It's about them." He moved his shoulders, apparently bothered by the microphone cord that snaked through his shirt.

"When the cameras go on, I'm going to ask you the questions I mentioned before." Moore leaned forward. "But the important thing is your appeal for information about the girls—that's going to be very powerful."

"Okay," Stevens said, his voice shaking.

Moore smiled and tapped Stevens on the knee. "That's the ticket."

Ten minutes later, KPAR-TV introduced Moore's segment.

"Good day, Port Angel. I'm here today with Rory Stevens. He's the *actual* father of the two missing girls, Alicia and Lacey. Mr. Stevens, I'm sure it's been difficult with your daughters missing."

"It's been tough, worrying about them, yeah."

"And have you had the chance to speak with their mother, Ms. Stevens?"

"Only a little. We rarely talk. Plus, there isn't much to talk about. We don't know what's happening."

"I understand, Mr. Stevens, and that's something that's frustrating many of us, too. Now, if you look at the camera, what would you tell the people of Port Angel?"

"Um, if you have any information that may help us find my girls, please call the tip line. I don't have the—"

"The KPAR-TV tip line is 541 555-7871. Let's bring these girls back to their parents."

"Thank ... thank you."

"And before you go, Mr. Stevens, what do you think of the fact that Mr. Martinez has a police record from Illinois?"

"Uh, I don't know anything about that. I mean, I just want to get the girls back. I don't know anything else."

"That's fine, Mr. Stevens. Please, Port Angel, help us get these girls back by calling our tip line. These girls need to be with their parents. Thank you, Mr. Stevens. Our thoughts and prayers are with you."

Moore released the interview back to Chad and waited until the commercial break. She looked at Stevens again. "That was great, Mr. Stevens. I hope that will get us more information about your girls."

"Sure," said Stevens, standing and waiting for the staff to remove his microphone. "Like I said, I don't know much about Alex, he's—"

Moore waved him away. "No problem, Mr. Stevens. You got the message across just fine. You were great!" She smiled at Stevens again as he left the studio. She exchanged glances with Chad, who gave her a thumbs up. *Oh yes, by Father's Day, if not sooner.*

"My wife saw that protest action at the police station," the man said. He wasn't talking to Spool, but Spool listened in.

"What about it?" asked another man.

"Well, she was just talking about those two girls and worrying about what's happening to them."

The other man shook his head. "It's usually my wife who worries too much about shit like this, but I have the same worries. There's no telling what's happening to those girls."

"I agree. They seem like nice girls, too."

"You never know," Spool chimed in, uninvited.

"What?"

"I said you never know. Those girls might be in a better place."

"How do you figure?"

Spool shrugged. "What I mean is, who says the parents were so good? They already think the stepfather is a rapist or something. All I'm saying is the girls might be in a better place is all."

The first man frowned. "Not sure I can agree on that, Spool. Having somebody kidnap them can't be good for them."

Spool turned back to his work. "Still, you never know. I mean, what did they have to live for?"

Perkins glanced at Shoemaker as his captain and other officers in the muster room watched Moore's interview of Rory Stevens. "This just keeps getting better and better, doesn't it, people?"

"Do you want us to answer that, Perk?" Boyd shook his head. "That woman is a menace."

"Ha!" Mike Canady said. "Are you just figuring that out?"

Perkins stood. "Doesn't matter." He looked to Shoemaker. "But Jackie Moore won't be the only person who interviews Rory Stevens. I'm calling him in."

"Do you think that's wise?" Elliott asked. "Do you want him to get upset and run crying to Jackie Moore?"

Perkins' mouth set in a line. "I don't care about Jackie Moore. And this man may not have any additional information, but it's my turn to ask the questions."

Perkins hung up the phone and turned to Kat Neely. "Lucky break. Rory Stevens was already off work today, so he's got time. He should be here in an hour." When Stevens arrived, Perkins met him at the reception area and escorted him back to the interview rooms. Stevens was nervous and intimidated by Perkins' demeanor, and he sat at the table like a child waiting to meet the principal.

"Mr. Stevens," Perkins began, "this is an informal interview, so you're not in custody at all. However, sometimes people are more comfortable with an attorney present. So, before we begin, are you willing to answer questions from us without benefit of counsel?"

"A lawyer? Yeah, I don't need one."

Perkin smiled. "Well, if you decide you'd like a lawyer, just tell me and we'll stop the interview and get something arranged, alright?"

"Sure. I'm good."

Perkins opened a small notebook with his prepared questions. "Let's start." Perkins asked many of the same questions the other detectives had asked Stevens to relax the younger man and set the tone. After three questions, Perkins leaned in. "Can you tell me the reason you were on TV with Jackie Moore today, Mr. Stevens?"

Stevens sat back. "What? Oh, that. Well, Jackie Moore thought going on the show to talk about the tip line and the girls would help, you know. I mean, I know that Patty and Alex did it a few days ago, but she thought I might get even more people to call the tip line."

I bet, Perkins mused. "It's been a few days since we interviewed you, Mr. Stevens, and sometimes we remember things after the shock wears off. What's been happening with you, and have you remembered anything, anything at all that we might use to find the girls?"

Stevens looked away for a moment, then back at Perkins. "No, I'm ... I'm not too involved with them." He sat back. "I work a lot, and I mean we're divorced, and I only see them every once in a while."

"Has that posed a problem?"

"Not seeing them a lot?"

Perkins nodded.

"No." Stevens laughed. "Truth is, I'm not the best father figure in the world for Alicia and Lacey." He looked up again. "I'm not a bad guy or anything, but being a parent has always scared the shit, um, crap out of me."

"You can say shit in the police station, Mr. Stevens."

"Oh. Yeah."

"Let me ask you something else about Mr. Martinez. What's your relationship with him?"

Stevens frowned. "I don't have one. I see him sometimes when I visit with the girls, and I've gone to Lacey's soccer games when she asked me to, but everything with Alex is cool, we just don't talk much."

"You don't argue, or—"

Stevens smiled. "Nah! Alex is a good guy. You don't expect a father to say that his kids' stepfather is a good guy, but that's true about Alex." He leaned forward. "That's why I didn't like that question Jackie Moore asked me about Chicago. Alex doesn't deserve that."

"Huh. You mean Moore didn't ask you that question beforehand?"

"No. It was out of the blue, and I didn't like it."

"I got that impression."

Stevens shook his head. "You know, once I saw something—it may have been how Alex coached Lacey and how they got along—I don't remember, but watching him, I think he's the best parent of the three of us, Patty, Alex and me. But my girls are special. I only went on the show to help get them back."

"Well, maybe having you on the show will help." Perkins stood. "Thank you for coming in, Mr. Stevens. I'm sorry this has been so hard for you. And I assure you, we're doing all we can."

In the observation room, Shoemaker turned to Boyd. "I think he's right—Martinez is the best parent of those three."

"And right now, he can't do any parenting at all," Boyd agreed. "And I bet it's just tearing him up."

CHAPTER TWENTY-NINE

Danny Novak took an earlier shift at the Stevens and Martinez home, showing up at 1300 hours during his regular patrol shift. After relieving Angela Marin, he entered the home to speak with Patty Stevens, her mother and her father, a compact bald man with a no-nonsense face. The man approached Novak and shoved out a businesslike hand.

"Brian Jones," the man said, inclining his head toward the women. "I'm Patty's father."

"Please to meet you, Mr. Jones," said Novak. "Have you been here when any other officers were here?"

Jones shook his head and leaned in closer to Novak. "To be honest, Clarise thinks she's Patty's only parent—that's not a problem most times." He brightened. "But I'm here because I'm concerned about my grand-daughters."

"I understand," Novak said. "I spoke to Officer Marin. Is there anything you want to tell me about the morning? How has Ms. Stevens been?"

Jones sighed. Instead of answering, he turned toward his wife. "Clarise, I'm going outside to get some air with this officer." Clarise Jones looked up, nodded, and went back to her magazine. "Let's go."

Jones was quiet until he and Novak were outside and the door was closed. "Is there something wrong, sir? Do I need to call in another offi-cer?"

"No, I ..." Jones hesitated. "Well, you can do something about investigating Alex Martinez." Novak tensed but Jones noticed and laughed. "And my reason may surprise you."

"What do you mean?"

Jones turned toward the house again. "I've never been mean or condescending toward Alex, Officer. But I have to admit, I may not—no—I have *not* treated him the way I should."

"I don't understand."

"It's one of those 'no one is good enough for my little girl things'. If you had daughters, you'd understand. That's how it was with Alex. And being Hispanic, too. I wasn't outright mean to the man, but I should have treated him a lot better."

"Why are you bringing this up now?"

"That's complicated."

Novak shrugged. "I have the time."

Jones laughed again. "Yes, you do. Okay. Rory called here twice today, once while I was here." He looked up at Novak. "Rory is a decent enough guy, but even he would admit, fatherhood is not his thing. His calls to Patty are nice and focused on the girls, because he and Patty will never get together again. But after seeing him on TV and hearing him now, then comparing him to Alex, I feel like a fool. Alex has been a great husband and stepfather, and I wish you'd finish your investigation, exonerate him and let them get on with their lives."

Novak nodded, choosing his words with care. "I understand he has a restraining order and a separation notice against him."

"Yes," Jones said with a bitter edge. "He does, doesn't he? And that's courtesy of my wife. She has some romantic notion that this will bring Patty and Rory together again. I doubt that, and if that did happen, we'd have to do a lot more with and for the girls than we'd like to at our ages."

Novak scratched his head. "Let me sum this up, sir. You'd like us to complete our investigation of Mr. Martinez soon so he and Patty can get back together?" Jones nodded. "But that's not what your wife wants, I gather. What does Ms. Stevens want?"

Jones sighed and shook his head. "I don't know what Patty wants," her father said. "But she sure was happy with Alex a few days ago."

Stephanie Hart drove down the street from the home of Nadine Delaplaine and her husband and parked in front of the Stevens' house, behind another cruiser. Novak was standing beside his cruiser and smiled at her. He appeared exhausted, and Hart could read the emotion on his face. "This is supposed to be easy duty, Danny."

Novak looked around and nodded. "So they tell me." He pointed to the house behind him. "There's still the same tension in the house, the same everything, including—"

"Mrs. Jones and Nadine Delaplaine, I imagine. I've read the reports."

"So you have." Novak sighed. "Let's go inside the house so we have the right bearings." Novak rang the bell and smiled at Clarise Jones. "Mrs. Jones, this is Officer Hart, another of the officers assigned to be here with you."

Jones looked at Hart and frowned. "Oh. Another female officer? I wish you would assign men to help protect us."

Novak smiled. "Officer Hart is quite accomplished, Mrs. Jones. I was her last field training officer, and she's one of the best. You'll be in excellent hands."

"I was also here before, Mrs. Jones."

Jones looked back to her daughter, then back to Novak and Hart. "I suppose it will be all right. Let's go inside."

Jones led the way to her daughter, who was standing in the kitchen making coffee. She looked up and smiled at Novak and Hart. Hart smiled, noting that Stevens seemed to have shrunk into herself, with little life in her eyes. Yet she still tried to be gracious.

"Officer Hart, may I get you some tea?" Stevens asked. "Officer Novak always refuses. And I feel like I'm not a good host."

"You don't have to be a good host, Patty," Jones said. "We're not having a party."

"Your mother is right, ma'am," said Hart. "But I'll take a cup of tea if it's no trouble."

Stevens smiled. "I'll have that for you in a minute." She faced the living room. "Won't you sit down?"

Hart glanced at the living room, then back at Novak. "In a moment. I'll be back after Officer Novak and I do the formal hand-off."

"Okay."

Hart and Novak left the house and Hart walked Novak to his cruiser. "I'm aware of the normal drama between these two, but is there something else I should know?"

"That's the tough one, Steve." Novak scratched the back of his head. "Between Jackie Moore trying to make a name for herself on the backs of these people, and activists like Nadine Delaplaine who won't leave anything else alone either, this is far more difficult than it should be."

"Will Delaplaine be a problem tonight?" Hart shook her head. "Doesn't that woman ever sleep?"

Novak settled against his cruiser. "You got me. I know nothing about her home life, nor do I want to know. She has no young children and my guess is whether she doesn't like her job or husband, or whatever, she's never had a purpose, something she could fight for."

Hart sighed. "Great. I guess I can't fault her for trying to make a difference. But does she have to fulfill her destiny with this family? They don't need any more outside intervention—that's how Martinez and Stevens got split up in the first place."

"You're not telling me something I don't already know." Novak stretched. "But this is your problem for now, Steve. My bed is calling my name."

Hart punched him in the arm. "Fine. Go on and abandon your friend in her hour of need." She turned back to the house. "With any luck this will be a quiet night."

Novak drove away, and Hart called into her precinct. "This is Unit 214 to Nine Central."

"Central," came the voice of Louise Forest. "What's up, Steve?"

"Reporting in at the home of Martinez and Stevens. Novak is relieved."

"Got it. You're there until 2100?"

"That's the plan."

"Enjoy. Hope it's quiet."

"You and me both—214 out."

Hart leaned into her cruiser, took out a book she had been reading, and locked the door. She turned and came face to face with three men. "Is there something I can help you with?"

One man stepped forward, his arms at his side but hands halfway to fists. He looked at his colleagues before he spoke. "You can tell me what you're doing with that rapist. We've heard nothing and we're tired of this 'investigating' shit."

"What would you like to know?" Hart asked. "Whether we've strung the man up yet?"

"Don't get smart with me," said the man.

"I'd never do that to you, sir." Hart bowed her head slightly. "My apologies." She stood erect again. "Now, to answer your question—though there's little I can tell you—the department and FBI have completed their investigation of Mr. Martinez. And while I can't tell you much more than that, if there's anything they need to do with him, they're on it."

"Are you *serious*?" The man turned around to look at his friends. "A rapist is loose and you just blow it off like that? You obviously don't have any children, lady."

Hart smiled. "I can understand that you're frustrated, sir." She took out her notebook. "Do you have a special interest in the Stevens girls? Do you know them or do your kids know them?"

"So now you're going to interrogate me rather than that wetback who could have raped our children?"

"Not at all, sir. But I don't know if any other officer has talked to you about the Stevens girls. You may have information that can help us figure—"

"Put the man in jail!" screamed one of the other men. "Just arrest his ass and put him in jail! What's so hard about that?" The man approached Hart as he talked, getting louder with every step.

"Sir, please don't walk toward me like that."

"Don't order me around!"

Hart looked to the first man, who hesitated. She nodded, hoping he'd get the message. "Can any of you tell me about the girls, their habits, or what you've observed about them before they disappeared? This can be important, in case you saw something that no one else has told us."

The second man threw up his hands. "I don't fucking believe this! Marty," he said to the first man, "why are you letting this bitch push you around?"

"Joe, we don't have—"

"Marty, we have a right to protect our kids!" He turned again to Hart. "And you're supposed to be protecting us, not interrogating law-abiding citizens!" He advanced again, and Hart put her notebook away.

"Sir, please stay back." Hart smiled to reduce the tension. "If you don't want to talk with me, that's okay." She gestured to the house behind her. "I'm here to help Ms. Stevens and in case something breaks. We've had police here twenty-four seven since the girls disappeared, and this is my shift. My focus is on the girls and Ms. Stevens, that's all. Please let me do my job."

"And they put a damn girl here to 'take care' of Patty? What's this city come to?"

Marty had taken Joe's shoulder. "Joe, let's go. We can deal with this—"

Joe threw off Marty's arm and shook his head. "I should have done the talking all along." He turned again to Hart. "Sweetheart, you don't know who you're dealing with."

Neither do you. Hart took out and extended her asp. "Your friend had a good idea, sir. I just want to go inside and help Ms. Stevens. If you want to come to our station to give us more information or make a complaint, please do that." She raised her hand. "I may not understand all that comes with being a parent, so I—"

"You're damn right you don't!" screamed the man as he approached Hart again. As he pushed toward her, Hart shifted her weight and moved forward to her left, extending her arm. She kept her arm steady as the man lunged forward and ran into her, his momentum preventing him from stopping. He let out a loud "oof!" and doubled over, holding his stomach and moaning. Hart turned to the other two men. "Stay where you are!" She held the man down. "Breathe. Not shallow breaths, as deep as you can. Don't come up yet." He started to rise. "It's going to hurt more if you get up. Stay down longer. Deep, slow breaths." Hart looked again at the other two men. "I assume you don't want the same treatment?" They both shook their heads.

"Good decision." She turned her attention back to Joe. "Unfortunately, your lunge at me constitutes assault on a police officer, sir. I hope you had nothing else planned for tonight."

Hart had another officer arrive to take the arrested man in and to take statements. Once they dispersed the crowd, she was walking back into the house for what would be cold tea when a voice behind her made her jump.

"Officer?"

Hart shuddered, then turned with a smile. "You surprised me."

The woman who faced her was in her forties, of average build and hair color. She looked uncertain.

"Ma'am, what can I do for you?"

The woman pointed to the Stevens house. "Are you one of the officers staying with Patty?"

"I am. And probably with her mother, too."

The woman studied Hart, swallowed and said, "I'm Kris Allen from two doors down that way." She indicated her house, then turned her attention back to Hart. "You've heard a lot of bad things about Alex, I'm sure." Allen pointed to the Delaplaine house. "Nadine is loud, but she means well."

"I see."

"But the fact is, she doesn't speak for the entire neighborhood."

"No?"

Allen shook her head. "No. The fact is, many of us lived here when Patty Stevens first moved in with the girls. She's a sweet woman, and the girls are well behaved." She looked up again. "But they became a genuine family when Alex Martinez married her."

Hart smiled. "We've heard more negative or neutral things about Mr. Martinez."

"I understand that," Allen said. "That's why I wanted to talk to you." She smiled again. "Because I have to say, Alex is the best thing that ever happened to Patty Stevens or those girls. And you can take that to the bank."

Hart smiled at Allen and leaned forward. "Off the record, I'm inclined to agree."

Alicia looked up again at the window, which was eight or ten feet above the floor. She looked around the bare room for something that would allow her to get out or open the window. She hoped that by making noise, someone might hear her and get her and Lacey out. She spotted the bucket and got on her knees, shuffling her sister toward the wall, with Lacey holding on to the bucket/toilet, hoping they could stand on it.

Alicia had just placed the toilet under the window and was standing on it when the cellar door swung open and the man walked in. "What are you doing?" His voice was menacing as he approached them. "I said, what are you doing?"

Alicia sat and pulled Lacey behind her. She looked up at the man, who stopped in his approach. He lunged fast toward Alicia and slapped her, knocking her down and overturning the bucket. Alicia struck out to protect herself and felt rather than saw the scratches she put on his face.

"See what you made me do?" Spool recoiled and turned away. "I'm sorry you made me do that. We're supposed to be a family, and—"

"I want my *old* family!" Lacey screamed. "I want my mom and my dad. I want to go home!"

"Right," the man snarled. "You want to live with a rapist for a stepfather when I can offer you a—"

"My dad is not a rapist!" Lacey screamed.

"Lacey," said Alicia, further shielding her sister. "Not now."

Lacey pushed Alicia's arm away. "My dad is not a rapist. I'm only eight and I know what that is!"

The man stood and walked toward the door. "You don't understand yet, but you will." He closed the door, leaving Alicia and Lacey behind, crying.

Hart arrived early for muster the following morning but before she could enter the muster room, Andrew Shoemaker pulled her into his office.

"Trouble last night, Hart?"

"No trouble at all, sir. And I wasn't looking for a fight, either. Those three men confronted me, and the one wouldn't back off. He wasn't even the ringleader."

Shoemaker held up his hands. "I wasn't accusing you of anything." He smiled. "I wondered how it felt to let out some of that tension."

Hart sighed. "Not good at all. I also didn't 'strike' him. I just let him run into me. I still feel bad about what happened."

"Not bad enough to forget the charge."

"Nope. I asked them two or three times to stop approaching me, and when he lunged, I felt I was within my rights. His buddies even said so last night." Something in Shoemaker's eyes told her something. "Wait, are they changing their testimony now?"

"No, but they're suggesting you escalated the situation in ways you shouldn't have. Have you turned over your body camera evidence to records?"

"First thing today. Those three came at me with an agenda, with the original leader, Marty, I think his name was, giving me shit from the get-go. It's only when I asked if they had any information we could use that he backed off, but Mr. Cowans saw red. I think I was within my rights, sir, especially since I only used the asp and nothing more lethal."

"I'm inclined to agree with you." Shoemaker sat on his desk. "Just in case, be ready to provide more info if necessary. Do you have regular patrol today?"

"Yep. Nothing special that I know of."

Shoemaker placed his hand under his chin. "Tell you what, why don't you hook up with Fair and Shore, and with all the detectives to get them in the loop? That way if they have questions you can answer, you're already available."

"Do you want me to find them after muster?"

"No time like the present."

Early the following morning, a call awakened Martinez. "Hello?"

"Alex?" Martinez heard the voice of Bill Cook, his boss.

Martinez yawned and shook his head to wake up, then looked at the clock. "Hey, Bill, what's up?"

"Oh, I'm wondering when one of my best troubleshooters can get back to work?"

Martinez sat up. "Are you serious? I mean, what about the background check?"

"You weren't worried about that and neither was I—you passed it with flying colors. In fact, the company running the check said we wasted our money, since they hit all the sources hard, and found out that your record is squeaky clean."

Martinez laughed. "You sound like you're surprised by that."

"Oh, no," said Cook. "And it didn't take them long to find what they needed."

"Are your bosses satisfied?"

"Ha! I think they're just embarrassed or annoyed that we didn't have some details about your background that were beyond our control." He sighed. "That's how corporate works. Are you ready to come back?"

"That's the best news I've had in a while." He checked his clock. "You want me in at the regular time?"

"That would help. The new contract with Birch Industries is kicking our butts."

"Hey, that's why you call the best, right?" Martinez got off the couch and started toward his friend's bathroom.

"Hey, don't take it that far, Alex," said Cook, who laughed. "See you in a bit."

Martinez reported to work at TJX smiling and ready to see his work colleagues. He entered his office to the welcome of the other senior consultants. "I guess you're happy to see me?" he asked as he sat.

"Nah, we're just tired of doing your work for you, man," said Ty Barnes.

"Yeah—what he said," said Sienna Hayes, the lone woman on the senior team. "But it's good to see you." She pointed to Martinez' desk. "We left the tough parts for you."

Martinez looked at the file, an inch and a half thick, and opened the cover, paging through the specifications. He exhaled, locking eyes with Jeffrey Frye. "No wonder you wanted me back."

"Yeah, it wasn't for your wonderful personality," Frye said. All the team members laughed.

At 10:15 that morning, Cook sat in his office, worried. He was thrilled to get Alex Martinez back; he was an excellent worker, easy to work with, and he made a great impression on their customers. Cook recalled the last two conversations he'd had with employees. Two were worried about having a rapist or suspected rapist (one made air quotes when she said "suspected") and thought the company should make him leave. Cook had countered with Martinez' performance on several contracts and his reputation in the company. One woman, Brenda Keene, looked at Cook surprised. "But his reputation isn't very good now, Mr. Cook," she'd said. This was the first time Cook realized that Martinez' suspension with pay had a dark side for the company because it suggested the company believed the allegations against him.

"What would you like me to do?"

"You can't fire him? I don't think people will feel safe with him here, and—"

"No."

"No? But we—"

"Brenda, we won't fire one of our best employees because some television person says he did something in Illinois twenty years ago." Cook stood. "This company ran the background check a second time, even deeper than when we hired him before, and it came back clean. Do you understand that? Clean. What Alex did in Chicago was to call the police on his brother when the brother was involved in a crime. He called the police on his own brother to make him stop: *that's* what happened in Chicago." He sat on the edge of his desk. "Brenda, the company made him leave and humiliated him so they could run this second check." Cook saw Brenda's eyes, even as she tried avoiding his. "We spent extra money for this, too, money we shouldn't have had to spend. And this because some news reporter smeared a good man." Cook stopped and lowered his voice. "This is the man you want me to fire?"

Cook waited and Keene said nothing. "Brenda?"

Keene looked up at Cook. "People are still going to talk. It's not …" she hesitated. "Well, just because they didn't find anything doesn't mean nothing's happened."

Cook rolled his eyes. "And that's a reason to fire Alex? We could say the same things about you, or me."

"Maybe not fire," said Keene. "But some people don't want to work with him anymore, Mr. Cook. You can't make that go away by telling them about the background check."

Cook stood. "What do you believe?"

"What?"

"I said, what do you believe? Is Alex a hardened criminal or the man you've known here for eight years and depended on and trusted?"

"Well, I—"

Cook sat again. "Because I know Alex and I trust him a hell of a lot more than I trust some television personality I've never met and never worked with. Think about that."

"Okay," Keene said. "But will you think about what I said? It's real, Mr. Cook, and you can't ignore it."

Cook sighed again. "I understand, and I will." He watched Keene leave and picked up the phone to call their general counsel. But before he could make the call, his secretary walked into his office and closed his door.

"Sorry to interrupt you, Bill, but there's someone here to see you."

"I didn't have any appointments."

Cook hesitated. "She didn't have one."

Cook sighed and stood. "Who is it?"

"It's Jackie Moore—from TV?"

"Here?"

The secretary nodded.

"Damn." He looked at his secretary. "That can't be good, but I guess it's better to see her than not, huh?"

The secretary looked away. "I suppose so."

"Give me a minute." Cook called the corporate law office and asked to speak with his usual contact. Told that she wasn't available, he asked for anyone else who could give him quick advice. A minute later he heard, "This is Jon Cummins. How can I help you?"

Cook quickly explained Alex Martinez' status, then mentioned the visit by Jackie Moore.

The lawyer cursed under his breath. "Tell you what, I'll pass on the situation—with Martinez, was it?—to Caroline, though I have a few questions she might ask you. For that Moore woman, I've heard of her, and we don't want our people talking with the press unless they're prepared for it. You're not.

"My advice is to meet with her and tell her that you're happy to respond to written questions. Also, tell her that you'll forward most questions to counsel for review before answering them. And do not allow yourself to be taped—make that clear up front."

Cook chuckled. "It still sounds tough."

"Working with the press can be tough if you're not prepared. My partner is a reporter, and he tells me this stuff all the time. Their job is to find things that no one else can and, to be honest, I don't want them around any of our facilities, even when we have nothing to hide or worry about."

"That's why I called you."

Cook could hear Cummings laugh. "Which is also why I'm glad you're the one facing her now. You'll do fine. Just remember what I said." Cook ended the call, then turned toward his office door. *No time like the present.*

As Cook reflected on his brief encounter with Jackie Moore, he was impressed, though still concerned. Moore walked in like she owned the place and appeared the way she did on TV—put together and in command. She walked with her hand extended. "Mr. Cook. Thank you for seeing me on such brief notice."

Moore walked in without her camera or other recording equipment, though he saw a man waiting in the outer office. Moore followed his eyes.

"We thought it better to be clear before bringing in our cameras."

Cook nodded. "Thanks. Our company doesn't like people speaking with the press unless they clear it first. This visit wasn't cleared."

Moore smiled. "I understand that, and I won't take up too much of your time."

Cook nodded and ushered Moore into the seat in front of his desk. "So what can I do for you today?" he asked, adding, "Please understand that some questions I may have to run by corporate before answering them."

Moore waved her hand. "That's what I expected. We wanted to ask you about Alejandro Martinez."

"Okay."

"Our viewers want to know whether Mr. Martinez is still working at TJX Technologies. We heard a rumor that he was either laid off or suspended. Can you confirm that?"

"I can't, Ms. Moore. We're not allowed to confirm or deny personnel actions, since they're considered private and between the employee and the organization."

Moore smiled again. "That's standard for most companies."

"I'll take your word for that."

"But he is still employed at TJX Technologies, correct?"

"I can confirm that he is an employee here."

Moore smiled. "And what can you tell us about him?"

"That's about it: he is employed here. On a personal note—and this is all I'm going to say—I believe Alex is a good man and a good worker. I have complete confidence in him."

"Even with these allegations against him?"

"Correct. We came to our own conclusions, using our own resources and outside ones to confirm or deny the allegations made by people against him. That's private company information, but no one has told me anything else about Alex, so—"

"So no other job action?"

"No."

Moore stood. "Then Mr. Martinez must be here. Can we speak with him, either on or off camera?"

"We can't allow that, Ms. Moore," said Cook. "This is still a place of business and Alex has a great deal of work to do."

"I only need a small bit of his time."

"I understand that, but he's very busy, as am I. Best of luck to you Ms. Moore." He extended his hand, and Moore shook it before leaving the office, picking up her cameraman on the way.

Cook sat down again and pondered what Brenda Keene had said and about Moore. He decided another call to the corporate law office was in order.

Right before the end of the day, Cook asked Martinez to stop by the office on his way out. Martinez arrived at 5:15 and was smiling more than he had two days before when he was suspended.

"Jackie Moore came by the office today."

Martinez deflated. "I heard a rumor and hoped that wasn't true."

"It was."

"What did she want?"

Cook stood and cursed. "To make trouble. She doesn't care about you or your girls. She asked if you still worked here, and if we were happy to have you."

"What did you say?"

"I gave her the HR line that we can confirm that you're employed here. I didn't say more because the lawyers told me not to." He smiled a Martinez. "I told her you're a great guy, however."

Martinez sat back in his seat. "Something tells me the lawyer wouldn't have wanted you to do that."

"I wouldn't know. I didn't ask him."

"You didn't ask?"

"Nope. And if he had, I would have balked. You're being painted with a bad brush, Alex, and I won't feed into that." Cook fell silent, searching for what to say.

Martinez leaned forward. "What do you need to tell me, Bill?"

Cook sighed. "There are employees who aren't happy that you're still working here. They're worried because they believe whatever television tells them and can't think on their own."

"Don't blame them, Bill. They're good people, just scared is all."

"But of you? I thought better of them."

Martinez sighed. "So did I. Now I'm not so sure." He looked up. "What are you going to do?"

"I'm not going to fire you."

"But they don't want me at the office or in the building, I assume."

"Correct."

"So?"

Cook sat back again. "I'd be happy to have you here doing your job." He paused. "But I also have another idea to run by you."

CHAPTER THIRTY

Alex Martinez smiled when he arrived at the precinct. Kat Neely rose to greet him and returned the smile. "Hello, Mr. Martinez. May I call the captain or lieutenant for you?"

"That would be nice." Martinez' voice was hollow, and he appeared even lower than before to Neely, if that were possible. She called Andrew Shoemaker, who met Martinez in less than four minutes.

"Hello, Mr. Martinez," Shoemaker said. "Why don't we go back to my office?" As Shoemaker led the way, he noticed Martinez' pain.

When they arrived at the office, Shoemaker asked, "Shall I call in Lieutenant Perkins? He may have something to share with us I'm not aware of."

Martinez looked away. "Sure."

Shoemaker called Perkins, who came into the office two minutes later. He exchanged a glance with Shoemaker once he saw Martinez. The younger man sat in the overstuffed chair with Shoemaker behind his desk and Perkins sitting on its edge. "I have to tell you, Mr. Martinez," Perkins began, "that I'm concerned about you. I know being out of work is stressful for you, but—"

"Work?" Martinez exhaled. "Well, my boss called me today and asked me to come in."

Shoemaker frowned. "Wait, he didn't fire you, did he? I thought you were on paid leave."

"That's what it was, pending successful completion of the second background check." Martinez looked back and forth between the two men. "I passed."

Perkins and Shoemaker exchanged glances again. "Let me guess," Perkins said. "Either the boss doesn't want you there regardless of the background check or some employees believe Jackie Moore and not the background check results."

Martinez stared, then shook his head. "You've seen this before, haven't you?"

"A few times," Shoemaker said. "But that doesn't make it any easier. I'm sorry."

"Me too," Martinez said. "There are positives, though—my senior consultant coworkers and my boss are all supportive. When I told my team what happened, they were ready to take my boss to task, but it isn't his fault."

"So it was other employees, not your boss?"

Martinez nodded. "Right. Bill told me what happened, though he wouldn't tell me who complained. Their logic, as he called it, is that they've found nothing bad about me 'yet,' like somehow a bad thing is going to appear magically from Illinois or the Navy or some other stupid source." He shook his head again. "My whole conversation with my boss was surreal. He told me even the people above him who ordered the second background check were pissed now, since I'm good at my job and they thought the background check would be the end of it."

Perkins crossed his arms and sighed. "Unfortunately, good people get hurt far too often. Given that, what are you going to do? You don't strike me as a person who gives up when things get tough."

Martinez sighed. "My boss said he'd support me if I decided to stay here, but I don't have the best reputation in Port Angel at the moment, so getting another job is out of the question."

"And nothing with your current company, like in another office?" Shoemaker asked.

"Well, that I've got. My boss was on the phone before he called me in and offered me a promotion on another team. But that job is in Springfield, so about ninety miles away. I can't live in Port Angel and take it."

"You won't stay here instead?" Perkins asked.

"I can keep working here until we get the girls back. My boss promised I was good until then, if I choose the new position."

"I wonder," Shoemaker said.

"What?" asked Martinez.

Shoemaker smiled and screwed up his face. "I wonder if Jackie Moore has ever had her reputation destroyed by a stray comment or baseless allegations? If she had, I bet—never mind."

"That's another thing," Martinez said. "Jackie Moore visited TJX today."

"Jesus!" Perkins turned to Shoemaker. "Just give a reason, Shoe. That woman is a menace."

"Who skirts the edge of the law but is just inside it, Perk."

Perkins looked at Martinez. "Do you think she had something to do with your being pushed out of your job?"

"She may have. But it may be for the best. It takes years to build an excellent reputation, yet no time to shatter it into a million pieces. That's how I feel now."

Perkins leaned toward Martinez. "But I bet you'd give up your reputation for good if it would get Alicia and Lacey back."

"You're right," Martinez said, fighting tears again. "I'd do it in a heartbeat if I could just see them safe again." Martinez looked into his lap, blinking his eyes.

"Do you plan to go to work tomorrow?" Shoemaker asked. "And is there anything we can do to help you?"

"I'm going to work. We made significant progress today on a couple of new contracts. Normally, we'd be in and out of the office working on projects like this. But we're staying in longer until I get the girls back, then we'll decide who goes to visit the clients. I'll be on the field team for sure."

"And when this part of the project is over, you'll head to Springfield?"

Martinez nodded. "Most likely. That'll be a big change. I settled in this state because of Port Angel. Life will be different there."

"I never asked you what brought you to Port Angel?" Shoemaker said.

"Oh that," Martinez said. "My Master Chief is from here and his favorite childhood memories were made in Port Angel. When he heard I was getting out and wanted to settle far from Chicago, he suggested I search for jobs around here." He smiled. "There are a lot of tech jobs here, and a nice Hispanic community. I found a good job at TJX and the rest is history."

Shoemaker paused then spoke again. "We're sorry you have to go through this, Mr. Martinez."

"I don't know why I'm complaining. My, uh, the girls could be anywhere and may be in much worse shape than me right now. I feel selfish for complaining at all."

"But understandable." Perkins consulted silently with Shoemaker. "Have you told your wife?"

Martinez started. "About my new job?" Perkins nodded. "No, I mean, I can't even call her with the restraining order in place. Oh, and I need to get more of my things from the house. I'll need a police officer to go with me."

"We'll take care of that," Perkins said. "But it might be good for your wife to know what's happening with your job. Our officers can tell her when you pick up your things, tonight if you wish."

Martinez stood. "I guess. This is so much to deal with." He looked at Shoemaker. "Moving wouldn't be so bad if I could just be with the girls again."

"You don't think that's possible?"

Martinez shook his head. "I could never adopt them, so I don't have any legal rights with them."

"Just the right every dad has—to worry about his kids," Perkins offered.

"Got that right," Martinez said, then he looked away.

"What?" Perkins asked.

Martinez sighed. "It's ironic. It just occurred to me that if we divorce, I may have to pay support for Patty, but not for the girls, because they aren't mine." He looked up again. "But if they're not my girls, why does it hurt so much?"

Spool was gathering his tools after the workday when a coworker furrowed his eyebrows. Spool looked at him. "What? What are you looking at?"

The coworker pointed to Spool's face. "It's the scratch—you got a big one."

Spool gave a nervous laugh and looked away. "Hey, you know how it is. My girlfriend got rough with me last night."

The man laughed. "No shit! Damn!" He leered at Spool. "Does she have a friend for me? I could use some of that, too."

Spool shook his head. "Not this one. She's one of a kind." Spool smiled again and turned back toward his tools. *And I'm not into sharing, brother.* Spool started toward his truck when he saw two other carpenters pointing at him and laughing. Spool saw their reaction and got red. He jumped into his truck and took off for home.

Spool's home was on Foster, about seven miles from the work site, which was near City Center. Still reeling from his coworker's teasing, he wasn't watching his speedometer until he saw flashing lights behind him. Spool looked down and cursed, then slowed and moved to the curb.

Officer Mike Canady exited his cruiser and walked slowly toward the truck's driver's side door. As he reached the door, the man inside lowered the window and faced the officer.

"I've got my license and registration ready."

"Thank you for that, sir." Canady looked into the truck and smiled. "You need to watch your speed, sir. I clocked you at forty-nine, and this is a thirty-mile-an-hour zone."

"Yeah, guess I gotta watch that. Sorry."

Canady returned to his cruiser and called in the license for previous violations. He turned the license over in his fingers, noting that it was issued just two months ago. He wrote out the citation, lowering the speed to forty-five, and exchanged idle chat with central, who confirmed that Caleb Spool had no previous or outstanding violations.

Once he finished writing the citation, Canady climbed out of the cruiser and approached the truck, noting the "Cheseldine Motors, Ames, Iowa" sticker on the rear. Ames, Iowa was quite a distance from Port Angel. Canady stood by the truck's window. "This is your citation, sir." Canady indicated parts of the citation as he spoke. "I've got your information here, and this is the date and time I pulled you over. Now, here is the speed that I'm putting in the system, which is forty-five." He looked at Spool. "That will lower your fine if you choose to pay the fine rather than go to court. The fine jumps quite a bit once you're fifteen over the limit. And here," Canady pointed to the fine amount, "you can see that the fine is seventy-five dollars. You can send that in within fifteen days or send in the citation by the same time to request a traffic court hearing." He looked at Spool. "Any questions so far?"

"No."

Canady turned back to the citation. "Okay, now we ask you to sign this. Your signature is not an admission of guilt—it's just your acknowledgement that you received the citation. And this is my name and signature, Michael Canady, and my badge number, 2021." Canady gave Spool a pen and the clipboard. Spool looked up at him, shrugged, then signed the citation. Canady tore off the original copy, giving it to Spool and collecting his pen.

"Please make sure you slow down, especially in residential areas, Mr. Spool."

"You bet," Spool said as he started the engine.

"Oh, and something else?"

"Yeah?"

"I noticed that the truck came from Ames, Iowa. Whereabouts in the state is that?"

Spool's eyes widened. "Is something wrong?"

"No. Just wondering."

"It's in about the middle of the state. Iowa State University is there."

"So you're new to Port Angel?"

"Uh, yeah. I work construction. Got to go where the jobs are, you know?"

Canady smiled. "I hear you. Take care." And Spool drove away.

Stephanie Hart pulled up outside Martinez' former home, Martinez behind her. Nadine Delaplaine, her husband and four other people lined the driveway. Hart angled out of her cruiser and looked back at Martinez. His expression was blank.

Hart approached Delaplaine. "Ms. Delaplaine, we're coming in to get more of Mr. Martinez' things, so I would appreciate—"

"This is unbelievable!" Delaplaine screamed. "Now you're harboring this man?" She pointed to the people standing with her. "Patty told us he was coming, and we're here to say we don't want him in our neighborhood." She approached Hart, who stood her ground. "We want you to escort him away. Now!"

"Not gonna happen." Hart inclined her head toward Delaplaine's husband. "That gentleman can tell you I won't hesitate to protect people from mob violence, which is what this is." She glanced at Martinez. "Come on, Mr. Martinez." She returned her gaze to Delaplaine. "Ms. Delaplaine, Mr. Martinez is complying with the terms of the restraining order. He had an officer call here in advance and he is being escorted by me and another officer inside so there is no misunderstanding. When he is finished collecting his things, he will leave. That's the law, and I'm here to enforce it. Do you have any questions?"

Delaplaine had questions, but while Hart was speaking, her husband stepped behind her and whispered in her ear. Delaplaine nodded and stepped away from the driveway.

Hart smiled. "Thank you. Come on, Mr. Martinez." Hart rang the doorbell and greeted Carson Poole. "Hey, Carson."

"Hey, Steve. Are you ready?"

Hart glanced at Martinez. "As ready as we're going to be. Lead the way."

Hart and Martinez followed Poole into the home, and Martinez saw several plastic bags and four boxes stacked in the kitchen. He looked at Poole and pulled him aside. "Did you watch them pack those boxes and the bags?"

"I did. Is something wrong?"

"No, I mean, you don't know what belongs to me, so—"

Poole pointed toward the living room, where Patty Stevens and her parents were sitting. "But *they* do, and your father-in-law was very specific about how they packed the boxes and bags."

Martinez frowned. "What do you mean?"

Poole looked at Martinez and pointed to the front door. "We'll be right back, Steve." Once outside, Poole smiled at Martinez. "I gather you didn't always get along with your father-in-law."

"That happens."

Poole laughed. "You're being generous, but while your mother-in-law wanted to throw your things in the bags as haphazardly as possible, he put his foot down. Your clothes are either folded or rolled nicely in the bags and the boxes. It took them over two hours. You also have a bunch of suits and dress clothes upstairs, on hangers."

"Brian did that?" Poole nodded and Martinez laughed. "I would have never put it past him."

"That bad, huh?"

"No. But whether bad or good, I got used to it." He turned to Poole. "When you marry someone, you marry their family, for better or worse. Brian wasn't the tough one. Clarise was. I'm sure she's having the time of her life now."

"But your wife isn't."

Martinez looked at Poole and sighed. "Neither am I. But I can't do anything about that, now, can I?"

Martinez and Poole reentered the house and, with Hart's help, took the boxes and bags to Martinez' car. In between their two trips, Brian Jones brought the hanging clothes and carried them to the car. When he finished, Jones pulled Martinez aside. "Um, can I talk to you?"

Martinez glanced at Hart and Poole for help. "The restraining order only applies to Ms. Stevens and the girls, sir," Hart said.

"Right." Martinez turned to Jones. "What did you want, Brian?"

Jones exhaled and looked down, then back up at Martinez. "I wanted to tell you how sorry I am about the girls, about losing them, I mean." He saw Martinez' confusion and continued. "What I mean is, everybody is pointing fingers at you and raising a stink, so you've got to feel real bad about that. And with the restraining order and all, I …" Jones sighed again. "Well, I wanted to tell you I was sorry, and that I know this has been hard on you. You don't deserve this." He pointed back at the house. "I don't know if I'll be able to change anything. But maybe I can get Patty to see reason if I can get her away from Clarise or Rory, and—"

Martinez held up his hand. "I-I understand what you're saying." He cleared his throat. "I guess we never got off on the right foot, did we, Brian?" Jones shook his head. "But I appreciate you talking to me now." He gave a nervous laugh. "It's ironic, but during all of this, the only people who have been decent to me are the police, my work team and my boss. I haven't had that kind of support from Patty, and I'll certainly never get it from Clarise." He looked behind Jones to the six people still camped by his former driveway. "And not from this neighborhood, either." He smiled at Jones. "So what you said means a lot." He offered his hand and Brian Jones took it.

"Thank you, Alex. Like I said, I can talk to Patty, because I know she—"

Martinez shook his head. "Patty has to decide what she wants. And I have to decide what I want, Brian, and I don't know what that is yet. But it won't be here."

"What do you mean?"

"Oh, I'm going to be working in Springfield once the girls get back." He smiled. "It's a promotion, with more money and more responsibility leading my own team."

"But that's two hours away. No one in their right mind would commute from all the way ... Oh." Jones paused. "You're moving there?" Martinez nodded. "And I'm guessing by yourself?"

"That's how it looks to me."

Jones sighed again. "I wish you'd reconsider that. I mean, once the girls are back home, I'm sure Patty will change her mind."

"She might," Martinez said. "But this is bigger than Patty. I don't want to get into it now, but I don't really have a choice, at least in the short term."

"I'm sorry."

Martinez shrugged. "So am I, but it might be good to get a fresh start." He pointed to the neighbors. "It's hard to imagine dealing with these people after this."

"Them? You think those people matter?"

Martinez stared hard at Jones. "Oh, they matter, Brian, and people like that all over Port Angel and at my company matter. Look, this is not the best time to talk. I need to get my things back to where I'm staying. You can tell Patty that I'm checking in with the police every day, and she can call them if she wants. A lot of them, like the captain and lieutenant, are good people."

Jones smiled. "I will. Sorry again, Alex."

Martinez closed the trunk of his car. "Thanks."

CHAPTER THIRTY-ONE

Thomas Fair watched Danny Novak get into his car to drive home. "Danny, got a minute?"

"Sure. What do you need?"

"It's Dinah. She received a call from an informant, Sledge, and he says he knows you."

"Sledge." Novak shook his head. "Yeah, I remember him from the neighborhood. We went to high school together. What did Dinah see him about?"

"What else have we been working on for the last few days?"

Novak's eyes widened. "Really? What could Sledge know?"

"He didn't say, but he called the precinct asking to speak with the detectives. He didn't want to use the tip line."

Novak laughed. "He likely needs money. Sledge is always tapped out. Where are you meeting him?"

"Dinah didn't want to drive all over creation, so we picked him up with cuffs like he was being arrested."

"To maintain his street cred?" Novak asked. "I doubt Sledge is connected to anything big."

"I agree, but he's been reliable over the last year or so. He appeared nervous, so we decided we'd bring you in with us."

"Okay. Then what are we waiting for?"

Novak and Fair met Shore outside Interview Room 1. "He's inside," Shore said. "Do you remember him?"

"It's been a while, but yeah."

Shore pointed to the door. "Shall we?"

Fair opened the door and gestured toward a man who appeared much older than Novak. Novak and Fair entered, and Novak saw his former classmate for the first time in five years. Sledge had a lopsided smile that suggested missing teeth and looked the worse for wear.

Novak sat across from him. "Joe."

"Hey, Danny. It's good to see you."

"Thanks, Joe. We're glad to see you, too, if you have something we can use."

Sledge twisted in his chair. "I'm not in these chairs too much now. Got me a decent job at the insulation plant on Central Avenue. But helping you guys helps too, you know?"

"Right." Novak leaned in. "Joe, you called us about those girls, and this is important. Detectives Fair and Shore will do what they can to help you out, but we want to get the girls back. What can you tell us?"

Sledge twisted again. "Well, what I got isn't about the girls, exactly." He met Novak's eyes. "I mean, it still might be good, but what I got is about a guy, hasn't been here long, who a buddy of mine said was kinda weird."

"What about this guy?" Fair asked. "What can you tell me, and have you seen him?"

"I haven't. No. But my friend, he works construction and works on a bunch of projects, mostly in City Center."

"What projects?" Fair asked.

Sledge shrugged. "I don't know the exact ones, but my friend is a foreman, so he goes to more than one a week. But the guy we're talking about works on one of them."

"What's his name?" Shore asked.

Sledge frowned. "The weird guy? I don't know his name."

"No. Your friend," Shore asked, an edge to her voice.

"Oh, that's Jonny Spots, and he's, oh."

"What?"

Sledge looked up, sheepish. "That's not his regular name. It's just what we call him." Sledge set up straighter. "But I'm sure you can find him. Like I said, he's working a lot of the projects in the city right now."

Fair rubbed his temples. "Fine. What is Jonny Spots' trade?"

"He's a carpenter," Sledge said. "So is the guy he told me about."

"A carpenter?" asked Fair. Sledge nodded. "So why does your friend think this guy is worth our time, or worth looking at?"

"Well, he acts kind of strange, you know, about the missing girls?"

"Strange how?" Shore asked.

"Well, you know this is a big case, and everybody is talking about how terrible it is—you know, the missing kids, the rapist stepfather—stuff like that." Sledge licked his lips again, looking up. "Anyway, this guy was sayin' that the girls might be in a better place now. Strange."

"Could he have meant they were dead and with God?"

Sledge shook his head. "That's not what Jonny thinks. He told me this guy said they didn't have much to live for with a rapist stepfather and maybe they were better off where they are now. I ain't heard nobody say that. I mean, even some really hard guys I know feel bad for those girls. And this guy is just making like they're better off now. Who says shit like that?"

Fair's eyebrow furrowed. "What can you tell me about this guy?"

"Not a lot. Jonny says he's always appeared odd, like I said, but he's new in Port Angel. Came from the Midwest—Illinois or something. Something else Jonny said: the guy turned up today with scratches on his face, said his girlfriend got a little crazy on him, you know?"

"It happens," Novak said.

Sledge shook his head. "I don't know. Jonny said he doesn't think this guy *has* a girlfriend—he's too creepy."

"To each his own," Novak said, then he frowned. "You said Illinois?" Sledge nodded. "Where in Illinois?"

"I don't know. I only know Chicago."

Fair noticed Novak's eyes. "You have an idea?"

"Hard to say. But Chicago isn't very far from East Chicago or Gary, Indiana." He turned to Fair and Shore. "And that might be important."

Thomas Fair asked Samuel Perkins to meet him in the bullpen along with Shore and Novak. Another officer held guard over Sledge until they updated the lieutenant. "We don't say it's much, Perk," said Fair. "But we think we ought to check it out."

Perkins listened to the summary of the interview and turned to Novak. "What is the thing with Illinois that you mentioned?"

"It's not much, sir. But we all default to Chicago when we think of Illinois, and if this oddball is from that area, he could be our guy."

"What's this informant doing now?"

"He's trying to get a line on his friend, but he doesn't have his phone number," Fair replied.

"How about his name? Is that so hard?"

The officers looked at each other and shook their heads. "Sledge only knows his nickname, sir," said Novak. "He refers to him as 'Jonny Spots,' but that's not his name, nor is his first name Jon."

"Nor his last name 'Spots,' I imagine?"

"Nope."

Perkins sighed. "Of course not. Alright. Let's speed this up. If we have this much information, we should jump on it."

"We've got the calls in," Fair said. "We've also called O.C. and Brownie, but this Jonny Spots isn't someone on our radar like Sledge."

"Why not?"

Novak shook his head. "It sounds like he's a master carpenter who's on the straight and narrow." He laughed. "We don't see people like that too often."

Perkins rose from his chair. "Shoe's already left the office, but I doubt he's home yet. I'll fill him in. Can you stay a little longer?"

Fair laughed. "Are you giving us a choice?"

Hart left the Stevens house to clear her head. Once she got outside, her phone rang with a call from Danny Novak.

"Hey, Danny. What's up?"

"Are you outside?"

"Of the house? Yeah. You got something?"

"Maybe. How are things in Stevens' land?"

Hart told Novak of her encounter with Nadine Delaplaine and her group that evening and how Brian Jones apologized to Martinez.

"Wow! I would never have guessed that. I thought both Stevens' parents couldn't stand Martinez. This is a surprise."

"It surprised Martinez, too." Hart laughed. "When Mr. Jones told his wife he believed Martinez was a good husband and father, I glanced at his wife. I could almost feel the frost coming off Clarise."

"I'd love to have seen that."

"Hey, did you know he's leaving the city?"

"Yeah. He told us this afternoon. The guy's stuck, and probably depressed. But I called to tell you we just interviewed an informant—Sledge."

"Who is that?"

"I went to high school with him." Hart chuckled. "What?"

"You went to high school with everybody in Port Angel. You'd think we only had one high school in this city."

"Fine," Novak said. "But the point is he's got a friend who's encountered a really odd person."

Hart waited, but Novak said nothing else. "That's it? Do you know how many odd people I see every day in this job?"

"Ha! I knew you'd say that. Anyway, he was saying things about the girls in ways that implied they're in a better place now than before, and he wasn't saying it because they were dead and in heaven."

"That sounds strange, I suppose, but did this informant say much else?"

"No, except that the odd guy is a carpenter and is working on some active projects in Port Angel."

"But we don't know which one?"

"Not yet. Sledge is trying to contact his friend but only knows his nickname, doesn't have his number."

Hart paused. "Can we find out which projects are at the carpenter stage?"

"What do you mean?"

"Well, you don't need carpenters all the time on construction jobs. Sometimes you need only excavators or masons, then carpenters, and you've got to sprinkle in the electricians and plumbers, too."

"I kind of get that."

"Sure," Hart continued. There are lots of construction projects going on in Port Angel at any one time, but if it's a bigger one, like a housing complex or industrial park, we should have some clue which ones would need carpenters. We can get lists from the union."

"That's true," Novak said. "But their list of people is huge. It would take us too long to track them down."

"Right. So what about—"

"Wait. I've got an idea."

"What is it?"

"Well, you remember the perp from Indiana and Ohio?"

"What about him?"

"Would the union know if someone is a transplant from another state?"

"Beats me," Hart replied. "But it makes sense regardless of where they got licensed."

"Right. We can't say much else to the family now, but Perk and Shoe may have some new orders for us soon."

"Good," said Hart. "Make sure they include me."

Novak's smile came through the phone. "I'm on it."

CHAPTER THIRTY-TWO

Spool drove back to his house, shaking. His speed surprised him. His encounter with the officer had rattled him, but *no harm, no foul,* he thought. No one suspects anything, and he dodged a bullet. He entered his home after checking outside. It wasn't much of a building; it was a rundown shotgun-type house at the edge of an isolated street. But it suited him fine. Spool went into the kitchen and pulled out his second-to-last beer from the refrigerator. There was still enough lunchmeat for sandwiches for him and the girls. They might be getting tired of the sandwiches, but he wasn't much of a cook. Maybe one of them will do better. That was it. One of them could take over the cooking soon, and they could all eat better.

They just needed to hold out a little longer.

"Who are we calling again?" Moody asked.

"We're calling construction companies about current projects, trying to find where the carpenters are," Shore said. "This is going on the hunch from the informant last night."

"You think they're in the office already?"

Shore shrugged. "The lieutenant said call, so it's possible. These companies start early in the morning."

Moody rolled his eyes. "But we don't have to start so early." Moody talked a good game, but got on his calls quickly. No one answered the phone at the first two companies he called. At the third, Quality Built, he got an answer.

"Hello, this is Detective David Moody from the ninth precinct Port Angel Police."

"Yes, Detective," the voice said. "What can I do for you?"

Moody checked his script. "We're looking into any large construction jobs you have that are using carpenters right now." Moody could hear the confusion in the other person's voice.

"Uh, most of our jobs require carpenters throughout much of the work," the woman said. "And if one particular job doesn't need them, another within the company does. It's very fluid."

"When you look at your jobs, are there any you would classify as large—you define what large means."

"Well, our work is primarily residential," the woman said. "We specialize in single-family homes, but also build and renovate apartment complexes. We don't have any of those right now, though."

"Oh." Moody's voice fell. "So only smaller jobs?"

"Right. We have nothing starting that I would classify as large until a couple of months from now."

"Right. Well, thank you ... could you point me to any companies that are doing bigger jobs right now?" Moody paused. "Ma'am, what we're trying to do is to locate someone—a carpenter—who might be involved in illegal activity. In fact, we wonder if he might have abducted those two missing girls."

Moody heard an intake of breath. "Oh. The Stevens girls? Wow."

"Right. And we have information that suggests that this person may be a carpenter working a large job in Port Angel. Do you know what those jobs might be?"

"That's a tough one," the woman said. "But I can think of two jobs that are big right now. There's a mixed-use project in City Center called the Mandrake. The other is near the airport where they're renovating an old business park. That depends on what you define as a 'big' job."

Moody was scribbling as the woman spoke. "This is very helpful, ma'am. Can you tell me the names of the general contractors for those jobs?"

"Hold on."

Moody turned to Shore. "I've got two possibilities here, Dinah. The lady on the line is getting me the names of the general contractors for two big jobs going on right now."

"Sweet."

A minute later, the woman returned to Moody's call. "Here you are. The GC for the industrial park is J. R. Snyder, and the GC running the project in City Center is Schreiber Construction."

"Great. And they're in the book?"

"Should be. I don't have the numbers."

"Great. Thanks again."

"I hope you find the girls."

Moody hung up and turned to Shore. "Have you had any luck?"

Shore shook her head. "Not yet."

"Okay. Here," Moody said, handing Shore a company name. "You check out Snyder. I'll call Schreiber."

Hart and Novak met for coffee when their shift began. Because of the on again, off again rain, they were standing in the gazebo at Dolman Park while Novak filled Hart in on the progress of the case.

"They're calling the companies now?"

"That's the plan," Novak said. "They're calling construction companies and the union hall hoping to find out more information. When I left last night, Sledge was heading home. What I was hop—" Novak looked down and saw that he had a call. "Hold on."

"Novak."

"Danny?" came the voice of Sharon Shore.

"Hey, Dinah. What's up?

"We've got some minor hits on the companies and we've identified two that are ripe to check out."

"Awesome!" Novak gave Hart a thumbs-up sign. "I hope you're calling me so I can go with you."

"Yep. We're going to visit one of two companies. One is J. R. Snyder, working on a business park project. The other is Schreiber—they're working in City Center. Even though both projects are at the edge of the ninth or out of it, we're still the leads."

"What do you need me to do?"

"Moody is heading to the Schreiber one at 500 Vine. I'm going to the business park. That's at Twelfth and Central Streets. Join me at the business park."

"Got it."

"And have Steve meet up with Moody at the Mandrake project." Shore paused. "She is there with you, isn't she?"

"Well, yeah, but—"

Shore laughed. "We could set our watches by your early morning coffee and tea routine, Danny. But we should get there as soon as we can for those girls."

"We're on it." Novak hung up and looked at Hart. "They've identified two extensive construction projects we're checking out. You're to meet Dave Moody at a project in the City Center. It's at 500 Vine Street."

"Isn't that in the 3rd?"

"Right. But we're still the lead, so—"

"Never mind—you don't have to ask me twice."

Hart arrived at the main gate for the Mandrake project twenty-five minutes later, stopping by Moody's unmarked car. She got out and walked over to Moody. "You have a contact here?"

"Yeah." Moody took out his notes. "It's Chuck Bell." Moody pointed to the construction trailer. "Over there, I'd guess." He and Hart walked over to the construction trailer and knocked on the door.

"Yeah?"

Moody looked at Hart, who shrugged, then opened the door. Only one man was in the trailer, a man of about fifty, overweight and wearing blue work clothes. Moody took out his shield. "Mr. Bell?"

"Right." Bell rose. "You must be the Detective Moody who called."

"Yes, and this is Officer Hart. We're here to ask about your carpenters."

"Right," Bell said again. "But I don't know what you need them for."

"I understand, Mr. Bell," Moody said. "But it's vital. May we sit?"

"Sure." Bell pointed to chairs at the folding table. "How can I help you?"

Hart and Novak explained what they were looking for, and about the odd statements by one carpenter, and Bell shook his head. "Are you serious? It doesn't sound like your informant knows much of anything. And you're driving all over the city following up?" Bell shook his head. "You have nothing better to do?"

"It's more than that, Mr. Bell," Moody said. "Like we said, this concerns the two missing girls. We can't leave any stone unturned for this. It's too important."

Bell nodded. "Yeah. That's true. But I doubt I can help you. We've got lots of carpenters on site, and they're working all over the place. How would you know where to start?"

"It might be easier if we could talk to a guy who goes by—" Moody scanned his notes "—'Jonny Spots.'"

"Oh shit, what has Reggie gotten himself into?"

"Reggie?" Hart asked. "What's his full name?"

"Uh, Reggie Stigall, but I can't imagine Reggie would do anything to those girls."

Hart held up her hand. "We didn't mean that, sir. Our informant didn't know his contact's proper name. We're sure his contact was Mr. Stigall. He's the man who told our informant about the other carpenter saying odd things about the girls and the whole situation."

Bell relaxed. "Well, that's okay then. I can't imagine Reggie doing anything bad to anybody. He's supervising the carpenters here and at one of our projects in Overbrook."

"How is that possible?" asked Moody

"Reggie's got lead carpenters at both sites. He goes in and checks on them and works himself on the harder tasks when they come up." Bell frowned. "I'm not sure if he's here, but he should be."

"We don't have to wait for him," Moody said. "We can talk to the carpenters now."

Bell stood and approached the far wall. "You'll need hard hats to walk on the site." He reached for the hats, handing one to each officer.

Caleb Spool looked over the construction site and saw the police cruiser and another car that had to be an unmarked police vehicle. *Not now.*

Spool turned to his lead carpenter, doubling over. "Hey, Bob?"

Bob looked over and raced to Spool. "What's the matter?"

"I'm not sure," Spool said with a grimace. "It might be something I ate earlier, but I can hardly stand. I may have to head out before I either fall or screw something up."

"That's okay, Caleb." Bob laughed as he pointed to the open room. "The work will be here when you get back."

"Thanks, Bob. I should be back by tomorrow."

"Can you get home okay?"

Spool nodded. "I'll be careful. If something bad happens, I'll pull over. I've had this kind of stuff before, and it's just sharp pains that come and go. I don't think it's dangerous."

"Just an unholy pain, huh?"

"Yep. See you tomorrow." Spool left his work area, walking slowly to avoid attracting attention. He had no idea why the police were there, but felt he couldn't take the chance. The rain had just started when Spool raced back to his house. He had to be careful and not draw too much attention to himself. He had to leave before the police put two and two together. That was what got him into trouble in Ohio the first time.

Once he was away from the site, he pushed harder on the gas pedal. Ten minutes later, he saw the flashing lights in his rearview mirror again.

Bell led Hart and Moody to the three suites where carpenters were working. The first had only two carpenters working there who hadn't been on the site until two days before. They knew nothing about the backgrounds of the other carpenters and seemed annoyed that Hart and Moody had interrupted them.

As Hart and Moody walked to the second suite, Reggie Stigall intercepted them. "I understand you're looking for me." Stigall held out his hand to both officers. "Is something wrong?"

"We hope not, sir," Moody said. "We're here because of some comments you made to a gentleman who goes by the name of Sledge."

Stigall rolled his eyes. "Sledge? That was a few days ago. What, did he get hurt or something? He's always too close to the edge. We were just talking, and I bought him a drink is all."

Hart shook her head. "No, sir. It's about comments you made to Sledge about a conversation you had with another carpenter. This other carpenter made some strange comments about the girls who were abducted."

Stigall frowned and nodded. "Yeah. Yeah. I remember mentioning that as an afterthought. We were sitting in the bar when a report came on. Everybody was talking about the girls, and whether they thought the stepfather had done anything to them." He looked up. "And that's when I remembered another conversation I had at lunch."

"Tell us about the conversation."

Stigall shrugged. "There isn't much to tell. We were sitting at lunch talking about lots of things when the missing girls came up and Spool said stuff that seemed off to me."

"Can you tell us his exact name?"

"Sure. Let me look at the roster." He walked over to a wall, picked up a clipboard, and pointed to a name on the list. "Yeah, I thought so. It's Caleb Spool. Good carpenter, very precise. He's a natural." He passed the clipboard to Hart. "Like I said, it just sounded odd since everybody else was worried about the girls or mad that you haven't arrested the stepfather yet. But no one was saying the girls are better off now than with their parents. I mean, who says that?"

"That's a good question, Mr. Stigall," Moody said. "Can you take us to Mr. Spool?"

Stigall led the officers into the second suite where they'd met with Bob, only to be told that Spool had left minutes earlier. "He said he had some intense stomach pains. So I sent him home."

"Do either of you know where Mr. Spool came from? Is he a Port Angel native?"

"No," Stigall said. "He's from Illinois and got here maybe two months ago? He didn't have any trouble finding work. Spool had good references, and his work is top-notch."

Bob nodded. "Yeah, he's one of our best. Dependable, too."

"Did you hear any of these comments from Mr. Spool about the missing girls?" Moody asked.

Bob looked first to Stigall, then to the officers. "Yeah, and it was weird. My wife and I discussed the girls the day before, then Spool comes out of left field with a whole new perspective, something you want to ask about, but you were too creeped out to ask?"

Hart closed her notebook. "I do. But it was important we asked. Can you get me his address from your records?" Stigall nodded. Hart turned to Moody. "We ought to get on the horn and spread the word, at least to bring him in for questioning. Somebody's got to ask him about those comments."

Officer Patrick Weiss approached Spool's car with the citation. "Now, Mr. Spool, I notice that you had another citation yesterday. Is there something I need to know?"

Spool smiled. "No, officer. I don't hardly drink at all, and certainly not this early. I, uh, had a lot of my mind and wasn't paying attention." He smiled again. "I do promise to do better."

"All right." Weiss explained the citation, took Spool's signature and handed him the original before releasing him. Weiss got back to the car to finish his notes as Spool drove away into the last of the rush hour traffic. Six minutes later, as he was finishing, he got a radio call.

"This is unit 188. You got a job for me?"

"Pat, you just called in a warrant check on a Caleb Spool for speeding, is that right?"

"Correct. Is something wrong?"

"No," Kat Neely said. "But is he still there?"

"No, he drove away five minutes ago. I gave him the citation and sent him on his way." Weiss sat up straighter in his cruiser.

"Pat, Moody issued a BOLO call to find and hold Spool as a suspect in the missing girls case."

"Shit!" Weiss said, and placed his cruiser into gear.

CHAPTER THIRTY-THREE

At the ninth precinct, Samuel Perkins directed the detectives to look into Spool's background in Illinois and wondered if he had a record in Ohio. "Make it fast, Thomas," Perkins said to Thomas Fair. "But don't make any mistakes."

"Yes, sir." Fair and Porter had been working the angle with the union halls while Moody and Shore visited contractors. While Spool was their best lead so far, they couldn't assume he was the only one. They found through the union hall that Spool was from Illinois and was a finish carpenter with an excellent reputation, but restless. Their records said he had lived in West Virginia, Ohio and Illinois, though he also worked at jobs in Indiana.

"What about Iowa?" Perkins asked. "Didn't we hear about something to do with Iowa?"

"The botched attempt, right?" asked Porter. "I remember that." He frowned. "But wasn't that vehicle a Ford F-150?" He looked at a copy of Spool's traffic citation from Weiss. "This is a Dodge Ram."

"People do buy new cars, Siem."

Porter nodded. "Sure, but most people are creatures of habit. They often buy the same makes and models."

"I agree," said Perkins. "But remember, the authorities listed the Ford as belonging to the child abductor. If Spool is our guy, he may have seen that and ditched the truck."

"True," Porter said. "We'll keep going on Ohio and Illinois, Lieutenant."

"Thank you." Perkins left the bullpen and had entered the reception area when he saw the drawn face of Alex Martinez. He hesitated before deciding. "Mr. Martinez. Do you have a minute?"

Perkins called Paul Andrews, who was working in the Stevens home and suggested she bring Patty Stevens to the precinct. Andrews brought Patty Stevens and Clarise Jones into the conference room forty minutes later. Alex Martinez sat in the room with Thomas Fair, and when Jones locked eyes on him, she froze. "I won't be in the same room with that man."

"Mom, please," Stevens said. "If you don't want to be in here, you can leave."

Jones flared. "Young lady, you will not speak to me in that tone of voice."

Stevens pushed her away. She stood less than a foot away from her mother, teeth clenched. "I don't like this any more than you do, Mom. But this is about the girls, not about you, or Alex, or me. We've excluded him from everything else we've done or talked about. And he's surrounded by police. You need to give it a rest."

Jones bristled again and looked between the door and the conference table.

"Your choice, Mom."

Jones shook her head and left the conference room.

Stevens deflated, as though the effort of being decisive with her mother was too much for her. She turned back to the conference table and took the seat farthest from Martinez. "You said you had something to tell me?"

"We do," Perkins said. "I want to caution you that this isn't definitive, but we are focusing on a single suspect."

When Perkins said that, Stevens looked at Martinez. "Is it somebody we know?"

"I doubt it," said Perkins. "He's someone we've identified through an informant, and we're checking into his background now." Perkins leaned forward. "What I can tell you is that we think he may be the child abductor from Ohio and Indiana."

Stevens' hand flew to her open mouth as she suppressed a sob.

Perkins brought Jones back into the conference room and brought her up to speed. Later, he asked Fair to stay with the family. Fair noticed the strain among the three and said little except to explain the investigative process to them. He also called for coffee and tea while they waited. When Mike Canady and Susan Elliott entered with the refreshments, Fair brightened.

"I'll need one of you to remain here with me while this is going on."

Elliott and Canady looked at each other. Both shrugged. "Lieutenant Perkins told us we were here on temporary duty," Elliott said. "We can both stay if you need us."

"Why don't you stay now, Susan? Mike can help Kat with communications."

"Right," said Canady, who left the room.

"Folks," Fair continued. "This is Officer Elliott."

"We've met," Jones said.

"Officer Elliott will stay with us today while things are going on. We hope things will resolve themselves quickly, but this may take a while." Fair turned to Jones. "Mrs. Jones, do you want to call your husband?"

Jones nodded. "I should do that." She pulled out her cellphone and called him, asking him to join them at the precinct. When she finished, she looked up. "He's on his way." She looked at Martinez and her daughter. "What are we going to be doing here?"

"Ma'am, we're going to be strong for your granddaughters by waiting and remaining as calm and focused as we can," Elliott said. "That will be tough, but that's all you're able to do right now. We plan to be with you."

"We, uh, I appreciate that," Martinez said, looking straight at Elliott. "I really do."

Spool had finished making sandwiches for the girls and himself when he got an idea. *If he's still at the house and that cop who pulled him over comes by, he could be screwed.* The more he thought about it, the more scared he was of staying in the house. He finished making the sandwiches and placed them into plastic bags. *Why not take the girls and head out of town for a couple of days until things cool down? If he drove over the bridge to Riverside, he'd give himself time and let things blow over in Port Angel.*

Spool walked downstairs, making more noise than usual. When he got to the basement, instead of using the light from the single bulb in the corner, he turned on the fluorescent. Alicia and Lacey screamed and huddled together as the brightness blinded them.

"What?" Alicia asked.

Spool walked over to the girls, tense but smiling. Alicia saw the scratches on his face and knew she had put them there. "We have to go."

Shoemaker stood behind Neely. "All right, send the BOLO to their laptops. I want anyone who hasn't gone home yet on tap, Kat. We need to send the right people to the house."

"Everyone's here, sir, even people from midnights. It's your pick."

"Fine. Send O. C. along with Porter and Moody to Spool's place. He's only one man, and we shouldn't need anyone else. If they think they do, send ..." Shoemaker searched his brain. "Is Brownie on?"

"Yes."

"Send Brownie along with them. Four officers. If he's not there, we'll decide on another plan." Shoemaker stretched to his full height. "Make sure the vehicle description is clear—there are a lot of Dodge Rams out there."

"Yes, sir."

On routine patrol, Stephane Hart received the ping telling her a new notification had come through on her laptop. She pulled over to check the full notification, including the vehicle description and a copy of Spool's picture from his driver's license. The man looked nasty, and Hart could imagine him doing terrible things to little kids. His face gave her a chill, but she pressed her lips together and put everything else out of her mind as she looked for a white Dodge Ram. She put the cruiser in gear and started her search.

Two police cruisers and an unmarked vehicle arrived at 441 Foster. They approached the house with caution, their sidearms drawn. Brown and Porter moved around to the rear entrance, keeping a bilco basement door in view while Moody and Boyd went to the front door. They sensed no movement or sound in the house, and Boyd knocked on the door, standing to the side.

"Port Angel Police! Caleb Spool!" Boyd waited ten seconds. "This is the Port Angel Police! Open up!" He and Moody waited again, then Boyd used his radio. "On my mark—three, two, one, go!" Boyd and Moody crashed through the front door as Porter and Brown entered the rear. They stopped inside the entrances, listening and treading carefully. Brown and Porter took the second floor, going through the two rooms there, finding nothing.

Brown called down to Boyd and Moody. "Second floor clear!" They went down to the first floor again, noting that lights were on throughout. They looked at the kitchen, at the bread and mayonnaise on the table, touching nothing.

Boyd's voice came through their radio. "First floor is clear. Come on downstairs." Porter and Brown descended the narrow stairs into the basement. Boyd was standing near the rings on the walls that held the rope. Porter and Brown looked around, saw two backpacks in the middle of the floor and smelled the toilet bucket in the corner. Brown approached Boyd and noticed the rage in his colleague's eyes. "This is bad, Brownie." Boyd keyed in his microphone "Unit 109 to Nine Central."

"Nine Central. What's the status, O.C.?"

"Spool is the guy, or else we have somebody else tying people to the walls in his basement." He could hear Neely's intake of breath as he locked eyes with Brown. "We also found a few items that belong to the Stevens girls." Boyd wiped the back of his neck. "This guy is sick and needs to be stopped."

Patrick Weiss was not the department's brightest star. He was a competent officer, but not very creative or ambitious. But Weiss could follow orders with the best of them, plus he'd seen the truck. After receiving the BOLO, Weiss started driving on Pleasant from Twelfth. He was waiting at the intersection of Pleasant and Seventh when he looked in the distance and thought he saw a large white truck that could be a Dodge Ram. Protocol told him to follow and examine rather than chase. Weiss followed protocol, but he would not let this man squeeze through his fingers, not after stopping him only a short time before.

Spool drove down Sixth Street toward the bridge. He didn't want to get chased on Central, now that the roads were slick with rain. He was careful to drive at the speed limit going west on Foster before turning to go south on Sixth. In the back of his mind, he heard the girls making noises, but he ignored them as he tried to develop a plan. And while he watched his speed, he ran through the light at Stevens as he continued down Sixth.

Weiss saw the Dodge go through the light and turned on his lights, just as two cars crashed in the intersection because the Dodge had run the lights. Weiss hesitated for a second, then he stopped. He drove to the accident site, cursed, and keyed in his radio.

"Unit 188 to Nine Central."

"Hey Pat, what—"

"Kat, possible sighting of the Dodge Ram heading south on Sixth Street. I am at corner of Sixth and Stevens at an accident site and unable to pursue."

"Oh," Neely said. "Anyone hurt?"

Weiss chuckled as he got out of his cruiser and shook his head. "Other than my pride, I hope not. I'll update you."

Stephanie Hart was driving on Oak heading west and had stopped at a light when she heard Neely through her headset. "All units, all units. Be on the lookout for suspect noted in BOLO, Caleb Spool. Suspect is believed to be heading south on Sixth Street. Last seen passing intersection of Sixth and Stevens. He may have the Stevens girls with him. Use extreme caution."

Hart thought for a moment, then turned on her flashing lights and drove forward, looking to make a U-turn and head east on Oak toward Sixth. "This is Unit 214 responding to BOLO. Turning onto Sixth and in pursuit."

"Acknowledged, 214," Neely said. "Be careful, Steve."

Hart saw the truck turn onto River Road.

"Continuing pursuit. Suspect has turned off River Road onto Anders," she announced.

Spool drove down Anders and found it led to footpaths that would take them through the woods and to the bridge. He stopped the truck by a clump of trees, then turned to the frightened faces sitting behind him. "Time to go, little ones."

Hart saw him. "Suspect is stopped by the woods leading towards Tannock River." She looked up and saw that the rain was building. She left her cruiser and pulled on a poncho to start the foot pursuit as she heard "wait for backup" in her earpiece.

Hart touched her microphone. "He has no weapons visible and the girls are right with him. Weather is not good for these girls. I will maintain safe distance." She took off.

"I will not argue with you, Hart," came the booming voice of Samuel Perkins. "Maintain a safe distance or you will answer to me."

"Yes, sir. Received." Hart continued running into the woods, then stopped as she tried to get her bearings and see where Spool had gone. She glimpsed him in the distance, running hard and urging the girls on, too. As she followed their direction, she realized they were headed toward the Tannock River and toward one of the higher drop-offs. It was dangerous in clear weather, but with the rain continuing and already threatening flood conditions, dangerous was an understatement.

CHAPTER THIRTY-FOUR

Captain Andrew Shoemaker looked up from the reception desk and saw Nadine Delaplaine walking toward the reception area and approaching him.

Shoemaker opened his mouth to speak, but Delaplaine took out her cell phone and held it out to him. "Before you say a word, Captain, I have Jackie Moore on speed dial."

"Are you serious?"

"Well, she's the only one who is helping to protect us here, unlike you and your officers!"

"Oh really?" Shoemaker said. "We're on the way right now to get the suspect. He was holding the girls at his house on Foster."

Delaplaine shook her head. "What do you mean?"

Shoemaker stepped toward Delaplaine with his nostrils flaring. "You didn't listen to me when I walked you through this the first time. I took your insults and accusations before, but I won't now." Shoemaker noticed Delaplaine's confusion, and it pleased him. "Yes, the suspect was holding two girls in a house on Foster and we're on the way to apprehend him now."

Delaplaine held the side of her head. "I don't understand." She looked up. "You had Martinez, and we thought—"

"No one *had* Martinez," Shoemaker said. "Mr. Martinez was never a suspect in this case, and he did nothing wrong in Chicago except call the police on his own brother *hoping to prevent a crime*!" Shoemaker shook his head in disgust. "Yes, for a twelve-year-old trying to prevent a crime, you've painted him as an out-of-control menace to society. You've also helped ruin the reputation of a good man and break up his family. Are you happy?" Shoemaker turned away again. "I'm done with you."

"But Jackie Moore, we ... we were on TV today, and—"

Shoemaker flared again. "You're telling me you were on the TV with Jackie Moore? *Today*?" Shoemaker crossed his arms. "You want to tell me what you said to Ms. Jackie Moore?"

Delaplaine looked away. "We ..." She looked up at Shoemaker. "We talked about how the police were letting a dangerous rapist go free and shirking their responsibilities. Oh my God. Are you sure this man took the girls?"

"A hell of a lot more positive than it having anything to do with Alex Martinez." Shoemaker shook his head again. "Jackie Moore is out for herself. She doesn't care about the girls, or anything about this city if it doesn't help her or her ratings." He gestured toward the phone. "Go on, call her and ask what she knows about the status of this case and the suspect. But don't take too long. Next thing you know, it will be your reputation she's destroying as the community busybody who wrecked a family. And you know what? I bet more people will believe her than you."

Shoemaker turned to Neely. "Kat, I want you to call the department's general counsel and make them watch the noon report from Jackie Moore today. You watch it, too." He turned to Delaplaine with a grin. "Let's see if we're able to take legal action against Jackie Moore and all of her tribe. Now, if you'll excuse me, Ms. Delaplaine, I have work to do."

Shoemaker shook his head but before he left the building, he saw Delaplaine turn back towards the main reception area as Alex Martinez appeared from the hallway. She looked at him, then lowered her head and turned away.

Shoemaker and Perkins could hear the exchange between Hart and Novak as they raced toward the scene.

"Steve? Are you there?" Danny Novak's voice jarred Hart.

"Danny? Where are you?"

"I'm near you but took a different direction," said Novak. "Driving down from the River Road heading south. I just saw movement to my right. Wait, I think ..."

"You're on my left, Danny. Stay with me

"That does not mean to take unnecessary action!" said Andrew Shoemaker, speaking for the first time. "Is that understood?"

Hart and Novak shook their heads in unison and continued moving. In his command cruiser, Perkins cursed, then turned to Shoemaker. "Is that why we love these two so much?"

Shoemaker smiled. "And why they're also a pain in the ass. Glad they're on our side."

Chapter Thirty-Five

Spool was out of options, except to keep running and hope to get away. The girls were still ahead of him, running for all they were worth, with surprising speed. *I don't know whether they're running with me or from me,* he thought as he barreled through the trees.

Hart remembered the way the terrain changed from a hiking outing with Novak and his wife months ago. Instead of running toward Spool, she shifted to her right and sped toward where the river bent hard toward the south and the terrain dropped off even more. She hoped to intercept Spool there and cut his escape short, or failing that, to get to the girls before he could do anything else to them.

Alicia kept running, and while she thought Lacey would be slower, her sister's fear and energy carried her far ahead. They couldn't see where they were running, but had to keep going. Alicia looked around to see if the man was close, and turned just in time to see Lacey fall out of sight.

Hart heard a girl's scream but didn't know who it was, and kicked her running into high gear. Spool was ahead and to her left, slipping slightly in the mud. It was enough for Hart to gain purchase, then motivated by anger, she made a last push, deciding at last to use her extendable baton rather than her sidearm unless conditions changed. She hoped that wouldn't be a fatal mistake for her or for the girls.

"You have nowhere to go, Spool!" shouted Novak, distracting the man and giving Hart the chance to get to him.

"On the ground! Now!" Hart shouted. Spool looked around, and Hart continued to advance. "On the ground, Spool! It's over!"

Spool noticed the asp but kept running teeth bared as he launched himself toward Hart, who stepped to her left and plowed her right arm and the asp into Spool's gut. He collapsed like a rock onto the ground, moaning and grabbing his stomach.

Hart switched to her sidearm and shouted, "Do. Not. Move." She watched Spool writhe on the ground until Novak arrived, his weapon raised.

"Cavalry's here."

"So I see." She holstered her weapon and placed Spool in cuffs, lifting him to his knees. "Stay on your knees unless you want more of what I gave you earlier."

"What did you give him?" asked Novak.

Hart smiled. "I used his weight and force against him. He deserved it." She turned toward the river. "But one of the girls screamed, and—" Just then, a second, louder scream echoed across the valley.

Shoemaker's voice came over the radio. "Hart and Novak, confirm location!"

Novak took out his phone and keyed in his microphone. "We're in from the river, Captain, can't say by how much, but I'll radio out the GPS coordinates in a second." He called up his app, located the reading and read it to Shoemaker over the radio. "This is accurate to within ten feet, sir."

The radio was silent, and then Shoemaker said, "We've got you. It's about a five-minute walk. What about Spool?"

"In custody."

"And the girls?"

Novak looked at Hart. "That may be a problem."

The police converged on the site after taking Spool into custody. Besides the search-and-rescue certified officers, they also had harbor police in the river. Hart pointed to the girls, who were on a five-foot-wide ledge on the side of the hill. But it was crumbling with the rain pummeling it. The alternative was a thirty-foot fall to the shrinking riverbank.

"All right, people," said Shoemaker. "We have two options here, and neither of them is any good. The first is to rappel down to the girls and somehow get them up."

"What's wrong with that?"

"Danger of mudslide, falling, and the difficulty of getting the girls up once we attach them," Hart said. "We could try to lower them to the ground, but that isn't any easier."

"Can't we get someone from the harbor patrol to come in on their side?" asked Boyd.

Perkins shook his head. "That's possible. But the current has picked up, and it's hard to get a boat beached in this area safely. They're going to try, though."

"Damn!" Novak said. "So close."

"Don't remind me," Hart replied. She looked up at Perkins. "I've got lots of experience rappelling, sir, and—"

"I realize that, Hart," Perkins said. "But we may have to bring up the girls or at least one girl along with an officer. No offense, but you're a bit heavier than we'd like to use."

"I'm not," Marin said. "And I've got experience and certification, too." Marin didn't wait for approval before removing her belt. "You get me the equipment and I'll go down and get them."

Marin had her Swiss seat in position and attached the carabiner and ropes for rappelling down the hill. The plan was for Marin to stand on the ledge, affix the horse collar to one girl at a time, and have them hoisted by the other officers.

Marin started down foot by foot as Hart talked to the girls.

"Alicia, Lacey, we're going to help you. The man who took you is going to jail. The woman on the ropes is Officer Marin. You can call her Gee. She's going to help you." Marin looked up at Hart. *Keep talking to them, girlfriend.*

"Alicia, when Gee gets to you, I want you to help your sister, okay?" Alicia nodded. "Good."

Marin continued her descent, watching her footing to prevent excessive mud sliding. "I'm twenty feet away!" she said. "Girls, I want to get you both out, but I can't take you both at the same time. Lacey, can you be brave for me today?"

Lacey nodded her head, but Marin saw that her heart wasn't in it.

Marin smiled. "Now, your sister is going to help you, so you don't have to worry. But I want you to hold on to Alicia. I'll place this collar around you so we can lift you. Can you help me do that?"

Lacey nodded.

"Awesome!" said Marin. "I'm going to get closer." Marin touched down on the ledge and looked up at the other officers. "I'm getting Lacey out of here first," she said as she took the horse collar, wrapped it around Lacey's tiny frame and snapped the harness shut. Marin knew the little girl wouldn't be hard to lift up the hill. Once the collar was on, Marin looked up again. "Start a slow pull." She looked at Lacey. "You just hold on and if you have to close your eyes on the way, it's okay. They've got you."

Lacey nodded and said, "Okay." The officers began lifting her.

Marin turned to Alicia. "You've been brave too." Alicia nodded and looked alternately relieved and even more frightened. "The man is away and gone, now. We'll take care of the rest. Don't worry."

Lacey was taken out of the horse collar and it was lowered again to the ledge. Just before Marin grabbed it, two feet of the ledge slid away again, and she barely maintained her balance as she grabbed the collar. She breathed out and placed the collar and harness around Alicia. It was a snugger fit, but for a ride of twenty feet, it would work. Marin secured the harness and turned to call up. "You can start," she said, but realized that when the ledge had crumbled, their lines had gotten tangled. Marin couldn't go up or down, and the officers couldn't lift Alicia either.

"Damn!" shouted Marin.

"What's wrong?"

"The ledge is almost gone, and our lines are crossed. We can't untangle them ourselves!"

"Hold!" Perkins said. "You mean we need to put somebody—"

"No, no," said Marin. "I've got to attach her to my line somehow, but that's going to be a lot to lift at one time."

"Would a third pair of hands help?"

Marin looked at Alicia. "You all right, girlfriend?" Alicia nodded, and Marin turned to look up the hill. "Try it."

Perkins turned to ask about the lines but Stephanie Hart was already in her Swiss seat ready to descend the wall. "Am I still too fat, sir?"

The goal was for Hart to lower herself down, attach Alicia to another line, then have her pulled up as she and Marin lowered themselves to the riverbank. Hart figured going up would be impossible and even riskier. She lowered herself, watching her footing and keeping her location and her lines away from the others. She saw a frightened Alicia trying to keep her balance on the shrinking ledge as Marin talked to her. Marin was doing a good job, but Alicia was becoming nervous and jittery. Hart planned to attach the fourth line to Alicia's collar, then cut the line tangled with Marin's. Her colleagues would lift Alicia once they secured the lines.

Hart perched on the tiny ledge and smiled at Alicia. "Good to see you again, Alicia. We're going to get you out of here soon." Hart attached the second line to the horse collar and was raising her head to tell the officers to raise Alicia when the ledge gave way. Marin was safe once they cut Alicia's first line, but Hart, with neither hand on her lines, couldn't grasp her rear line and place it behind her back, and she fell thirty feet to the riverbank below.

CHAPTER THIRTY-SIX

Novak ran to the trailhead and found the stairs to the riverbank. He vaulted down twenty stairs, slipped and then fell for ten more, skinning his knee and banging his arm on a rock. He cursed, got up and picked his way through the brush to get to the riverbank. The bank was narrow, but he could walk on it. He used the side brush to stabilize himself as he walked north toward Hart. He was emerging from the last clump of trees when he heard Marin. "The river caught her! She's floating down!"

Novak ran up the bank, hitting the trees in his way, trying to get to Hart. He spied her moving quickly with the current. He ran forward to grab her arm, slipped and fell face first into the mud. When he got up less than a second later, she had moved past his reach and was floating faster down the river.

"I couldn't grab her! Are the harbor—"

"They're on it, Danny!" Perkins cried. "Go south on the riverbank to assist."

Novak raced down the bank, keeping Hart in sight as he dodged the brush and tried not to slip again. Thirty yards away from where he had missed her, a harbor patrol boat motored across from the other bank. Hart seemed unconscious, and couldn't help her rescuers, but soon got stuck on a tree branch that had fallen into the river. The harbor patrol people shouted to Novak, who turned around and saw Marin stumbling toward him. The harbor patrol gestured for them to move to the side, then tossed a heavy object toward them. It was the weighted end of a heavy rope; Novak grabbed it, pulling it taut, and wrapped it around a tree. He turned and gave the patrol a thumbs up as a man jumped from the boat and approached him. The boat winch pulled the boat up, beaching it.

Novak turned to see another man tethered to the boat grab Hart, attach a line and collar to her and pull her clear of the tree.

"Coming aboard!" came the shout of the skipper.

The man who'd jumped off the rescue boat turned to Novak and Marin. "Are you coming?"

"Damn right," said Novak.

The rescuer retrieved the anchor line as he, Novak and Marin boarded the boat. The harbor patrol had Hart on her side, getting water out of her lungs. Novak knelt as the patrol checked for vitals. Worried, Novak prepared to start CPR, positioning his hands for chest compressions, when Hart coughed, then turned around to look at him.

"If you think you're going to be touching my chest, Danny Novak, you've got another thing coming."

Novak smiled and touched his microphone. "We've got her, and ... she's back."

"Damn it, Danny. I do not need a nursemaid." Hart didn't relish staying in the hospital for observation and to get her wrappings changed. "I doubt a couple of broken ribs and minor sprains means I have to eat rotten hospital food."

"We'll smuggle in some better stuff for you, Steve," Novak said. "You just rest and enjoy a few days off."

Hart crossed her arms, wincing from the pain in her ribs. "I don't like sitting and resting."

"No choice this time," Sheryl Novak said. "Doctor's orders." Sheryl took out her phone. "I recorded this for you, Steve, but you're not going to like it." Sheryl pressed a few buttons and gave the phone to Hart. It was the KPAR-TV news.

"And Jackie, we've heard congratulations are due to you for your excellent reporting on the Stevens girls and their abduction. You want to tell us about it?"

"It's not about me, Chad. It's about how KPAR-TV is a community partner here in Port Angel. We've just received special recognition from our regional broadcast journalist association for our work in helping to root out the kidnapper—Caleb Spool—using our KPAR tip line. The Stevens girls are fine and are now receiving treatment. We're all thrilled with the outcome."

"Thank you, Jackie. And congratulations to you. I understand you'll be moving on to our affiliate in Seattle-Tacoma?"

"Well, I wasn't going to announce it yet, but yes, Chad, they have asked me to move to the Seattle and Tacoma affiliate. You know I have family there, so this is a welcome move, though I will miss my time here. My thanks to our team here at KPAR-TV and our viewers in Port Angel."

"Good news all around, then. And that's our news today in Port Angel. You have a great day."

Hart shook her head. "Turn it off, Sheryl. That woman disgusts me."

Sheryl Novak frowned. "I don't know how she can take credit for helping to catch Spool when she kept pointing the finger at Martinez. Did their tip line produce anything that helped you?"

Novak laughed. "Not likely, since KPAR never sent us anything—not a single tip or item of information."

"So how could she?" Sheryl shook her head. "And I thought only politicians got away with lying and making it sound real."

"They're no better." Hart shook her head again. "That's not fair, I guess. There must be good reporters out there, so I shouldn't paint them with the same brush." Hart frowned. "But Jackie Moore is the lowest of the low. Getting her out of the city is a win for us."

Novak agreed. "Right, Steve. So, do you really want to watch the news again today?"

"I'm a glutton for punishment." Hart fumbled on the remote for the television and turned it on.

They watched a report on damage from the flooding and about a minor scandal in the state capital before Chad Roberts faced the camera.

"Now that the suspect in the Stevens abduction is in custody, KPAR-TV wants to clear up any misunderstanding. Some people believed we said Alejandro Martinez was responsible for the girls' kidnapping. That is not the case, but because of that, citizens have called for him to be arrested, which was never our intent. KPAR-TV regrets the misunderstanding."

Hart turned the TV off. "Their intent?" She shook her head. "Do they think that absolves them of all responsibility? Get real!"

"That *is* real," Novak said. "And this shit doesn't get any better with time. What's also real is that Martinez lost his family, the girls lost their father, and Jackie Moore got to a market that's more than twice our size. Yeah, that sounds like a great ending to me."

"I agree," Sheryl said. "Those girls deserve a good family, and now the best parent they ever had won't be around anymore."

Hart rubbed her temples. "You're right. At least with him in their lives, they had a fighting chance."

Samuel Perkins sat with Andrew Shoemaker chatting about the case over coffee. "Were you really going to sue Delaplaine? That was gutsy of you."

Shoemaker laughed. "Nah. I just wanted to gauge her reaction and get her out of the building."

"It worked. Kat said she stood there opening and closing her mouth until her husband pulled her away." Perkins chuckled. "I don't think her husband has ever seen her so quiet."

Shoemaker exhaled. "Well, she caused enough damage when she talked. It's time she shut up."

Chapter Thirty-Seven

Martinez stood outside the door to Alicia and Lacey's hospital room, looking glum. O. C. Boyd saw him and approached. "Mr. Martinez. I would think you'd be much happier now."

"What? Oh, yes, I am." Martinez smiled. "They're safe and they're going to be okay." He glanced in the small window. "It's just that I'd like to see them."

Boyd frowned. "Why don't you?" Then he remembered the restraining order. He looked inside the room and saw Patty Stevens and her parents along with Alicia and Lacey. "If you're with me, you can be in there."

Martinez' eyes lit up. "I can?"

"Oh yeah," Boyd said. "And I doubt Ms. Jones will mind at all, especially when I give her 'the look.'"

"Yeah, she buckles when people do that to her." Martinez turned toward the door. "You should go in first."

Boyd knocked on the door and peeked in. "I'll be accompanying Mr. Martinez and supervising while he's here."

Stevens rose. "Um, okay. Come in."

Martinez entered and Alicia threw off her covers. "Dad!"

"Hey, wait right there," Martinez said. "You shouldn't be out of bed yet." He held out his arms to both girls. "I'm so happy to see you! We were so worried, so worried." He squeezed Alicia, then pulled back, wiping tears from his eyes, and turned to Lacey. "And here's my Pumpkin!" He hugged Lacey and let his tears flow.

Boyd saw the joy and relief Martinez felt and the brightness in the girls' eyes. He couldn't help noticing the simmering anger mixed with embarrassment on the face of Clarise Jones, and the deep sadness on Patty Stevens'. *A real waste.*

Another knock on the door interrupted them. "Hi, everyone, I'm Jewel, and I have to take Ms. Lacey down for some tests." She turned to Lacey. "Are you ready? We won't take long, then you can get back to your family."

"What are you testing for?" Martinez asked.

Jewel looked at her clipboard. "It's a CT scan." She looked further down in the document and turned to Lacey. "Did you have some belly pain?" Lacey nodded. "That's it—they want to be sure there's nothing going on in there."

Martinez smiled. "Thank you, Jewel."

Jewel pulled the wheelchair to Lacey's bed. "I'm going to help you in, okay?"

"Okay."

Jewel helped Lacey into the wheelchair and turned toward the door. "Now let's how fast we can go. Put on your helmet!" Lacey laughed and Jewel whisked her away through the door.

When they'd left, Alicia looked at her parents and asked, "How did we get here? The last thing I remember I was standing on the ledge and those ladies were trying to pull us up."

"Well, they did it," said Boyd with a laugh. "But it wasn't as easy as we expected. One officer fell down to the riverbank and she had to be rescued, too."

"Is she all right?" Martinez asked.

"Hart? Are you kidding? She does this kind of stuff all the time. No, Hart's the original Iron Woman. She has a few broken ribs and major sprains in her shoulders and one leg. She's a few doors down the hall if you'd like to talk to her."

"I would," Martinez said.

"Me too," said Stevens.

"Okay. I'll pass that on."

"Can I see her, too?" Alicia asked.

"Of course, honey," Stevens said. "If this officer says it's all right."

"Hart would like that," Boyd said.

Alicia looked at her parents again, then to her grandmother, who kept looking out the window. "What's going on?"

Stevens frowned. "Well, you're safe from that monster is what happened, and—"

"That's not what I mean." Alicia looked back and forth between her parents again, noting that each lowered their gaze as she looked at them. "What's going on?" Martinez looked to Stevens, who turned back to Alicia.

"Alicia, the focus needs to be on you and Lacey right now. Nothing else matters," Stevens said. "We've got to get you both healthy and back to school soon, okay?"

Alicia's eyebrows furrowed, then she looked at Boyd. "Are you here because that man is still out there? Is he still looking for us?"

Boyd was emphatic. "No. He's behind bars, and he's not being offered bail. You don't have to worry about him."

Alicia frowned. "Then why are you here?"

Boyd turned to the other adults in the room. Martinez cleared his throat. "Honey, I ... I took a new job." Martinez smiled. "It's a promotion, so I'll make more money, which will be great and I'll supervise a team of my own. It's just that ..." Martinez stopped because he was tearing up.

"What?"

Martinez turned back to Alicia. "Well, it involves more travel to more worksites, and the job is based in Springfield, so I won't be around much, even on weekends."

"But that's far from here," said Alicia, trying to remember how long it took to drive from Port Angel to Springfield. "Would you have to live there?"

"Yes, honey. I'll have to get an apartment there, you know, a little one."

"You won't be around?" Alicia looked at Stevens, who looked sad.

"No. Like I said, I'll be living out of or at least close to Springfield for this new job."

Alicia held her head in her hands. "I don't understand. This is …" She looked at Martinez. "When will we see you?"

Martinez looked at Stevens, who said, "We'll have to work that out."

Alicia opened her arms and hugged Martinez hard. Then she looked into his eyes. "Can't you just forgive her, whatever it is?"

Martinez kissed her forehead, then broke the hug. "It's not that easy." He stood tall and looked down at Alicia again. "Look, you stay good for your mother, and I'll see you as soon as I can."

Martinez left the room as Boyd said, "Excuse me."

Boyd stepped into the hallway with Martinez and found him standing by Brian Jones.

"Alex, you don't have to go."

"Yes, I do, Brian. I have to work and that's where they're sending me. I doubt things will ever settle down for me at my old place again, nor would I have the promotion they gave me."

Jones held up his hand. "Let me ask you this: if you could be with the girls again, would you give up the promotion?"

"You know the answer to that, Brian." Martinez sighed. "But I don't much believe in miracles." He chuckled. "You're only allowed one in your lifetime and getting the girls back safely was mine. I won't get any more."

"So you're just going to quit?" Boyd asked. "I didn't think you were like that."

Martinez didn't rise to the bait and shook his head. "I'm not quitting. I'm working with the hand I was dealt and trying to make the best of it."

"But what about your girls?" Jones asked. "They need you."

Martinez shook his head. "Well, I guess they're not really my girls anymore, are they?"

After Martinez had left, Alicia turned to her mother, staring. "Mom, what did you do?"

Stevens stood. "What did I do? Why is it always something I did?" She collapsed in her chair, crying.

"Mom, what happened? Why is he leaving?"

"You heard him," snapped Clarise. "He got a new job, and he's taking it. What does that have to do with your mother?"

Alicia shook her head. "Grandmom, Dad would never do that. He would never just leave us." She looked at Jones. "Did you make him go away?"

"*Me*? Why do you think that?"

Alicia ignored her grandmother and turned back to Stevens. "Mom, I remember how things were before you married Dad, but he's really the only full-time dad Lacey knows. What's she going to do?"

Stevens smiled through her tears, trying to soothe her older daughter. "It will be all right, honey, you'll see. It will be almost just like it has been."

Alicia lay back in her bed and turned away, her voice quiet. "No, it won't. It won't ever be the same again."

Boyd saw Brian Jones deflate and Martinez touch his father-in-law's shoulder. "Look. Brian." He sighed. "This project in Springfield is for a minimum of eighteen months. A lot can happen in eighteen months."

"So, maybe you and Patty—"

Martinez held up his hand. "You asked about the girls, Brian. I've realized that ..." He paused. "That I've been doing a lot of the heavy lifting in this marriage for a long time, and that's okay. But after all that, Patty believed the worst of me without a second thought." He shook his head, and Boyd saw his eyes welling with tears. "I can't forget that." Martinez looked back and forth between Boyd and Brian Jones. "So yeah, a lot can happen in eighteen months, and a lot can't. We'll see."

Also By F. J. Talley

Flight of the Raven
Twin Worlds
Desert Son

Stephanie Hart Novels
Take Hart
Standalone
21 Things Parents Wish They Knew
Before Their Kids Went Off to College

Send in a review using this QR Code:

Watch for more at fjtalley.com and collegeandparents.com